"Solotaroff's sympathies for writers and writing, his self-assessing autobiographical reflections, his probing excursions into publishing mores, and—above all—his pressing candor, all display a mind . . . constantly re-forming and redeeming its vantage points. There are stimulating openings here for every sensibility—and plenty of opportunity for political and cultural argument. In Solotaroff's pages, even biblical characters jostle elbows with the contemporary and the controversial."

—Cynthia Ozick

"Ted Solotaroff is a witness, wonderfully honest, of the state of literature today, of cultural hazards, of the struggle for quality in an inimical society. His testimony gives enlightenment and reassurance to the rest of us."

—Stanley Kauffmann

"No one has survived the publishing wars of the past thirty years with more humane and stalwart vision than Ted Solotaroff. He has been in the thick of the battles, fighting for all of us who take literature seriously; he has observed our tremendous losses, studied the tactics of our enemies, and has been responsible, directly or indirectly, for a remarkable number of our successes. At the same time, he is a writer himself and a fine one."

—Hayden Carruth

"Ted Solotaroff once again gives evidence of the range and acuity of his literary sensibility. These essays are marked by the courage and sincerity of a seasoned critic who has that rarer quality—generosity of spirit. A wonderful book."

—Richard Selzer

"Ted Solotaroff is one of the most astute, humane and knowledgeable observers of literature—and life, too, for that matter—we possess. Beyond fashion, without axes to grind, he does for our culture what only the very best critics are able to do: *place* things, reveal them, relate them to each other, and to our lives."

—Richard Gilman

Also by Ted Solotaroff

The Red Hot Vacuum

An Age of Enormity: Life and Writing in the Forties and Fifties by Isaac Rosenfeld (editor)

Writers and Issues (editor)

Best American Short Stories, 1978 (editor)

Many Windows (editor)

A Few Good Voices in My Head

Occasional Pieces on Writing, Editing, and Reading My Contemporaries

Ted Solotaroff

A Cornelia & Michael Bessie Book

Harper & Row, Publishers, New York
Cambridge, Philadelphia, San Francisco, Washington
London, Mexico City, São Paulo, Singapore, Sydney

For information address Harper & Row. Publishers, Inc., 10 East 53rd Street, New York, N.Y. 10022. Published simultaneously in Canada by Fitzhenry & Whiteside Limited, Toronto.

FIRST EDITION

Designer: Erich Hobbing
Copy editor: Marjorie Horvitz
Indexer: Olive Holmes

Library of Congress Cataloging-in-Publication Data

Solotaroff, Ted, 1928–
A few good voices in my head.

"A Cornelia & Michael Bessie book."
1. Literature, Modern—20th century—History and criticism. I. Title.
PN771.S618 1987 809'.04 86-46101
ISBN 0-06-039075-1 87 88 89 90 91 MPC 10 9 8 7 6 5 4 3 2 1
ISBN 0-06-039078-6 (pbk.) 87 88 89 90 91 MPC 10 9 8 7 6 5 4 3 2 1

For Isaac, Jason, Ivan, and Paul
and to Virginia

Defenceless under the night
Our world in stupor lies;
Yet, dotted everywhere,
Ironic points of light
Flash out wherever the Just
Exchange their messages. . . .

W. H. Auden

Contents

Preface

Most of the pieces in this collection were written for or grew out of a particular occasion—a book to review, an anthology to edit and introduce, a talk to give. I've selected those that seem to have survived their occasion because the points they make still seem worth making. They are also occasional in the sense that they were intermittent, at most two or three a year. I developed them in the midst of my work as an editor and like to think of them as a corollary effort to "do something for the hive," as Robert Bly once put it, by presenting writers, books, and ideas that I felt were worth public attention, and personal experience that seemed useful to pass along. Written, too, in the midst of a time, East and West, that has been mostly devoted to "the scrimmage[s] of appetites behind the hedges of privilege," in Delmore Schwartz's words, they represent work that has helped me to understand and withstand the institutionalized stupor, mediocrity, mean-spiritedness, and brutality, and to think beyond their dominion.

As such, these pieces generally, sometimes eventually, strike an affirmative note, their criticism meant in a positive spirit, more or less like an editor's regarding the manuscripts he or she chooses to publish and work on. Since *The Red Hot Vacuum,* my previous collection, which dealt with American and Western European writers of the 1960s, I have been particularly drawn to writers from the other Europe, because their words, even when comic or satirical, have the gravity of necessary speech. Their work makes the writer's vocation continue to matter in both public and personal ways. Several of the other pieces reflect my interest in Jewish culture, which awakened in recent years. Two essays, "The Telling Story" and "*American Review* Fiction," were initially efforts—the former a recently rethought, reshaped, and expanded one—to understand the premises and slant of my judgment of fiction, which both as an editor and reviewer I was imposing on writers and readers. The several essays on the literary vocation and its various contexts, from the campus to the publishing business and from the personal to the public, began as talks, generally to students in writing programs, in which I tried to tell one or another of the truths I've wished had been told to me when I was starting out. Though each of these subsequently developed well beyond the point of its occasion once the village explainer and reformer in me took over, I still see them as being finally addressed to the young writers I like to find and publish, and to their better hopes.

In selecting these pieces, I've taken the liberty throughout of touching up the prose, cutting and adding material, restoring what had been altered or cut in their magazine publication, here and there even allowing myself the benefit of second thought. In arranging them, I've let them fall together in the common interests and preoccupations they sustained.

I would like to thank the editors who have sponsored my writing, particularly Jack Beatty, Leon Wieseltier, and the late Robert Evett at *The New Republic,* Harvey Shapiro, Richard Locke, and Charles Simmons at *The New York Times Book Review,* Gordon Lish when he was at *Esquire,* Elizabeth Pochoda at *The Nation,* Bill Buford at *Granta,* and Stephen Berg at *The American Poetry Review.* Also Austin Olney and

Robie Macauley at Houghton Mifflin, Hugh Van Dusen at Harper & Row, and David Godine, who has kept *The Red Hot Vacuum* in print these many years. I am especially grateful to my two friends and publishers, Simon Michael Bessie, who saw there was a book here, and Cornelia Bessie, who persuaded and helped me to improve it.

Finally, I have a special debt to Helen Wolff. She once said, after receiving the Publisher's Citation of the American Center of PEN, that she has never thought of herself as standing in the shadow of her husband, Kurt Wolff (who was one of the towering publishers of our century), but in his light. For twenty years now, I have been standing in her light.

Part One

Silence, Exile, and Cunning

I

My idea of being a writer was formed during those strenuous years after World War II, when the modern tradition came into its own in America. Though I was at ease as an English major, and though the way ahead to graduate school had been paved, I knew that if I was "serious" (that somber password of my generation) about writing, I would have to put aside my prospective fellowship and go forth, naked and uncertain, into the world. Not just the world, though: rather, to a place that would lie at the necessary distance from my middle-class background and from the normal course of a professional career. Where this place might be geographically was less to the point than where it was, as we had begun to say, existentially. It was the place to which Sherwood Anderson had gone after walking out of his marriage and paint factory, the tenement on a lost street where Thomas Wolfe had set his bank ledgers on an icebox, the boiler room where Faulkner wrote *Sanctuary,* or the cork-lined bedroom where Proust wrote his *Remembrance.* Preeminently, it was the home of "silence, exile, and cunning"—the remote, "alienated" community of the modern artist.

Stephen Dedalus's instructions to himself were like a

beacon to a fledgling literary type like myself. This was not only because he was such a hero to me, the prince of my desires and disorders, but because his counsel made sense. After four years of steadily overreaching myself as a literature major, I was quite mixed up, and the air I breathed as a writer was so rarefied that it supported very little life.

Hence, silence. But Joyce's word meant more than just starting over again. Part of my grandiose practices as a student had stemmed from a passionate response to the artistic and intellectual grandeur of modern literature, and even when I realized that the practices were self-alienating, I didn't doubt for a moment that the passion was well-placed. To become a modern writer was an awesome calling, one that required huge reserves of learning and craft. Take Thomas Mann. That mighty line of Knopf books on my shelf was said to have been produced by a trickle of prose during a few hours each morning, while the rest of Mann's day was spent in reading and contemplation, so that the great reservoirs of information and intuition would remain full. How much mastery of the sources had gone into works such as *The Magic Mountain* and *Joseph and His Brothers!* How much power of judgment, both daring and steady, was required to create a Leverkühn! That amazing resonance of stories such as "Mario and the Magician" and "Disorder and Early Sorrow" came from the sense that behind what Mann chose to tell you were the rich implications of what he didn't: like islands, they went down and down. Proust, Valéry, Gide, Kafka, Rilke, Joyce, Yeats, D. H. Lawrence, Eliot, Pound, Auden, Henry James, Wallace Stevens . . . wherever one looked, the answer was the same: the exemplary modern writers were men of learning, critics as well as creators of culture, and, characteristically, architects of a worldview.

Moreover, they were artists. They didn't write to produce the obvious point, the immediate effect; rather, they slowly, patiently built up intricate, impersonal structures of meaning. For most of them, the slower, the better. The archetypal modern novelist was Flaubert—"our Penelope," as Pound said—who wrote to a friend that he had slaved all day and produced a single sentence. Or it was Stephen Dedalus giving himself ten years in which to "forge" his first book. The discipline of the novice writer, therefore, was not so much in writing as in preparing himself to write, of locating himself in something called "the tradition" and submitting to its authority. This he could afford to do, because literature, in the prevailing view, was not an expression of his personality but, in Eliot's famous phrase, an escape from it. What Stephen Daedalus was to create in the smithy of his soul were not romantic (chilling word) visions—"spilt religion," as Hulme called it—but the veritable "uncreated conscience of my race." A wholly impersonal creation toward which he would be as indifferent as God was to His. Far from being the object of art, the writer's self was not even the source. According to Eliot's classic formulation, one's ego was merely a catalyst that enabled emotions and images to fuse, and should itself be made up in good part of the tradition. Indeed, if one subscribed to "The Impersonal Theory of Poetry," the tradition was a more vital force than even an individual's talent; at least, so one was encouraged to interpret this famous essay that summed up the aesthetic of the great moderns. And though Eliot was talking about poetry, the force of his argument applied to fiction and drama as well, for poetry then was the queen of the literary arts, and to its regime of complexity and order the other genres were thought to aspire.

Since Eliot wrote so much criticism, and since it was so articulate and striking and unyielding, his tended to be the main voice of authority one carried in one's head. It also encouraged silence. "Teach us to care and not to care/

Teach us to sit still." From Eliot also emanated much of the sacerdotal aura that hovered about the vocation and study of literature. But there were many other sources and exemplars: the Christian mysteries and austerities were the "something in the air" by the early fifties. A particularly telling case was that of Auden: he was the poet one read by the yard, the chief witness of contemporary consciousness, whose verse had lit up the age on all sides and at the center:

> But ideas can be true although men die,
> And we can watch a thousand faces
> Made active by one lie:
> And maps can really point to places
> Where life is evil now:
> Nanking; Dachau.

But by the time of *Nones* and of Auden's Oxford lectures, it was clear that he was in retreat (in both senses of the word) from the postwar world and devoting himself to the rigors and consolations of faith and art. These two realms moved closer and closer together in the New Criticism, whose vocabulary itself, featuring terms like "ritual," "sacrament," "anagogic," and "heresy," expressed its penchant for Christian mystery and orthodoxy.

All of which created a great deal of cold water—valuable for tempering style, for sobering imagination, but also dampening to one's enthusiasm for writing and for the world. I would spend days rewriting a paragraph of description, as a sailor works on his shoes, polishing, burning off the wax, and repolishing, trying to give the words that quiet, impassive gleam through the ordinary of Flaubert's "Un Coeur Simple"; I would spend months revising a ten-page story so that it might come out like the poem Yeats dreamed of, "as cold and beautiful as the dawn." These values of "art" persisted, and in the five years after I left Ann Arbor, I wrote exactly seven stories. In terms of experience, they were probably the richest years of my life: I was engrossed in a young, deep, complex, and stormy marriage; we lived mostly in the Village but also in Berkeley and in Maine; I worked in innumerable restaurants and a few gambling houses and racetracks as a waiter or bartender; I was also a psychiatric attendant, a temporary office worker, an eradicator of gooseberry bushes in the Sierras, and an assistant to a Japanese gardener; I twice started graduate school, read a great deal, and even taught myself Latin and German. Virtually none of this went into my writing. Instead I labored on my few ironic tales of empty lives, all turning upon the theme of initiation and resignation; never realizing the irony was on me, that my theme was mostly an unconscious parable of the experience of writing, while my life itself was one virtually constant, varied—and unexplored—initiation.

Now and then I would try to capture what was happening around or within me, but would soon abandon it: The material just didn't seem sufficiently "literary." That is to say, it wouldn't hold still, wouldn't fit into the oblique, gray vision of things, the austere cadences, which had become as much a part of writing as my typewriter and cigarettes. The more something touched me, the more life there was in it, the more expressively it came out, the less eligible it seemed to achieve that sacrosanct condition of a self-contained work of art. Like Hemingway, I wished to be commended for my reticence, for that single, taut line of narrative strung across an abyss of feeling; like the Joyce of *Dubliners,* I wanted to write in a style of "scrupulous meanness," subtly awaiting and anticipating that muted lyrical moment of "epiphany" at the end, which delicately completed and illuminated the meaning.

There was little excitement in writing such decorous

realism, which came out much more pallidly than it did in Hemingway or Joyce. But though I squirmed and wrestled to get out of my corner, I was stuck there by the concept that form was everything—surface, meaning, expressive power. Anything merely vivid and direct would be a false element that detracted from the quiet, impassive working of the total effect; form was nothing if not a ruthless subordination of the parts to the whole. The result was that content followed form: spare, elegiac stories about my childhood or about other lives that struck the same note of muted life. My childhood had hardly been muted (it had been mostly one long struggle to escape from others' designs on it), but through the operation of the reticent style, it came out that way, which accorded with my longstanding grievance of stifled superior sensitivity and helped to maintain it.

Now and then I dimly sensed the characterological evasions that made this narrow conception of fiction so compelling. I kept my journal filled with injunctions to "be myself" in my writing—though with the restraint proper to the "classical" mode. The trouble was that there was nothing very classical about the striving and strife of my marriage; or the frenzy of the kitchen at the Oyster Bar in Grand Central Station, which made me so comically hapless; or the spic-and-span brutality of the psychiatric ward in Berkeley, where the only treatment was different modes of shock therapy; or the revelation of the maniac in myself that occurred during six weeks of working in a gambling house in Lake Tahoe, where the only greenness that attracted me was the felt of the crap tables. These and other interesting matters were the ground of my present self—except when I was writing. Without their raw, immediate, vexing concreteness they were toneless; but writing about them was "self-indulgent" without the cool, rigorous detachment of art. So I went on compulsively choosing the latter way and sparing myself the actual conflicts and illuminations I experienced in the world. Needless to say, growth was difficult.

Yet there was a side to me, God knows, that was irreverent and outspoken enough, and it is strange that this gap of silence I had opened between self and art and self and life should have been taken so much as an article of faith. From year to year, from story to story, I could tell that it was doing real damage. At the very least it took away my early joy in writing (even now that word seems a little frivolous) and suppressed most of the personal quest which, however naive, had provided natural energy and tension. Nor was the case for impersonality all that self-evident. Had modernism itself really been founded on the "escape from personality"? Did the young Baudelaire or Lawrence or Kafka or Hemingway follow this discouraging and possibly perverse idea? Did Eliot himself?

> Should I, after tea and cakes and ices,
> Have the strength to force the moment to its crisis?
> But though I have wept and fasted, wept and
> prayed,
> Though I have seen my head (grown slightly bald)
> brought in upon a platter,
> I am no prophet—and here's no great matter;
> I have seen the moment of my greatness flicker,
> And I have seen the eternal Footman hold my
> coat, and snicker,
> And in short, I was afraid.

Contrary to popular critical opinion, that was no mere "persona" speaking there, but rather a man in very precise and painful touch with himself and emboldened to put his judgment of his existence on the line. The main aspect of his personality that Eliot was escaping from in his early poetry was his fear of asserting it.

There is much to be said for the intellectual endeavors of the "Age of Criticism," but, given the creative situation, it possessed little active cause for its doctrines. Romanticism was hardly a threat to American writing during the 1950s; indeed, as time was to prove, it was more like a scarce specific for the malarial formalism and the heavy congestion of aesthetic and cultural opinion that burdened it. For the most part, modernism was no longer a movement of opposition and innovation but was rather a revolution that had long since prevailed and was now being canonized in the universities, where it was institutionalized, becoming genteel, fetishistic, repressively normative. The literary situation still existed mainly in the trails blazed by the giants, some of whom were still walking the earth, and the arbiters, whether they wrote for *Partisan* or *Kenyon* or *Hudson*, were preoccupied with analyzing the substance, force, and permanent relevance of the towering dead and the last few survivors.

In sum, the literary atmosphere was thick with authority. But why was I, like so many other young writers, so susceptible to its dicta? The trouble was not so much, I think, the eminence of the masters: one could love, say, Joyce or Chekhov or Kafka, be content to work for a good while in his shadow, and still grow. The cataclysms of recent history had certainly created enough of a distance between their world and ours to provide fresh material and scope—a new postwar mass society and man as well as the fall-out of WWII, the Holocaust, and the Cold War, were waiting to be discovered with their aid. The problem was that their work was, by now, so thoroughly mediated by the moral constructs and historical perspectives and aesthetic injunctions which had been placed upon it, by the sheer knowingness which surrounded it, that any personal attachment was bound to seem tenuous, derivative, and depersonalized. How does one model oneself on an institution? The passage of their achievement into the hands of the explicators and commentators tended to obscure the master value they could have communicated to the young: their example of fierce and unyielding individualism, their complete possession of their own faces.

So what I picked up instead from the literary atmosphere was mostly a certain vanity and despair of participation. I religiously read *Partisan* and *Kenyon* and *Hudson:* They were brilliant, learned, magisterial, full of principles and precedents, rather like the deliberations of the Supreme Court. They provided a fund of literary information, political and cultural bearings, fruitful debate: a quick indoctrination into both the radical and the conservative approaches to modern letters. They kept me on my toes—tiptoes—peering in. They produced their own lofty figures—Rahv and Trilling, Ransom and Tate, Blackmur and Kenner—the keepers of the shrine, the masters of the game. Into their deliberations very little new writing intruded, but that made them the more august. The pages of *Partisan* were particularly seductive to me: All my vague intimations of a potential background, position, fealty, style seemed embodied there and raised to a higher power. But this, too, was tiptoes behavior, which, like my fiction, kept my feet barely touching the ground.

II

Along with silence, there was "exile." Some of my contemporaries, such as the group that formed around *The Paris Review,* took the idea literally for a time, but there was something historically banal and frivolous about that course: what I called "Lost Generation stuff." The spell of the twenties—of Hemingway, Fitzgerald, Dos Passos, cummings, Gertrude Stein—was strong enough without trying to live at its source. Moreover, America in the early fifties was certainly turbulent and treacherous enough to keep one on edge. Finally, it was simpler and cheaper as well as more stirring to be an "internal émigré," whose isolation was more a matter of principle than of place. Why hang around Paris like Robert Cohn when one could hole up in New York like George Weber?

In 1952 I left Ann Arbor and came to New York, looking to sink as quickly as possible into poverty, loneliness, opposition, and whatever other challenges were necessary to prove my will to be an artist. I found them quickly. Within a month, we were living on East Twenty-eighth Street in a small "studio" with a skylight (but no windows), next door to a sweatshop that noisily manufactured wristwatch bands. Our other neighbors were the Gerundalos, a couple from San Francisco: he a pianist, she a painter, who supported them by working as a welfare investigator. Wearing an old pair of tuxedo pants, Robert would stay home all day perfecting his repertoire. Wearing mine, I would return from an "extra lunch" job at the Harvard Club or somewhere, or from another bootless morning at 80 Warren Street, a building full of sleazy employment agencies, where I waited around with New York's other nonunion and relatively unemployable waiters (their problem mostly being drink, mine mostly incompetence). Though one of the other mottoes I shared with Stephen Dedalus was "*Non serviam,*" I had somehow hit on the idea that a high-paying lunch job was the ideal one for a writer. My wife found one quickly at one of the Longchamps restaurants and held on to it, and I suppose I could have done so too, but what I secretly wanted was the full descent represented by 80

Warren Street. Trying to put a foot down in Bohemia, I had fallen through to the Depression. I even found a consumptive-looking Stalinist to argue with there, who regarded most modern writing as "decadent crap." Wishing to become a "marginal man," as they said in *Partisan Review*, one who lived at a "perpetual extreme," what more could I ask? In the afternoons, I retyped a paragraph of one of my stories, while in the next room Robert went over and over a passage of Tchaikovsky's Piano Concerto No. 1—both of us preparing for our debuts. On the landing outside hung his wife Mary's paintings, which appeared to be abstract but were really enlarged studies of stones. Through the thin wall, the productive stamping machines and their Puerto Rican operators chattered away.

So it went, more or less, for the next four years. Under my twin sign of alienation and integrity, I courted failure as assiduously as some of my classmates were courting success on Madison Avenue and Wall Street. Apart from my neurotic taste for it, I was sustained for a time by the endless modern legend of the artist as the outsider, the inspired dropout. Now and then I would weaken and try to drop back in by starting graduate school in Berkeley, or looking for a job in publishing, or, at one particularly desperate point, writing a TV script. But then the legend would sweep me up again, the affluent society that I was not of would fall away, a waiter's job would turn up that kept me going for a few more months, a favorable rejection slip would set me to work revising. If my life was still anxious, grim, and lonely, didn't this mean that I was still on the right track? Hadn't Chekhov himself said that to become a writer had cost him his youth, that he had had to squeeze the slave out of himself, drop by drop?

By 1954 I was living in Greenwich Village, an environment that I counted on to support my lean and deviant existence. In some ways it did, though not the ones I had anticipated. What I liked about living on Macdougal Street was that by day it was still an Italian working-class neighborhood: The tenements and stores gave off an earthy, dark, foreign sobriety that stimulated and settled me. By evening, though, and on weekends, it would be transformed, and I would sit on the windowsill of our sixth-floor walk-up, which we were continually "fixing up," and gaze down at the flocks of tourists, striding and craning, hoping, as I was, to breathe the air of liberation. Because of them, it was very easy to get work, and I bounced around the clubs and restaurants, a month or two here, a few weekends there, implementing my salary and tips by the various ways of earning "the smart dollar" that cabaret waiters practice.

This put me in the middle of the prevailing atmosphere, for what the neon lights along West Third Street and around Sheridan Square spoke of was the commerce of cultural voyeurism and its sad dissipations. Perhaps they always had. But whatever the Village had once signified, it was now mainly a fashionable place to live, to shop, to date, to cruise, to booze. As the lofts and studios were leveled and replaced by luxury high-rise apartments, I sensed the ending that was taking place, just as I did on Saturday nights at Café Society Downtown, where a sly Josh White sang his sexy ballads and anguished chain-gang songs to a rapt audience of suburbanites. Under the transforming spread of affluence, nothing was quite what it seemed. The sculptor across the street, who had once designed sets for Piscator, now spent most of his studio time giving lessons to ladies from the ILGWU to pay for his house in Woodstock. The Cuban painter downstairs had poured over five thousand dollars into his twenty-two-dollar-a-month cold-water flat. The wild-looking men I watched drinking at The Kettle and thought were painters turned out mostly to be Village moving men; and at the San Remo, the haggardly urbane types who were always talking about "Wystan" or "Delmore" or playing sardonic poetry games,

> Full fathom five
> Thy father lies,
> Among the fishes
> And the flies . . .

were teaching at the New School or working on Madison Avenue.

No doubt there were still writers and artists in Greenwich Village who lived mainly for and through their work, who might have fathered my own ambitions to do so, but the evidence of their existence was scarce. The *Partisan Review* group, the one I was particularly attracted to, was scattered among the various universities: Rosenfeld and Bellow at Minnesota, Rahv and Howe at Brandeis, Kazin at Amherst, and so forth. In fact, one of the regular features of this erstwhile school of alienation was a "Letter from the Academy." Even more disturbing was its famous symposium, "Our Country and Our Culture," in which the Cold War and a rising sense of cultural opportunity and well-being furnished the occasion and tone for the return of this family of prodigal sons. What slowly dawned on me was that the conflict I had taken for granted between the artists and intellectuals and bourgeois society was entering a wholly new phase, with a good deal of accommodation on both sides. It was evident in the dominant novel of this period—Bellow's *The Adventures of Augie March*—which opened with the image of an aggressive young man's fist, not raised in protest but knocking at the door. It was evident in the so-called paperback revolution—the first capitalization of serious culture—and especially in the collections of new writing—*New World Writing, Discovery, Anchor Review*—that it spawned. It was evident in a new periodical called *Perspectives USA,* a classy showcase of the higher orthodoxy. When I ran into Mary Gerundalo one day on Greenwich Avenue, she told me that Robert was now with a chamber music group that was giving a series of recitals in the suburbs. "It's for the Amana Food Plan," she said.

All of which meant that the ground I had chosen to stand on was shifting and that the bearings I had taken were now somewhat baffling. Instead of the avant-garde and the philistines, the rebels and the conformists, the marginal men and the solid citizens, there seemed to be some kind of synthesis taking place, or, at least, what one writer called "the shrinkage of extremes," which conferred on all of the surviving positions and doctrines a greater or lesser degree of acceptability. This was clearest in politics: Senator Joseph McCarthy's disavowal of the social attitudes of fascism enabled him to bestride the right and to traumatize the left; on the left, there was no fear of admitting to being a Socialist (even Sidney Hook said he was one) as long as your anti-Communist credentials were in order. By the middle fifties, a similar dull, cautionary mood had settled upon writing. The younger American novelists who had come on the scene during or just after the war—Paul Bowles, Eudora Welty, Carson McCullers, Tennessee Williams, Saul Bellow, Truman Capote, Vance Bourjaily, William Styron, Norman Mailer, James Baldwin, Ralph Ellison, et al.—were specialists in solitude, anxiety, violence, and terror, full of a profound uncertainty and dismay about the human condition. Similarly, the older American novelists who mattered most, such as Hemingway, Faulkner, Fitzgerald, and Nathanael West, were valued as the prophets of the broken moral order, of the nihilistic malaise that had been left by the destructive energies of World War II. By the middle fifties, most of this literary opposition to the confident, up-and-doing postwar ethos had weakened, and the novelists were dropping back into society or else remaining silent. The fiction of the sensitive private life was coming into vogue, carrying its burden of bittersweet resignation to things-as-they-are, its tone of civility, its modest complexities. The great iridescent visions of Joyce and Mann, Proust and Lawrence, began to fade into the common daylight of *The Catcher in the Rye.* The intransigent novelists and poets from the little magazines also turned up, wryly, in the pages of *The New Yorker.*

All of this mood of accommodation and adjustment came to me in the vague intimations in which the *Zeitgeist* speaks. But I knew from merely consulting my own growing despair that I was on the wrong track, or, at least, on a much more difficult one than I had bargained for. It was not so much a matter of being poor: my idea of being a writer was closely associated with the heroics of a meager income, which I had cultivated since childhood. A Depression kid, I had been a caddy at twelve, a bellhop at fifteen, and so forth; I had always worked because having a job was my primary form of independence and security: it was my way, in the fullest sense of the word, of *supporting* myself. This intimate relation between work and identity was, of course, hardly peculiar to me; indeed, it was particularly keen among members of my generation, whose "style," as the magazines kept pointing out, was that of early commitment to the responsible attitude, the modest career. What lay behind this drive for security was not just the desire to share in the affluence of the times but a deep jumpiness about careers, about being unemployed, which stemmed in good part, I think, from the *angst* of the thirties, which we had taken in with our mother's milk and father's table talk. If I was fascinated by 80 Warren Street and by all that faintly remembered yet familiar sense it evoked of dispossession and immobility, I could also feel myself sinking into a kind of fear, as I drew on my tuxedo pants and sash and alpaca jacket—all redolent of coffee, the waiter's cleaning fluid—that I was allowing myself to be left back, stymied, "screwed." I would work in a restaurant or cabaret until I had saved up enough money to stay home at the typewriter; and then my entailed and encumbered attitude toward writing, the rising cost of poverty, the guilt of staying home while my wife was out working, but mainly the ongoing failure to produce art, would drive me back into waiting or temporary typing or some other such job. I still held on to my hard, dry values, but I was losing what little conviction I had that I could ever make use of them. As for "alienation," I was learning about that from my fellow waiters, particularly the European refugees, and could see now that it was either a posture, fastidious and superficial, or else a fate—a slow crushing of the social bond, a cold remoteness and self-centeredness, of which no one could want more than his lot and which only some real achievement of art or intellect could possibly redeem.

I knew now that I could go that way myself: not toward the strength and courage to stand alone but toward the bitter, spiteful, barren sensitivity that was hardly in short supply in the Village. Was my quarrel with society really any different from that of the San Remo poets, or from the general malaise of the Eisenhower age? Did it have any more radical content, any more yield of boldness and sympathy and vision? Or was it merely a depressed vanity erected into a pretentious identification with the great outlaws of art? Two new ones—Beckett and Genet—were coming into view. In the face of their genuine deviance, their rock-bottom solitude, their strategy of constituting the self in the midst of its nullity, of grasping existence at its loathsome and precious extremes, I could begin to regard my running around New York in my tuxedo as a cunning but profitless form of self-abuse. Beckett and Genet were what it meant to take alienation seriously, to live it out, to invite its demons. I had merely cut myself adrift: a professional type without a profession.

I still said that I was a writer, but after four or five years and not many more stories, that hardly had much experiential meaning. I don't think it once occurred to me to look for book-reviewing work or to write a sketch, say, for *The Village Voice.* I wanted to be an artist, not just a writer. And the less writing I produced, the greater my vanity grew. And the greater my despair. I called it a writing block, but it felt more like a sieve through which my consciousness of anything soon disappeared between the punctilious words and sentences, the arch descriptions, the veiled dialogue.

As though to mock my pretensions and contradictions, life went on sowing the seeds of fiction all around me. A week among the stray souls in our building on Macdougal Street would have kept Chekhov going for a year, and almost any night at Marie's Crisis on Grove Street could have gone directly into a story by Saroyan. I watched Carmine DeSapio, the most powerful man in New York, at work and at play in the private room of The Duplex (with fifteen Village pols and somebody's girlfriend); I eavesdropped on the executives of a record company at a private lunch, nervously shooting their cuff links as they tried to figure out the best way to package Sammy Davis, Jr. I served Manhattans in coffee cups to nuns at the Oyster Bar in Grand Central Terminal, and held conversations rich in overtones with a number of priests there. In one Saturday at The Elegante, a supper club in Brooklyn, I could observe the whole pageant of Jewish family ceremonies: *bris,* bar mitzvah, sweet sixteen, engagement, wedding, silver and golden anniversary parties, or I could work in the bar and try to figure out what Paddy DeMarco, a famous welterweight, and a couple of famous Mafiosi were mumbling and grinning about. There was a night in a little delicatessen in Brighton Beach when, after waiting on a handful of customers, I was fed "specially made" blintzes, while the owner, a widow, furtively offered me first a partnership, then a steady job, then a "walk" with her dull but luscious daughter, who was sitting between us. Or a year later, I worked for two partners in a delicatessen in Astoria. Each had sunk his life savings into buying it and then watched the neighborhood shift month by month from Jewish to Negro/Puerto Rican:

"He wants to put in a telephone booth. . . ."

"Sure, it'll help business."

"And what do you think, you genius, they'll do in your telephone booth?"

"They'll make their telephone calls. How many of them you think have telephones?"

"I'll tell you what they'll do. They'll urinate in it. They'll do all kinds of filthy things in it. The smell of urine, that's all we need. . . ."

Who wrote about such people anymore? Did I want to imitate the social realism of the thirties, go back to my own square A? How could literature possibly spring from such banal, coarse stuff?

III

Eventually, my wife became pregnant, and I took a job that got me into the waiters' union. After a month of filling in here and there as an extra and of picketing the Stork Club, I was sent to the Blair House and fell into one of the most lucrative waiting jobs in New York. The manager was a Broadway character named Conny Immerman, who had owned the famous Cotton Club in Harlem, and had run the gambling casinos for Batista in Cuba. When he found out that I had gone to the same college as his brother-in-law Benny Friedman ("the first and the last, kid, of the great

Few Good Voices
My Head

me years ago, probably around 1971, a young writer me to see me. He wanted to write an essay for *American view* about the sudden decline of the counterculture, and talked about that for a while. He seemed both jaunty d troubled, as many young people were in that fading era fresh alternatives, but he didn't seem to have much of a ip on his subject. I suggested that instead of talking, he ight do better to sit down and write and see what he really anted to say. He said that that was the other thing he anted to talk to me about. He had been having trouble riting lately and he thought that writing for *American eview* might get him going. "I don't know who to write for nymore," he said.

I asked him whom he had written for in the past. Well, e'd started out as an English major at Yale and written nostly for his professors. "I came on as a sort of young Northrop Frye." After college he landed a job at *Time* and ecame a staff writer, which was a welcome change from ancy literary jargon, and he did it happily for a couple of years. But then, "I got tired of the *Time* style, of having to come up with clever locutions like 'sluburb' and 'peace-monger.' " Also, as he said, "My politics were changing and

Jewish quarterbacks"), Conny took me under his wing. I was to be his future biographer; in the meantime, he threw all the "live ones" my way that he could: Billy Rose, Fred Allen, Senator Lehman, David Sarnoff. "Take good care of him, General, he's the only Phi Beta Kappa we've got here." It was fun, and the money poured in. But when I went to a nearby cafeteria during the afternoon breaks to do my writing, nothing at all happened. I was now a professional waiter; each week confirmed that a bit more. I had even been approached by the shop steward at the Blair House about working as an organizer for the union.

As I sat in the cafeteria one afternoon, wondering what to write about, thinking of those lines by Sydney—" 'Fool,' said my Muse to me,/'Look in thy heart and write' "—two lines of Yeats rose in my mind: "Too long a sacrifice/Can make a stone of the heart." I wrote the lines down, closed the notebook, went out of the cafeteria, and walked through Central Park.

It was a nice day in early spring, one of those few days of the year when New York bears a tenderness toward life. The whole park seemed turned toward the sun; even the muddy, littered paths spoke of renewal. I thought of a line, probably translated from the Yiddish, that my father, another misemployed and locked-up man, had once spoken to me: "Alone is like a stone." Soon I would become a father, perhaps of a son. What example would I pass on? Everything in me that had wanted to be, like the young Henry James, "just literary," seemed to collapse against those hard words of Yeats, the sad ones of my father. It was as though the "madness of art"—a phrase by an older Henry James—had, for the first time, revealed itself. And something else. I was full of "doubt," but where was the "passion" for the "task"? Where had it gone? Probably into the stories I hadn't allowed myself to write. The simple truth of that brought me close to tears. I sat there on a bench and tried to contemplate, really for the first time, the "block," the "sieve," the "abyss" I had been cultivating as well as deploring for the past five or six years. No doubt some of the hole had always been there; indeed it was what writing was supposed to fill. For the first year or two, back in Ann Arbor, of unhampered feeling and expression and discovery, writing had filled it. This had led me on, "committed" me. But then I had opted for "art," which didn't merely fill the self but fulfilled it, made it admirable, redeemed it.

I could begin to grasp now the grievous mistake. Why hadn't I written about that funny and sad evening in Brighton Beach with that mother and daughter? Was it merely that Chekhov would have done it better? So what? Wasn't the truth rather that I didn't *want* to write about it, that what I wanted from writing was another self than the one that was implicated in such lives? Weren't the qualities of style I aspired to precisely those that enabled me to avoid the coarse and painful immediacy of my character, my work, my days, my thoughts, my hang-ups? In return, the impassive prose, the fiddling with form, provided an illusionary sense of mastery—control without confrontation, refinement of surfaces, mere gestures of good taste. No wonder I had been plagued by the guilt of being an impostor. There was an impostor in me, a false self that wished to stand above my groping existence and be admired for its cunning and grace. That was what I had meant by transcendence of the ordinary, by "art." No wonder the rest of me had become so stony and lonely.

I writhed for a time with the awareness from these thoughts, if not their precise sense, and then went back to the Blair House. That night I raced home, eager to put my new insight to immediate use. But there were only the familiar spasms of silence and then a trickle of the same old self-conscious words. For several months I struggled to break the habits of constraint and false pride. It was a desper-

ate, ghastly experience, dogged by t
years, of having run out of time. Th
of yellow paper and my wife's belly we
of that. So was our cold-water flat at
flights of stairs she had to climb, and w
giness we had never quite been able to
or paint away. Neither of us wanted th
had no future. The time had come to b
"mature."

One day a curious customer asked me w
side." Formerly, I would have been eage
now I said, "Nothing."

"I thought you might be continuing you
said with a knowing smile.

"Yes," I said. "I'm saving up for gradua

most of my friends were writing for *The Village Voice* or *Rolling Stone.*" So he began to moonlight for the underground press, and after a while he left *Time* and traveled around the country, writing reportage about the new street communities, communes, and so forth.

Why, then, didn't he write this piece for, say, *Rolling Stone*? He explained that writing for the youth culture had become like the flip side of writing for *Time:* you were just "enthusiastic and snotty about the opposite things." Also you had to deal with another standardized style—words like "downer," and "heavy," and "hassle," and spelling America with a *k.* That's why, he said, "I'd like to write for *AR*—you don't have any one style, any one point of view, and that grabs me. On the other hand, it's hard to know what you're looking for."

He was watching me carefully, as though I might inadvertently reveal the secret requirement. I said that *AR* published different kinds of pieces but mostly they were ones that seemed necessary for the writer to have written, which is why I suggested he try to find out what he really needed to say. He nodded but pressed on. "Okay, but look—you write yourself, right? Who do you write for?" I thought for a moment and said, "I guess I write for a few good voices in my head." At which point he suddenly smiled, relaxed, looked at me in a companionly way, and said, "A few good voices in your head—far out!"

Well, I've been thinking about that idea off and on ever since. I don't think it's as far out as the young writer found it. I think it's the way people start out writing—or painting, or composing, or doing scientific research: for one or two powerfully meaningful figures in their lives. And I think that those who continue as artists remain in touch with complementary and internalized versions of those early good voices. Needless to say, there are also bad voices in one's head—voices of doubt and despair and intimidation, particularly intimidation, which can also have a powerful effect early in one's career, and late as well. Harry Stack Sullivan calls these voices "supervisory presences" or "personifications of the self." They are evident in daily behavior; they prepare our faces for the faces that we meet, put us at ease or turn on the anxiety, tell us to be gentle or firm, or to keep quiet, or to cut out the crap. And so with writing. Sullivan describes his own writing supervisor as a "charming pill, bitterly paranoid, a very brilliant thinker and a wrongheaded imbecile, whose harassment in the name of an impossible clarity is all but entirely responsible for the fact that I almost never publish anything."

But to return to the benign voices. Literary scholarship, at least the more conventional kind, looks for another kind of supervisory presence, which it calls "influences." Thus scholars say that Hemingway was deeply influenced by Gertrude Stein and find the main import of this in Hemingway's sparse idiom, his use of repetition, his short sentence rhythms, his impassive point of view, etc. But such studies of stylistic influence or even of borrowings of content, of concepts, seem to me to focus upon the signs rather than the substance of the indebtedness, which has less to do with imitation than with validation. Perhaps what Hemingway got most from Gertrude Stein was confirmation—that his way of being a writer was all right, or rather that this way, one of several possibilities for him, was the right way because it brought out the precarious best in him. So I shall try to write about these matters in the spirit of Gorky's statement about Tolstoy: "As long as this man is alive, I am not alone in the world."

Actually, Tolstoy's role in Gorky's sense of self and vocation, his encouraging and confirming presence, probably came relatively late in Gorky's development, and was preceded by other good voices, good supervisory presences, beginning with his loving, storytelling grandmother, the one redemptive figure in that disaster area of poverty, brutality, and uprootedness that was Gorky's childhood. The reason a writer needs such presences is that they minister to the ongoing identity conflict, sometimes acute, sometimes dormant, but probably never resolved, that is characteristic of the literary vocation itself. A writer's identity, to paraphrase Erik Erikson, often begins to be formed in late adolescence, and points to the individual's unique core, and its intimate relation to his own group's inner tradition. As Erikson puts it, "the young individual must learn to be most himself when he means most to others, the others being those who mean most to him." A writer's "identity," then, involves a mutual relation, between what earlier ages would have called one's spirit or soul and the persistent ability to share it with kindred spirits. Without this early and then ongoing transaction, the problem of my young visitor is likely to arise, for he was trying to tell me he no longer knew who he was as a writer, so dependent had his identity become on a succession of immediate, receptive, but transient audiences, so removed had he become, in trying to accommodate them, from his unique core.

The young writer is typically beset on both sides of the issue—of "being most himself" and of "meaning most to others." On the one hand, he is likely to be just emerging from the adolescent warfare in which his creative self has been under attack from his conforming, socialized self for being freakish, timid, unpopular. On the other hand, he is also beginning the process, likely as not, of challenging the values of his home and community, which are felt to be inimical to a literary career but which are also connected to the "inner tradition" that he sooner or later finds he abandons at his peril.

Hence the importance of the right literary role model. "As long as this man is alive, I am not alone in the world." Such a figure nurtures the young writer in the estranged and divided state that William James calls being "twice born." Part authority figure, part ally, whether real or imagined, the right older writer confers upon the enterprise of writing a more powerful and refined version of *your* way of feeling, *your* sense of truth. His durable presence instills within you a hopefulness that you can somehow, someday, embody—not imitate but embody—the same felt values that this higher kindred spirit does. By being there, if only in your imagination, he prevents you from being an orphan as a writer—merely your parents' son, on the one hand, and your dubiously sensitive inner side, on the other. From this influence can come the beginnings of a style, because as you fall under the spell of the writer, you try to make the bond a little tighter and more intimate by being adopted, as it were, by his voice. But the durable influence, I believe, is from the kindred but refined attitudes and values behind the voice, which center and inspire you by evoking the new but "persistent sameness of self." It's not so very different from finding a best friend or a good psychotherapist who brings out and confirms your better nature, who prompts your calmest, most personal, most truthful voice. It's also not so very different from prayer.

Not all influences, as I've said, are centering and enabling ones. Erikson observes that the twice-born are particularly vulnerable to new ideologies that provide answers to those pressing questions that come with a new identity and also offer a way of repudiating the past life which nourished and frustrated the self. At the time, for example, that I was starting to think of myself as a writer, there was a prevailing literary ideology, known as the New Criticism. Its principal canon was that literature was best read hermetically and hermeneutically. The true meaning and emotion of a poem or story or a novel were to be found in the text itself, especially between the lines, where the deeper content was hidden away from common view in the form of ambiguity, irony, paradox. Literature was the Great Tradition of sacrosanct texts, and a literary vocation was like a priestly one, in which you first mastered these texts and the mode of interpretation before you were really entitled to practice the rites. There was even a recondite, mysterious language—"sacramental vision," "social anagogic," "the heresy of unintelligence," and so forth—which bespoke the hieratic aspiration. The New Criticism and its favorite texts and authors were suffused in a Catholic or Anglo-Catholic aura or an American Protestant one, and even had room in them for the anti-Semitism of Eliot and Pound. All of which I was caught up in by the time I was a junior at Michigan, and I was carried away until my coarse, practical, middle-class Jewish background and its heavyhearted liberal moralism were all but out of sight, much less reach.

Erikson observes that the twice-born does not necessarily solve his identity problem when he adopts a new ideology; instead he may well be creating a kind of pseudo-self and a subsequent crisis at the point when he "half-realizes that he is fatally overcommitted to what he is not." This was to be the story of my next five years: a pretentious literary self with fetishistic notions of detachment and purity of style and covertly placed meanings. Mostly I wrote stories over and over again, modeled on the austere surfaces of Joyce's *Dubliners* or Flaubert's "Un Coeur Simple," beneath which lay a circuitry that was switched on only at the end by an epiphany that was supposed to cast a subtle retrospective light. Or something like that. A full account of this dead end is in the previous essay, "Silence, Exile, and Cunning."

Fortunately, life did not leave my pseudo-self alone. While I was still at Michigan I wrote a review for the *Daily* of the stories of William Carlos Williams. Since he, too, was part of the modernist pantheon, I assumed that his stories were much more complex than they seemed and I gave them the exegetical treatment, as though Williams were Kafka, ambiguities and paradoxes everywhere, whereas his stories were really much more like those of his fellow physician Chekhov—all eyes and heart. The review was rejected as being too "obscure." At first this didn't dismay me. What would a newspaper editor know about symbolic meaning? Looking for vindication, I showed my review to my favorite English professor. He said that my writing style had certainly changed a lot since the last time he'd read it. He also said that reading my review made him feel as if he'd been hung by his suspenders.

His name was Herbert Barrows. He wasn't a New Critic either, but I took his response hard. He was the most civilized man I had yet met, a Boston bachelor who might have stepped out of the pages of a Henry James novel, one of those discreet tutelary figures like Ralph Touchett or Lambert Strether, who say little but understand everything. That Barrows had thought well of my writing had been one of my first and abiding incentives to become a writer. I'd also hung around him because he made me feel interesting to myself; there was a Jamesian encounter going on between us—between Cambridge, Massachusetts, and Elizabeth, New Jersey, as well as between a seasoned literary mind and a green one. I particularly loved his sense of humor, its wryness, freshness, accuracy—which was his way of relating to life while keeping his retiring distance. I once asked him, for example, if he'd been at Michigan when Auden was. No, he'd come there shortly after. "But you could pretty well follow his doings by the trail of sulfur he left."

Barrows had no literary method to teach me, other than to read a writer until you'd gotten "the hang" of his work.

He seemed to have the hang of everyone from Henry Adams to Henry Miller. What he had to teach me was more primary than method: it was literary taste, which he communicated with his whole being. For, being alone and rather reclusive, he was sustained by the arts and treated their works accordingly, as nutritive and pleasurable or not. Hence his judgments were unaffected by fashions, conventions, and pretensions and came directly from his character. He said that a good style was like a simple, expensive black dress that you could then make expressive in your own way: a bad style was like a gaudy dress from Woolworth's that you couldn't do anything else with. Perhaps he told me that on the day I sat in his office with my William Carlos Williams review and realized I was becoming not a little screwed up: i.e., "fatally overcommitted to what I was not." He said that he was going to try a course in something called "practical criticism" and suggested that it might be helpful to me.

It was a swell course or, better, group; even a kind of little community that assembled three times a week, so we could all learn from one another. The first thing Barrows did, for a while, was to read us a story or a poem and ask us to jot down what struck us about it. The first few times I was left at the post in a kind of panic. I could barely make out the lines on this one reading; how was I supposed to read between them? But this, of course, was the point of the exercise, which had to do not with ingenuity but with a kind of basic responsiveness known as paying attention, and with letting an impression grow inside you, and with articulating it. Clearly I had a lot to learn, beginning with the distinction between having an impression and making one. The pretender-critic—in me, the "pseudo-self," didn't have impressions, for that was to be impressionistic, which was the last thing a New Critic could afford to be in his pursuit of order and complexity. But someone with my name had better begin to have some impressions, if I was to stop handing in my desperate gibberish.

I had a lot of help from Barrows and from the group itself. There was one student who regularly came up with an amazingly sharp and interesting response. He seemed older than most of us, and he wore a hearing aid, which at first I thought might be really a miniature recorder, by which he would play back to himself what the rest of us had heard only once and were stumbling to remember. But as I began to see, his secret advantage lay elsewhere. Instead of groping about to describe or judge the poem or story—this poem is about X, what I like about it is Y, and so forth—he would find an image, which as he deftly developed it characterized the work and stated its appeal in such a way that it came back from his mind as freshly and distinctively as it had entered. I remember him speaking about a Yeats poem as being like a patch of ocean where two mighty warships had just fought and gone down, leaving a single empty lifeboat circling on the surface.

So I began to see that practical criticism was not only trusting your own impressions but also using your imagination to take the measure of a work, to turn it this way and that so as to locate it in the world of your own experience. As time went on and I got "the hang," it was like being let off a leash; my mind could nose around in a work, looking for its real interests, and respond with its natural energy. Criticism stopped being the ponderous, anxious task of lifting up the lines and sentences to see if you could find the structural grid underneath, or of injecting an image or a detail with added significance so that the work became like a chicken shot full of artificial hormones; instead criticism became more like play: i.e., making a piece of the world your own object, letting your response and the writer's work meet each other halfway.

Toward the end of Barrows's course, I wrote a review of e.e. cummings's collection *Xaipe*, which began:

> cummings is back again at his old stand, working this time out of a satchel with this cryptic Greek word pasted on its side. . . . Again one can watch adjectives dance into adverbs and participles put on weight and sit down as nouns, while the commas plummet and the clauses disappear and the parenthetical expressions get sawn in half. Whole mountains are again given the chance to dance and city pavements to grow flowers. The individual is sung back to significance and the social outcast to humanity.

I remember writing this for Barrows with a kind of "Look, Mom" élan. According to the English psychoanalyst D. W. Winnicott, who has a great deal to teach about these matters, that's how creativity begins: exploring, self-expressive play under the auspices of a mother who frees the child of anxiety; who is, in effect, one's first and determining audience. To Winnicott, psychotherapy is or should be a mode of play in this sense, and so are those other inventive activities that take place on the interface between one's inner and outer worlds. As the sort of "holding" figure Winnicott speaks of, Barrows enabled me to relax, to open up, to trust my imagination, and to stop pretending, which is really a form of compliance bred by anxiety. By his kindness and probity toward me as well as by his example, he helped me to see that I had to find some way to be literary and still be myself. But he could not lead me to my "inner tradition." A different figure was needed for that.

His name was Isaac Rosenfeld. I first met him through a story published in a *Partisan Review* anthology. This was in

1954, a few years after I had left college and was living in Greenwich Village, working occasionally as a waiter to support myself in my state of "alienation." Though I was where I was supposed to be, existentially speaking—that is, 180 degrees from the middle class—I was still writing stories so self-consciously posed they couldn't live. I was trying to be like the Joyce of *Dubliners* without his temperament, not to mention genius. Rosenfeld's story was called "The Hand That Fed Me" and tells of a young writer named Joseph Feigenbaum. It is set back in the early 1940s, when he has reached bottom. The WPA Writers' Project has folded, the war effort has passed him by, the last six women he has approached have turned him down. He receives a Christmas card from a Russian girl who flirted with him one day three years before, took him home for lunch, and then dropped him. Touched and wounded, hopeful and bitter, he writes one letter after another, none of which she answers. He becomes more desperate, even calls at her home, and is turned away by her brother. Finally, Feigenbaum comes to rest in his yearning and humiliation:

> For after all, what is humiliation? It does not endure forever. And when it has led us underground to our last comfort, look, it has served its purpose and is gone. Who knows when newer heights may not appear? I believe some men are capable of rising out of their own lives. They stand on the same ground as their brothers, but they are, somehow, transcendental, while their brothers are underground. Their only secret is a tremendous willingness—they do not struggle with themselves!

Here was Dostoevsky's underground man—but with an American-Jewish voice that I could immediately relate to. And not just his voice. Here I was, running around New York in a fake tuxedo looking for work as a temporary waiter. I, whose motto was Stephen Dedalus's "*Non serviam*"! Like Feigenbaum I was pretty confused, and like him I could no more stop struggling with myself than I could fly. But I had found someone who understood me, who knew better than I where I was coming from and what I was looking for. As Feigenbaum says to his beautiful, heedless *shiksa:*

> Be gentle to the unfulfilled, be good to it. We are accustomed to sing the joys of the happy, the fulfilled men. Let us also sings the joys of the desolate, the empty men. Theirs is the necessity without fulfillment, but it is possible that even to them—who knows—some joy may come.

This heart-flooded story that somehow managed to soar at the end—at least in my lofty mind, busy with its own unwanted offerings and resignations—was the first thing that fastened me to Rosenfeld. A couple of years later, when I decided to try graduate school, I chose Chicago, partly because I'd heard he was teaching there. He died before I met him, but that made him even more of a shining presence to me. I'd slip away, now and then, from the scholarly grind in the library stacks to hunt up his pieces in *Partisan Review, New Republic, Commentary,* et al. He had much to teach me, not the least of which had to do with my false consciousness of "alienation." One of his essays dealt with Sartre and the underground and began with the thought that modern writers like to believe they stand at a necessary remove from society, resisting, if passively, its disorder, amorality, and so forth.

> This has put a high value on confessions, disclosures of the private life and its feelings, usually revulsions, which earlier ages have found neither interesting nor tolerable. The tone of very much modern writing is,

> accordingly, one of malaise. But we are so accustomed to it, we are seldom aware of it as such; and when we do take this malaise into direct account, we readily mistake it for what it is not—a report from the underground.

The burden of this passage—as relevant today as it was thirty years ago—is that writers have no more right to their disaffection than anyone else, particularly in view of the self-preening uses to which it is put. This was a good thing for me to hear; it was also exhilarating to see Rosenfeld arraign Sartre for taking the view from the café—"its contactlessness, the emptiness and superfluity of existence, the sexual miseries and perversions, violence and self-destruction"—as the leading truths of existence. Sartre, after all, was the leading intellectual in the West at the time and existentialism was everywhere in vogue. Yet here was Rosenfeld, in his calm, clear way, exercising his right, as he would say elsewhere, to "take a good look" at the attitude with which Sartre approached experience and to weigh it on a firm, moral scale.

This was not like the New Criticism at all. Rosenfeld's criticism was full of immediate encounter and judgment ("I should like to say what I must about Jean Malaquais' war diary with the humility owing to a man who has been through hell"), yet was lucid and even-tempered and steady. I knew in my Jewish bones, well before Matthew Arnold confirmed it, that literature was first and last a criticism of life, and now I had found a voice that embodied this viewpoint in a warm, masculine, somehow familiar way. It was less like discovering a writer than like finding a terrific older brother.

The first significant essay I wrote was done under his spell. The *TLS* was planning a special supplement on the American imagination and asked Philip Roth to write an essay on the Jewish role in American letters. He said that he didn't know much about it, but he had this friend in Chicago who did. What little I knew about it I'd already exhausted in a review of *Goodbye, Columbus,* which compared Roth to Bellow and Malamud as, not surprisingly, Jewish moralists. But there were professors of mine at Chicago who would have killed to get a letter to the editor into the *TLS,* and I was being asked to contribute three thousand words. If I didn't know much about the subject, I did know my way around a research library by then (I was doing a dissertation on Henry James), so I got a new bundle of three-by-five cards and camped out in the stacks. I read Rosenfeld's colleagues at *Partisan Review* and *Commentary* and *Midstream,* and as much as I could about the historical background of Jewish writing in America. I had six weeks, and in dutiful graduate student fashion, I gave myself five weeks to do the research and one week to write. And then toward the very end, just as I was beginning to do the writing, I broke a finger playing first base for a local tavern. It seemed like a judgment. I could barely type, which was the way I wrote, and the whole project, hasty and shaky at best, began to collapse.

I sat there thinking: Here's your big chance and it's all going down the drain. In despair, I picked up a posthumous essay of Rosenfeld's which had just come out in *The Chicago Review.* At one point, he talks about himself as being "uncertain, alone, and much of the time afraid," which was exactly how I felt, and about the importance of the attitude with which you approached experience. About the only thing I was sure of about Jewish writing was my attitude, which was one of enthusiasm for the contribution that so many novelists, playwrights, poets, and critics were making to American letters. Until now, I'd avoided Jewish chauvinism like the plague, but there was no getting around my discovery, amplified by my research, that the contemporary writers who interested and inspired me were Jewish—whether overtly so like Singer or Howe or Malamud, or more indirectly so like Trilling or Arthur Miller or Stanley Kunitz. What I could trust, then, was my own excitement that the Jewish sensibility, however broadly defined, had suddenly come into its own, that there was what Leslie Fiedler had called the "breakthrough."

That word, "breakthrough," began to resonate in my mind. I sat down again, with my broken finger, and my heart in my mouth, and began to write a passionate essay in real trembling. I sent it off, thinking it would be rejected summarily as being the babblings of an enthusiast. But it wasn't; it was published and was even well received. In fact, it got me a job at *Commentary*; Norman Podhoretz said that he could tell the writer didn't know what he was talking about, but had guessed right 90 percent of the time, and so would probably make a good editor.

I went to New York, became an editor of and contributor to *Commentary*, and a new nephew in what Podhoretz was to call the "Family." After a few months I met William Phillips, who asked me to write a piece for *Partisan Review*. If the *TLS* was august at that time, *Partisan Review* was out of sight for a young critic of my background. *PR* was the Castle. So I'd arrived. Or so I thought.

The truth is that virtually every piece I've written since has meant starting out again. At a certain point, the enterprise invariably breaks down and I don't see how I can write this review or essay; in fact, I shouldn't write anymore at all. Because I continue to lose confidence, including the confidence that may have accrued from seeing the last piece in print: the reasonably clear, coherent product of all that disarray. It's the ongoing identity crisis I mentioned earlier: this constant struggle, this manual and psychic labor we perform against our doubts and misgivings and sense of unworthiness, in which we do rely, at times quite desperately, on those good voices in our heads. I know this to be so because each time the crisis hits full force again—when I say I must abandon this, it's just too painful to go on, I'm too ignorant, too superficial, I don't have enough time, I can't write anyway—I'll open a book of literary pieces, *An Age of Enormity* by Isaac Rosenfeld, read a page or two, quiet down, gather myself, and say: Well, that's what it's all about, he's just telling the truth as best he can, get on with it.

(1982)

Some Words for Muriel Rukeyser

When I first met Muriel Rukeyser, in 1975 or so, she was a large, somewhat top-heavy woman in her early sixties with a broad, crafty Russian face—the kind you might see behind the counter of a Jewish deli—an infirm walk and a full heart. She was one of those people who come across immediately, which I remember thinking was surprising in a poet as famous as she was. Fame, at least literary fame, tends to make people cagey, not to mention the conflicts that maintain them as poets, so that, in person, they typically usually wear a sleeve on their hearts.

Not Muriel. She arrived before you on a wave of feeling each time you saw her, a bit disheveled from the ride. At least, that's how I remember our meetings. What first brought us together was a matter of literary politics. A faction at PEN was looking for someone to stand for president at the last moment. We felt we needed a writer of renown whose career would immediately have a commanding appropriateness for the post: a veteran literary freedom fighter. Some of us were also hoping for an activist who might get American PEN off the dime of a certain dated genteelness on which we felt it had been languishing and make it a center of literary community in New York.

For both jobs Muriel seemed a terrific choice. She was one of the few literary radicals from the 1930s who hadn't lost faith in her social conscience: that special blend of outrage and tenderness which was always on tap in her poetry—"the desperate music/poverty makes." Her radicalism still prompted her active engagement with the causes and movements of the 1960s and early 1970s, as it had in Spain and in the coal-belt factory and mining towns and in the Deep South thirty years ago. At the same time, she was already a kind of one-woman center of energy and community for poetry. She was a mainstay of the Translation Center, an organization that was trying to reclaim this wasteland sector of American letters. She was also a force for good in the 92nd Street Y poetry program, which was in several ways a model for what we wanted to do with American PEN. Muriel had a special workshop going there; instead of teaching poetry writing, as her peers did, she taught poetry reading. When her friend Louise Bernikow once asked her what she did besides writing, Muriel said she was "mainly reading poems with people: undergraduates; two year olds; dropouts; the old; the blind, etc." She was also reading a lot of poems by young poets; she was a rarity in that way too, a "name" who took the manuscripts that were thrust at her at readings and meetings, who tried hard to get the good ones published. She was genuinely approachable: that warm, steady look that took you in in just the way you liked to be seen, that smile which gave you welcome, one which could easily be taken for the smile of Fortune.

At the time we approached her on the PEN matter, Muriel was recovering from a heart attack, the latest of her cardiovascular problems, and looked it. Listening to her breathing, I wondered whether we were asking too much of her. Sitting there in her studio loft in the artists' housing project known as Westbeth (where else would she live?), surrounded and protected by the tools and arrangements and icons of a working literary life, what did she need us and our thorny issue and airy plans for? But she listened to us intently and then, I think, she held up her hand and said, "All right, I know what needs to be done now. I'll do it if you'll help me."

And so she did and so we did. The bureaucracy of PEN at the time didn't know what to make of her and gave her a hard time. She didn't go through channels and agendas very well; as Grace Paley says, "Muriel was like the ocean instead of a stream or a puddle." There was a poet, Kim Chi Ha, in prison in South Korea. Instead of sending letters and cables to Seoul, Muriel sent herself. She went to see the authorities and when they wouldn't let her visit Kim Chi Ha in his cell, she went to the prison anyway and stood outside in the mud and rain and bore witness. Back home at the executive board meetings, she also poured herself out. Somewhat indifferent to the housekeeping problems—to which her standard response was a wily "What is the board's pleasure?"—she pressed on to the heavy issues, such as decentralizing PEN through regional centers and creating programs for writers in the New York area. Her pet project was a conference on "the life of the writer," a topic that had a kind of numinous meaning for her but remained somewhat vague to the rest of us. Without much support, she persisted and brought it off in Washington, D.C. In her public actions, as in her poetry, she trusted her visionary gleam, a trust that made her, in the fullest sense of the word, undiscourageable.

Gallant Muriel. The final few years beggar description. Her health, which had always been precarious, was devastated by a serious stroke, by cataracts, and by her longtime nemesis, diabetes, "the Caligula of diseases," as Richard Selzer puts it. Still, as always, she did what she could, writing poetry and bringing out her *Collected Poems,* going her appointed rounds of literary panels and juries and conferences and keeping up her readings. As Grace Schulman tells it, "Whenever poetry was being celebrated, Muriel would somehow get there." At one such event, a group of poets was assembled on a stage; Muriel arrived and then, walker and all, virtually blind, she somehow hoisted herself up on that stage, for that was where she belonged.

In one of her late poems, "Facing Sentencing" (she was about to go to jail for protesting the war on the steps of the Senate), these lines appear:

> But fear is not to be feared
> Numbness is. To stand before my judge
> Not knowing what I mean.

Muriel was not a measured poet. Like Whitman, a powerful early influence, she was a sayer rather than a maker. Her mind ranged and ranged, from aviation to zoology, from the mines of West Virginia to the sacred caves of India, from the writings of Akiba to the speeches of Wendell Willkie. In her *Collected Poems,* there is a series of portraits, of the early physicist Willard Gibbs, the painter Albert Ryder, the aristocratic man of letters John Jay Chapman, the labor organizer Ann Burlack, and the composer Charles Ives. Her verse is typically open, notational, even documentary; its rhythm comes from the onrushing movement in her mind of the experience, from the flow of her passion for the object. There are transcripts of trials in her poems, the minutes of congressional hearings, detailed descriptions of silicosis. Her experiments tended to be on the side of plenitude rather than restriction, of inclusiveness rather than refinement. For she had much to clarify, much to keep alive. In her body and in her mind, in her life and in her art, she fought against numbness.

Muriel had a peculiar habit. She never said goodbye. You would call her up, an animated conversation would ensue, reach a conclusion, and then suddenly she would be gone. Now she's hung up for good, leaving her poems to speak from her silence to ours. One of her last ones, "St. Roach," seems to me pure Muriel.

> For that I never knew you, I only learned to
>   dread you,
> for that I never touched you, they told me you
>   are filth,
> they showed me by every action to despise your
>   kind;
> for that I saw my people making war on you,
> I could not tell you apart, one from another,
> for that in childhood I lived in places clear of you,
> for that all the people I knew met you by
> crushing you, stamping you to death; they
>   poured boiling water on you, they
>   flushed you down,
> for that I could not tell one from another
> only that you were dark, fast on your feet,
>   and slender.
>   Not like me.
> For that I did not know your poems
> And that I do not now know any of your sayings
> And that I cannot speak or read your language
> And that I do not sing your songs
> And that I do not teach our children
>   to eat your food
>   or know your poems
>   or sing your songs

But that we say you are filthing our food
But that we know you not at all.

Yesterday I looked at one of you for the first time.
You were lighter than the others in color, that
  was neither good nor bad.
I was really looking for the first time.
You seemed troubled and witty.
Today I touched one of you for the first time.
You were startled, you ran, you fled away
Fast as a dancer, light, strange and lovely
  to the touch.
I reach, I touch, I begin to know you.

(1980)

Art and Generosity

The novelist John Keeble told me this story. He was living in Seattle and working at an industrial job when he found out that he had been accepted at the Iowa Writers Workshop. It was a last-minute thing, classes were starting in a week, he was just scraping by and had no money to move his family. An older friend of his at Boeing offered to give him a hand. Working straight through the weekend, he built a frame for Keeble's pick-up truck to make it into a small van, then helped him to pack and load all his movables. By Sunday night the job was done, in time for Keeble to be on his way to his new prospects. His cup running over, he said to his friend, "I don't know how to repay you." "You can't," he replied. "You'll have to do it for someone else. Pass it on."

The story has meant a lot to me. It has taken me out of pettiness and selfishness at times in my work by reminding me of the obligation we all have to pass on the good that we have received. In so doing, it reaches into a part of the self that is not for hire and to another part that attaches one to the rest of humanity, and it makes a connection between them. It also provides an image to set against the calculation and greed that swell up in a society awash in self-interest and consumerism.

But I've recently come to see that the story goes well beyond the uses I've made of it. It's like a cutting from a vigorous, complex, and beautiful plant whose roots go wide and deep into the earth: in this case, the strata of human nature and experience. They ago back to societies whose whole way of life was built around gift exchange and to a folk wisdom contained in a global literature that deals with the nature of material and interior gifts, and to the religions, including our own, that began by thinking of little else. Some of this wealth of customs, sentiments, insights, and creeds survive in and illuminate our own gift exchanges; they also can be found at the heart of the highest mode of gift exchange that remains with us—the creative process itself. I've been learning about all this from a splendid new writer named Lewis Hyde, whose book *The Gift*, with its esoteric but perfectly apt subtitle, "Imagination and the Erotic Life of Property," seems to light up everything it touches, including the reader's mind.

I imagine that Hyde and Keeble and his friend would understand one another immediately. They come from the same place, morally speaking, and share a similar background, Hyde having worked as a carpenter and an electrician and a counselor on an alcoholic ward to support his literary interests. He also comes out of the 1960s, the foolishness and smugness of the counterculture stripped away, its articles of faith in nature, community, and spirit presented in an enlightened and tempered form; he seems like a young Robert Bly or Gary Snyder. Touch his sentences and you touch a man who is going his own way, traveling far, but who is glad to have your company. He will show you the wider vistas of otherness and credence to which we still belong once we get away from what he calls the "small ego" and the "commodity society."

Hyde tells us at the start that he came to his subject in

an existential way: that is, as a self-employed poet, translator, and scholar, he had gifts that the society he lived in didn't support and barely valued. Indeed, in its increasing reliance on forms of work that are highly rationalized, routinized, impersonal, and in its awarding of status not so much to what one contributes but to what one consumes, America today can be viewed as the antithesis of art. Sensing, too, that poetry and scholarship are gifts that must be bestowed, that the work of the imagination and the documented intuition are not completed until they are carried over, as he puts it, into "the real" by means of publication or its equivalents—that is, by public validation and use—he came to perceive the problem of the market for his work as doubly onerous, making him feel trivial as well as poor. Trying to think his way out of this impasse, he became interested in the anthropology, theology, and folk literature of gift exchange as a commerce within and between tribes, as well as with the natural and spiritual realms that completed and guaranteed the flow of the cycle.

He was particularly struck and instructed by the literature on the "spirit of the gift": the generative principle or "eros" that provided the increase and whose exchange and worship provided the "feeling bond" in the members of the group, the bond that protected the source, fostered solidarity in the group, and conducted its members beyond the personal and tribal ego, beyond nature itself, and into the mysteries of creation. Thus the Northwest Indian tribes treated the first-caught salmon as a visiting chief, then ate it, and then returned the bones to the sea to ensure the supply and its return; so, too, the Maori hunters gave some of their birds to priests, who brought them back to the forest to feed its *hau;* so, too, the Israelite priests burned the fat of the firstborn male sheep and cattle on the altar "as an odor pleasing to the Lord." The person or group that feeds

the hau and is fed by it thereby enters a realm of life that underlies creaturely existence and consciousness and endures beyond it. Hyde draws upon the distinction in Greek between its two terms for life:

> *Bios* is limited life, characterized life, life that dies. *Zöe* is the life that endures; it is the thread that runs through bios-life and is not broken when the particular perishes.

From this principle of generation and generosity in cyclical exchange, it is but a step to the creative cycle of the source gift, of the artist's generous and grateful labor by means of his imagination to shape and enliven it, and of its bestowal on his or her community, tradition, faith, and the race itself:

> A circulation of gifts nourishes those parts of our spirit that are not entirely personal, parts that derive from nature, the group, the race, or the gods. Furthermore, although these wider spirits are a part of us, they are not "ours"; they are endowments bestowed upon us. To feed them by giving away the increase they have brought us is to accept that our participation in them brings with it an obligation to preserve their vitality.

The artist, then, wishes to nurture, use, and bestow what he has been given: the gifts of his sources and of his talent. What he has to pass along are the fruits of this intercourse, the images, as Hyde finely puts it, which enable the rest of us to imagine our lives. Or, in the famous words of Joseph Conrad, which Hyde quotes twice as a kind of *ur*-text:

> The artist appeals . . . to that in us which is a gift and not an acquisition—and, therefore, more permanently

enduring. He speaks to our capacity for del
wonder and to the sense of mystery surroun
lives; to our sense of pity, and beauty, and pa
latent feeling of fellowship with all creation
subtle but invincible conviction of solidarity t
together the loneliness of innumerable heart
solidarity . . . which binds together all human
dead to the living and the living to the unb

As Hyde develops his vast array of sources t
ethic/aesthetic for the situation of the creative
cinating and compelling perspective comes in
the one hand, it functions as an incisive and
fresh critique of the commodity-exchange socie
rates and alienates its members from each ot
spiritualizes life and denatures the world, tha
greed, envy, competitiveness, and callousness
getting and spending we lay waste our powe
that exploits the essence and maldistributes the
the same time, Hyde takes literature out of the
various elites in which it has been languishin
identity and restores it to its rightful place in
community, the agent of its moral memory a
mover and movement of its spirit. He does so
of complexity and subtlety: his understanding
tive process is phenomenal, his portraits of W
Pound as the culminating examples of art u
gift exchange are models of critical imaginatio
and acumen. *The Gift* is a book about life and
one who knows and knows.

My one disappointment is that it doesn't co
ward into the present and deal with the actual
art in a commodity society and culture. At th
tells us that he has come around to believing th
if he watches his step, can make his way withou

slav, which he quotes, "have no cl
to one's fellows, there arises a simp
light." Buy two copies of this book:
with and the other to pass on.

Writing in the Cold: The First Ten Years

During the decade of editing *New American* (later *American*) *Review*, I was often struck by how many gifted young writers there were in America. They would arrive every month, three or four of them, accomplished or close to it, full of wit and panache or a steady power or a fine, quiet complexity. We tried to devote 25 percent of each issue to these new voices and seldom failed to meet the quota. Where are they all coming from? I'd ask myself, though more as an exclamation than a question. They came from everywhere: from Dixon, New Mexico and Seal Rock, Oregon, as well as Chicago and San Francisco, from English departments in community colleges as well as the big creative writing centers. They came amid the twelve hundred or so manuscripts we received each month. America in the late sixties and seventies appeared to be on a writing binge, and eugenics alone would seem to dictate that half of one percent of the writing population would be brilliant.

But what has happened to all that bright promise? When I look through the cumulative index of *NAR/AR*, I see that perhaps one fourth of our discoveries have gone on to have reasonably successful careers; about the same number still have marginal ones, part of the alternative literary community of the little magazines and small presses. And about half have disappeared, or at least their names are again as obscure to me as they were when they came from out of the blue. It's as though some sinister force were at work, a kind of literary population control mechanism that kills off the surplus talent we have been developing or causes it to wither slowly away.

Literary careers are difficult to speculate about. They are so individual, so subject to personal circumstances that are often hidden to the writer himself. Also, what is not hidden is likely to be held so secretly that even the editor who works closely with a writer knows little more about his or her sources of fertility and potency than anyone else does. And those writers who fail are even more inclined to draw a cover of silence or obfuscation over the reasons. Still, it's worth considering why some gifted writers have careers and others don't. It doesn't appear to be a matter of the talent itself—some of the most natural writers, the ones who seemed to shake their prose or poetry out of their sleeves, are among the disappeared. As far as I can tell, the decisive factor is durability. For the gifted writer, durability seems to be directly connected to how one deals with uncertainty, rejection, and disappointment, from within as well as from without, and how effectively one incorporates them into the creative process itself, particularly in the prolonged first stage of a career. In what follows, I'll be writing about fiction writers, the group I know best. But I don't imagine that poets, playwrights, essayists, will find much that is different from their experience.

The gifted young writer will say: I already know about rejection and uncertainty. I know what to expect. Let's get on to surviving. I have to reply: You know about them much as a new immigrant to Alaska knows about cold and ice and isolation. Also, if you come from an enlightened middle-class family that has supported your desire to become a writer and if you have starred in college and then in a graduate writing program, you are like someone who is immigrating from Florida.

Thirty years ago, when I came out of college and went off to become a writer, I expected to remain unknown and unrewarded for ten years or so. So did my few associates in this precarious enterprise. Indeed our low expectations were a measure of our high seriousness. We were hardly going to give ourselves less time and difficulty than our heroes—Joyce, Flaubert, et al.—gave themselves. Also it was such a dubious career that none of our families understood, much less supported, us. Nor were there any universities—except for two, Iowa and Stanford—that wanted us around once we'd gotten a B.A., except as prospective scholars. Not that we knew how to cope with the prolonged uncertainty, isolation, indifference, and likely poverty that faced us—who does until he has been through them?—but at least we expected their likelihood and even understood something of their necessity.

I don't find that our counterparts of the past decade or more are nearly as aware of the struggle to come, or have even begun to be emotionally and mentally prepared for it. As the products of postwar affluence and an undemanding literary education, most of them have very little experience with struggle of any kind. Also their expectations of a writer's life have been formed by the mass marketing and subsidization of culture and by the creative writing industry. Their career models are not, say, Henry Miller or William Faulkner but John Irving or Ann Beattie. Instead of the jazz musicians and painters of thirty years ago somehow making do, the other arts provide them with the model life-styles of rock stars and of the young princes of Soho. Instead of a Guggenheim or Yaddo residency far up the road, there is a whole array of public and private grants, colonies, writing fellowships, that seem just around the corner. And most of all, there is the prospect, no longer as immediate but still only a few significant publications away, of teaching, with its comfortable life and free time. As the poet William Matthews recently remarked, "What our students seem to mainly want to do is to become us, though they have no idea of what we've gone through."

I don't think one can understand the literary situation today without taking into account the one genuine revolutionary development in American letters during the second half of the century: the rise of the creative writing programs. At virtually one stroke we have solved the age-old problem of how literary men and women are to support themselves. Most fiction writers today mainly support themselves by teaching writing. To do so, they place themselves in an insulated and relatively static environment whose main population every year grows a year younger and whose beliefs, attitudes, and privileges become the principal reflection of the society at large. The campus writer also risks disturbing the secret chemistry of his gift by trying to communicate it in class as well as defusing and depersonalizing it in coping with student writing. Then, too, the peculiar institution of tenure prompts the younger writer to publish too quickly and the older one too little. It's no wonder that steady academic employment has done strange things to a number of literary careers and has tended to devitalize the relation between literature, particularly fiction, and society.

The graduate writing program is also a mixed blessing to career-minded young writers by starting them out under extremely favorable—that is to say, unreal—conditions. At a place like Johns Hopkins or Houston or Sarah Lawrence or the twenty or thirty others with prestigious programs, the chances are that several highly accomplished, even famous, writers will be reading a student's work, perhaps even John Barth or Donald Barthelme or Grace Paley. If he is genuinely talented, his work will be taken very seriously because his teachers need to feel that what they are doing for a living isn't entirely a waste of spirit. As well as a dazzling ally or even two, he will also have a responsive and usually supportive audience—the other writers in the program—and a small, intense milieu that envisions the good life as a literary career, particularly the model supplied by his teachers. And of course, he will have a structure of work habits provided by the workshops, degree requirements, and so forth.

For reasons that I shall come to, I think graduate writing programs are mostly wasted on the young. But at their best, they're often good correctives to undergraduate ones in giving the gifted a more realistic sense of where they stand among their peers (there are now three or four others in a class of fifteen), in guiding them in the direction of publishable writing, and in providing a certain amount of validation to a young writer's still green and shaky sense of identity. In general, these programs are a kind of greenhouse that enables certain talents to bloom, particularly those that produce straightforward, well-made stories, the kind that teach well in class, and, depending on the teacher, even certain eccentric ones, particularly those patterned on a prevailing fashion of postmodernism.

At the same time, the graduate writing program makes the next stage, that of being out there by oneself in the cold world, particularly chilling. Instead of a personal and enlightened response to her writing, the young writer now receives mostly rejection slips. Instead of standing out, she now finds herself among the anonymous masses. Instead of being in a literary community, she now has to rely on herself for stimulation, support, and discipline. Also she now has to fit writing into the interstices left by a full-time job or by parenting. In short, her or his character as a writer will now be tested—and not for a year or two but much more likely for five or ten.*

That's how long it generally takes for the gifted young fiction writer to find his way, to come into her own. The two fiction writers whose work appears to be the most admired and influential in the graduate writing programs just now are Bobbie Ann Mason and Raymond Carver. Mason spent some seven years writing an unpublished novel, and then story after story, sending each one to Roger Angell at *The New Yorker,* getting it back, writing another, until finally the twentieth one was accepted. In his essay "Fires," Carver tells about the decade of struggle to write the stories that grew out of his heavily burdened life of "working at crap jobs" and raising two children, until an editor, Gordon Lish, began to beckon from the tower of *Esquire.* (It would be another seven years before Carver's first book appeared.) Three novelists whose "arrival" I witnessed—Lynne Sharon Schwartz, Joan Chase, and Douglas Unger—were by then in their thirties and had already written at least one unpublished novel. My most recent find, Alan Hewat, the author of *Lady's Time* is in his early forties and has written two unpublished novels.

Why this long delay of recognition? Each of the above writers doesn't regard it now as a delay. All of them say the unpublished novel or novels shouldn't have been published. They were mainly part of a protracted effort to find a voice, a more or less individual and stable style which best uncovers and delivers the writer's material. This often re-

*In the three years or so since this essay was written, there has developed a wave of publishing fashion that favors the young fiction writer, in some cases the younger the better. But like the previous vogue, "the brat pack" is more a marketing than a literary development, I believe, and will soon be replaced by the next bit of trendiness. Further, the young writers in question will likely find that their flurry of fame and fortune will postpone and then further complicate the problems of a durable literary vocation that are discussed in the following pages.

quires a period of time for the self to mature and stabilize, particularly the part one writes from. The writer in his middle twenties is not that far removed from adolescence and its insecurities. Indeed the sensitivity he is trying to develop and discipline comes precisely from that side of himself that he likely tried to negate only a few years ago as freakish, unmanly, and unpopular. Hence the painful paradoxes of his new vocation: that his most vulnerable side is now his working one, the one that has to produce, the one that goes forth into the world and represents him; further, that from the side that had been the most uncertain, he must now find his particular clarity about how and why he and others live and his conviction about what is significant in their ways and days as well as in his own. If he is writing a novel, he must also develop a settled and sustainable moral point of view if its meaning is to cohere. And all this from a self that is likely to be rejected each time it looks for confirmation by sending out a manuscript.

The second difficulty is that the typical M.F.A. in creative writing has spent eighteen of his, say, twenty-five years in school. Thus he is likely to be still fairly limited in his grasp of how people live and feel and look at things other than in books and films, sources he still needs to sift out, and other than in his family and its particular culture, from which he is likely still rebelling in typical ways that lead to banal content. Throw in a few love affairs and friendships, a year or two of scattered work experience, perhaps a trip abroad, and his consciousness is still likely to be playing a very limited hand. (There appears to be a long-term psychosocial trend over the past fifty years or so in which each generation takes several years longer to mature: Many of the postwar generation of fiction writers, such as Mailer, Bellow, Styron, Baldwin, Bowles, Flannery O'Connor, Truman Capote, Updike, Roth, Reynolds Price, were highly developed by their mid to late twenties.) As often happens, a young writer's gift itself may fake him out of understanding his true situation by producing a few exceptional stories, part of a novel from the most deeply held experiences of his life. But except for these, he has only his share of the common life of his age, which he must learn to see and think about and depict in a complex and uncommon way. This takes much more time.

A young writer I know won a national award a few years ago for the best short story submitted by the various writing programs. It was one of a group of several remarkable stories that she published, almost all of them about members of her family, gray-collar people finely viewed in their contemporary perplexities from her observation post as the kid sister and the one who would leave. But almost nothing she wrote after that came near their standard; the new fiction was mostly about a difficult love affair that she was still too close to to write about with the same circumspection and touch as her family stories. After they were turned down, she was left low and dry; finally, she went to work reading for a film company and learning script development. Recently she sold an adaptation of one of her early stories, is writing another script, and is looking to take up fiction again. By the time she publishes her first collection, if she does, she'll be in her thirties too.

What she has been going through as a fiction writer is the crisis of rejection from both without and within, and more important from within. For writers are always sending themselves rejection letters, as the late George P. Elliot observed, to this sentence and that paragraph, to this initial characterization and that turn of the story, or, heartbreak time, to the story that has eluded months of tracking it, the hundred pages of a novel that has come to a dead stop.

The gifted young writer has to learn through adversity to separate rejection of one's work from self-rejection, and with respect to the latter, self-criticism (otherwise known as revision and what one might call re-envision) from self-distrust. For the inexperienced writer, a year or two of rejection or a major rejection—say, of a novel—can lead all too easily to self-distrust, and from there to a disabling distrust of the writing process itself. Anxious, depressed, defensive, the writer who is suffering this distrust, whether temporarily or chronically or terminally, gives up her most fundamental and enabling right: the right to write uncertainly, roughly, even badly. A garden in the early stage is not a pleasant or compelling place: it's a lot of arduous, messy, noisome work—digging up the hard ground, putting in the fertilizer, along with the seeds and seedlings. So with beginning a story or novel. The writer can't get her spadework done, can't lay in the bullshit from which something true can grow, can't set her imagination to seeding these dark and fecund places if she is worried about how comely her sentences are, how convincing her characters will be, how viable her plot. But the self-rejecting writer finds herself doing just that. Instead of going from task to task, she goes from creating to judging: from her mind to the typewriter to the wastebasket. In time, her mind forgoes the latter two stages and becomes a ruthless system of self-cancellation.

The longer this goes on, the more writing becomes not a process of planting and cultivating—or, perhaps more accurately, of mining and refining—but an issue of entitlement and prohibition. That is, what the writer sets down or merely thinks about must be so promising that her right to write is suddenly allowed again. But even if she hits upon an exciting first sentence or paragraph or even a whole opening development, just as surely as night follows day, the dull stuff returns, her uncertainty follows, and soon she is back in court again, testifying against herself. To stay in this state too long is to reach the dead end of narcissistic despair known as writer's block, in which one's vanity and guilt have so persecuted one's craft and imagination and so deprived them of their allies—heart, curiosity, will—that they have gone into exile and into the sanctuary of silence.

Unless he is a graphomaniac, the gifted writer is likely to be vulnerable to rejection from without and within, and how well he copes with them is likely to determine whether he has a genuine literary vocation or just a literary flair. To put the matter as directly as I can, rejection and uncertainty and disappointment are as much a part of a writer's life as snow and cold are of an Eskimo's: they are conditions one has to learn not only to live with but also to make use of.

The trouble with most talented first novels is that they lack a prolonged struggle with uncertainty. They typically keep as much as possible to the lived lines of the author's life, which provide the security of a certain factuality and probability but at the expense of depriving the imagination of its authority. Laden with unresolved conflicts, the voice is too insistent here, too vague there. Such a novel is also typically overstuffed and overwritten: the question of what belongs and what doesn't being too easily settled by leaving it in. The writer, particularly if he has some literary sophistication, may also try to quell uncertainty by allying himself with some current literary fashion. At the same time, the struggle with uncertainty may be here and there strongly engaged and won: The material rings true instead of derivatively, whether from experience or books; a power of understanding is abroad in the narrative, however intermittently. If there is enough earned truth and power, the manuscript is probably viable and its deadnesses are relatively detectable. The rest is mostly a matter of the writer's willingness to persist in his gift and its process and to put his ego aside.

This can take some very interesting and illuminating turns. Douglas Unger, whose first novel, *Leaving the Land*, was received with considerable acclaim in 1984, began writing it in 1976. He had already had a previous novel optioned by a major publisher, had rewritten it three times to meet his editor's reservations, only to have it finally rejected. "He literally threw the manuscript at me and told me to get out of his office. Since I didn't know what to do next, I didn't have an agent or anything, I enrolled at the Iowa Writers Workshop."

I met him there the following year when I used the opening section of his next novel to teach a workshop. It began with a young woman named Marge walking through a dusty farm town in the Dakotas, on her way to be fitted for a wedding dress by her prospective mother-in-law and barely able to put one foot after the other. It is just after World War II, in which her two brothers have been killed, and she has chosen the best of a bad lot of local men to help her father and herself to keep the farm going. Unger's writing was remarkably sensitive to the coarse and delicate weave of a farm girl's childhood and adolescence and to the pathos of her love life, in which her spunk and grace are manhandled by a series of misfits left behind by the war. At the same time, he wrote graphically about crops and farm machinery and the special misery of raising turkeys, and he brought the reader close to the local farmers' struggle with Nowell-Safebuy, a turkey-processing plant and part of a giant food trust that drives down their prices and wants their land. Marge's long reverie suddenly ends when a convoy of trucks transporting factory equipment rolls into town. In the midst of it is an attractive man in a snappy roadster. Sensing that her luck may have finally changed, she follows the newcomer into the local café. All in all, it was a terrific beginning.

About eighteen months later, Unger sent me the final manuscript. It was some seven hundred pages long. About one fifth was taken up by a separate story of German prisoners of war operating the turkey plant; the final third jumped ahead thirty years, to tell of the return of Marge's son to Nowell, which is now a ghost town, and then backed and filled. Along with its disconnected narrative line, the writing had grown strangely mock-allegorical and surreal in places, as though Unger's imagination had been invaded by an alien force, perhaps the fiction of Thomas Pynchon. Most disappointing of all, he seemed to have turned away from a story with a great deal of prospective meaning—the eradication of farmers and agrarian values by agribusiness—to make instead the postmodernist point of the pointlessness of it all. I wrote him a long letter, trying to itemize what had gone wrong, and ended by saying that I still felt there was a genuine novel buried inside this swollen one and hoped he would have the courage to find it. When he read the letter, Unger became so enraged he threw down the manuscript and began to jump on it, shouting, "But I've spent so much time on it already."

He didn't write anything for a year and a half. By then he was living on an unworked farm, owned by his wife's family, outside Bellingham, Washington, and had become a commercial fisherman. Then one night he woke up with the people he had written about on his mind, pulled out the manuscript, and began to reread it. His main reaction was a deep chagrin at the distortions he had made in telling their story. "I was running up against people every day who gave the lie to what I'd done to my characters. Then one day my wife's older sister turned up with one of her sons, to try to get the farm going again. I witnessed an incredible scene in which her will to revive the farm ran into his admission that he wanted nothing to do with it. This opened my eyes to the truth that the original version had gone off in the wrong direction. It was really about Marge's efforts all along—through her marriage, her staying in that forsaken community—to hold on to their land with the same tenacity her father had shown and pass it on to her son. Much of this material was already there, lying around undeveloped and untidy. In order to feel easy again, I had to rework it."

It took another three years to do so. I asked Unger what had sustained him, particularly in view of the crushing disappointment after revising his first novel. He told me that after he left Iowa City, he had spent some time in San Francisco with Raymond Carver, to whom he was related by marriage. "Anyone who knows Ray knows that you have to believe that if you write well you'll eventually get published. Also the one thing he kept saying to me was 'A good book is an honest one.' I knew that his whole career had been an effort to write honestly, so those words really sunk in. And they were just the ones I needed to hear. At Iowa I was so desperate to get published, some of the others already were or getting close, and I thought it would help if I put in a lot of postmodernist effects. Also, Barth and Barthelme and Pynchon were all the rage then and it was easy to be influenced by them."

He ended up with three novellas: Marge's early life culminating in her affair and marriage to the man in the roadster, who is the lawyer for the Safebuy Corporation and the farmers' immediate adversary; the prisoners-of-war story; Marge and her son twenty-five years later, her marriage long over, the farm and most of the area abandoned when the Safebuy scheme of "vertical ownership" fails, her life divided between the dying community and the bright lights of Belle Fourche, forty miles away, and her final effort to pass on the deed to her son, who can't wait to get away. A brave, sad, increasingly bleak wind of feeling blew through the final novella, joining it tonally as well as narratively to the first. Were they the buried novel? The prose of all three maintained the straightforward realism of the original opening, but Unger's style had grown diamond hard, with glints of light whichever way it turned. So the three were eminently publishable as they were. Unger decided to go for the novel and set to work revising the first and last to join them more securely together.

What enabled him to persist through all his rewriting and also to let one hundred fifty pages of very good writing go by the board? "By now I'd lost any egotistical involvement in the work. The book was coming together. I was very objective now, almost impersonally watching a process occurring. The book wanted to come together and I was the last person to stand in its way."

There are several morals for the gifted young writer to draw from this account. Perhaps the main one is that Unger needed a period of adversity and silence, not only to recover from my "litany of its flaws," as he put it, but also to reorient himself as a writer and to undo the damage that the frustrated false writer, who wanted to be fashionable and publish as soon as possible, had done to the uncertain true one who had started the project. Once that had been done, the characters, like rejected family or abused friends, began to return.

There is a theory, put forward by D. W. Winnicott and W. R. Fairbairn, that creativity is a mode of play which we do not only for its enjoyment but also to explore the interface of self and world and to make restitution for the damage we do to others and ourselves by our narcissism. The youth tuning up the family car, the man weeding his garden, the woman rewriting a description five times to get it right, are all involved, psychically speaking, in the same activity. Even more overtly was Unger's rewriting an act of restitution ("In order to feel easy again, I had to rework it") for the falsifications he had made about others, and for the harm he had done to his own craft and spirit.

Earlier I wrote of the time that the gifted young writer needs to strengthen and trust the self he writes out of. To put it another way, the struggle with rejection, uncertainty, and disappointment can help him to develop his main defense against the narcissism that prompts him to become a writer in the first place. Writing to a friend, Pushkin tells of reading a canto of *Eugene Onegin* that he had just composed, jumping from his chair, and proudly shouting, "Hey you Pushkin! Hey you son of a bitch!" Anyone who has written knows that feeling, but also knows how easily it can turn over into self-hatred, when the writing or the blank page reflects back one's limitations, failure, deadness. The writer's defense is his power of self-objectivity, his interest in otherness, and his faith in the process itself, which enables him to write on into the teeth of his doubts and then to improve it. In the scars of the struggle between the odd, sensitive side of the self that wants to write and the practical, socialized one that wants results, the gifted young writer is likely to find his true sense of vocation. Moreover, writing itself, if not misunderstood and abused, becomes a way of empowering the writing self. It converts diffuse anger and disappointment into deliberate and durable aggression, the writer's main source of energy. It converts sorrow and self-pity into empathy, the writer's main means of relating to otherness. Similarly, his wounded innocence turns into irony, his silliness into wit, his guilt into judgment, his oddness into originality, his perverseness into his stinger.

Because all this takes time, indeed most of a lifetime, to complete itself, the gifted young writer has to learn that his main task is to persist. This means he must be tough-minded about his fantasies of wealth, fame, and the love of beautiful women or men. However stimulating these motives may be for the social self, for the writing one who perforce needs to stay home and be alone they are trivial and misleading, for they are enacted mostly as fantasies that maintain the adolescent romance of a magically empowered ego that the writer must outgrow if he is to survive. And this is so even if the fantasies come true, and often enough, particularly if they come true. No writer rode these fantasies farther or more damagingly than Scott Fitzgerald did, but it was Fitzgerald who said that inside a novelist there has to be something of a peasant.

Rejection and uncertainty also teach the gifted writer to be firm, kind, and patient, a good parent to his gift if he is to persist in it. As he comes to realize, his gift is partly a skill that is better at some tasks than at others and partly a power that comes and goes. And even when it comes, it is often only partly functioning and its directives are only partly understood. This is why writing a first draft is like ice fishing and building an igloo, as well as like groping one's way into a pitch-dark room, or overhearing a faint conversation, or having prepared for a different exam, or telling a joke whose punch line you've forgotten. As someone said, one writes mainly to rewrite, for rewriting and revising are how one's mind comes to inhabit the material fully.

In its benign form, rewriting is a second, third, and *n*th chance to make something come right, to "fall graciously into place," in Lewis Hyde's phrase. But it is also the testing ground of the writer's conscience, on the one hand, and of his faith, on the other. One has to learn to respect the misgiving that says, This still doesn't ring true, still hasn't touched bottom, still hasn't delivered me. And this means to go back down into the mine again and poke around for the missing ore and find a place for it and let it work its will. Sometimes this may mean re-envisioning the entire work: that is, finding another central idea or image, a new star in the area of the former one to navigate by. Revision is mostly turning loose the editor in oneself, a caretaker who tinkers and straightens out and tidies up and has a steadier hand. At the same time, one must come to the truth of Valéry's remark that no work is ever finished, only at a certain point abandoned. One has to learn to recognize when that point has come from the feel of the work coming together once and for all and of the writing having to be what it is, more or less. For beyond that point, rewriting and revising can turn compulsive and malignant, devouring the vitality and integrity of what one has found to tell and say.

In sum, the gifted young writer needs to learn to trust the writing process itself and, beyond that, to love as well as hate it. For writing is not, of course, always stoop labor and second thoughts and struggling with one's tendency toward negation and despair and accepting one's limits and limitations. There are the exhilarations of finding that the way ahead has opened overnight, that the character who has been so elusive has suddenly walked into the room and started talking, that the figure has been weaving itself into the carpet. But if the gifted young writer persists in believing that for him the latter conditions should be the normal ones, otherwise known as "inspiration" or "natural talent," he will likely decide after a few years that he fatally lacks one or both or that he has developed a writer's block, and may well turn to a more sensible and less threatened mode of expression, such as teaching or editing or writing for one or the other of the media.

There appear to be better and worse ways to get through this long period of self-apprenticeship and to get the most out of it. Of the first novelists and story writers I've been involved with, virtually none of them were teaching writing, at least in a full-time way. Teaching offers the lure of relatively pleasant work and significant free time, but it comes with the snare of using and distorting much of the same energy that goes into writing and tends to fill the mind with the high examples of the models one teaches and the low ones of student work. Moreover, it tends to be insulating and distracting during the period when the young fiction writer should be as open as possible to a range of experience, for the sake of his character as well as his material. A job that makes use of another skill or talent and doesn't come home with one seems to work best over the long haul. It's also well, of course, to give as few hostages as possible to fortune.

What the gifted young writer most needs is time, lots of it. Bobbie Ann Mason says that when she is asked by writing students how to get published, she feels like saying, "Don't sweat it for twenty years or so. It takes experience at life before you really know what you're doing." She began writing fiction in 1971, after she got out of graduate school, and for the next five years or so wrote in a desultory way, finding it hard to get focused. In 1976 she finished a novel about a twelve-year-old girl growing up in western Kentucky who was addicted to Nancy Drew novels. "It took another two years before I began to find my true subject, which was to write about my roots and the kinds of people I'd known, but from a contemporary perspective. It mainly took a lot of living to get to that point. I'd come from such a sheltered and isolated background that I had to go through culture shock by living for years in the North to see the world of Mayfield, Kentucky, in a way I could write about as I was now—in a kind of exile. Also it took me until I was in my thirties to get enough detachment and objectivity to see that many of those people back home were going through culture shock too."

My own sense of things is that young fiction writers should disconnect the necessity to write fiction from what it is often confused with and by, the desire to publish it. This helps to keep one's mind where it belongs—on one's own work—and away from where it doesn't—on the market, which is next to useless, and on writers who are succeeding, which is discouraging. Comparisons with other writers should be inspiring; otherwise they're invidious.

Bobbie Ann Mason says that "the writer I was most involved with was Nabokov. It was because he was a stylist and had a peculiar sensibility. In some ways, comparing myself to him is like comparing Willie Nelson to an opera singer, but I felt connected to him because he had the sensibility of an exile, was working with two opposing cultures, which made him peculiar, the same way I felt myself."

If there is no necessity to write fiction, then one should wait and in the meantime write other things. Keeping a journal with some depth to it is a good way to discover and strengthen one's natural style and the best way to talk to oneself about the real issues of one's experience. My other suggestion is to look for other opportunities to write and publish and thereby give one's talent some chance of gainful employment.

Thirty years ago there was a great fear of "selling out," of "prostituting your talent," etc. It was as though your talent was like a beautiful pure virgin whom the philistine world was waiting eagerly to seduce and corrupt. Literary mores no longer place as much stock in the hieratic model of the writer, which is just as well. Unless one is good at self-sacrifice, is endowed with an iron will and a genius-sized gift, it's likely to be a defeating thing to insist on producing Art or nothing.

If one of the primary projects of the gifted young writer is to begin to create a neutral zone between his social self and his literary one, so that the latter can live in peace for a while, it is also true that both need exercise and some degree of satisfaction and toughening. Many novelists-in-progress find it helpful to take their talent at least some of the time out of the rarefied and tenuous realm of literature and put it to work in the marketplace to try to earn some of its keep. Even hack writing has the benefit of putting serious writing into its proper perspective as a privilege rather than a burden. At a respectable professional level, writing for publication makes one into someone who writes rather than, in Robert Louis Stevenson's distinction, someone who wants to have written. Writing without publishing gets to be like loving someone from afar—delicious for fantasies but thin gruel for living. It produces in time what Milan Kundera, in other contexts, calls "the unbearable lightness of being." That is why, to my mind, a strongly written review, profile, piece of reportage in *The Village Voice* or *The Texas Monthly* or *Seattle Magazine* is worth three "Try us again"s from *The New Yorker.* The young writer needs whatever grounding in the vocation she can get. Once in print, her words detach themselves from the fluttering of the ego and become part of the actual world. Along with the reality of type, there is the energy that comes from publication: the "let's see what I can do next" feeling. Unger found that once he began revising his novel, his other cylinders kicked over and he was soon partly supporting himself by writing theater reviews for the local paper and developed a piece for the stage with his wife. The reality of getting paid is also good for one's work habits.

By the same token, the first years the writer is on his own are a good time to let his imagination off the leash and let it sniff and paw into other fields of writing. From journal writing it's only a small Kierkegaardian leap into the personal essay. It's also liberating to get away from term-paper type criticism and begin to try to write about other writers in the way that other writers do, as, say, Updike or Mailer or Sontag does. There is also the possibility of discovering that criticism or reportage or some other mode is for the time being more congenial than fiction. A young fiction writer I know had about come to the end of his rope when he had the wit to turn one of his stories into a one-act play and has been flying as a playwright ever since. Similarly, inside a functioning poet there is often a failed fiction writer. One of the most deforming aspects of American literary culture is the cult of the novel. Another is the decline of the concept of the man of letters, which less specialized times and less academicized literary cultures than ours took for granted. And still do in Europe, where a Graham Greene, a Robbe-Grillet, a Grass, a Kundera, write in three or four modes, depending upon the subject, the occasion, and the disposition of his well-balanced Muse. Even if he doesn't become a triple-threat writer, experimenting with other modes frees up energy and also helps to demystify the writer's vocation, which, like any other, is an ongoing practice rather than a higher state of being. This is particularly so for a prospective novelist. He must get over regarding his medium as a tinted mirror before doing so fakes him out completely. Auden puts it very well when he says that the novelist

> Must struggle out of his boyish gift and learn
> How to be plain and awkward, how to be
> One after whom none think it worth to turn.
>
> For to achieve his lightest wish, he must
> Become the whole of boredom, subject to
> Vulgar complaints like love, among the Just
> Be just, among the Filthy filthy too.

Hence he must learn to think of his medium as not a flattering mirror but a lens that he must grind and polish himself so that he can see more sharply and closely and powerfully.

Virtually all the fiction writers I've been speaking to about these matters fix the turning point in their writing lives in the period when the intrinsic interest of what they were doing began to take over and to generate a sense of necessity. This is not to say they first had to renounce the world and its painted stages. A little support and recognition from outside tends to go hand in hand with the recognition from within. This seems to be particularly true of women writers. As Lynne Sharon Schwartz explained, "Most women don't give themselves the freedom to pursue their dream. Being brought up a girl has meant just that." She began to write stories when she was seven and did so again during and after college but without taking the enterprise very seriously. "I'd get a letter from *The Paris Review* inviting me to submit other work and I'd think, That's nice, and then put it away in a drawer. Writing fiction was one of several dreams that probably wouldn't be realized." She married, had children, went back to graduate school, which somehow seemed permissible, perhaps because no one does much dreaming in graduate school. "I found, though, that I didn't want to write a dissertation when I got to that point. I just couldn't face the library part of it. Going down into the stacks seemed so alien to my real sources. About that time, a childhood friend who also was married and had children told me she had resolved to give herself five years to become a dance critic. It was the way she did it, putting everything else to the side: it was her fierce tenacity that inspired me. I gave up graduate school and started to write fiction again." "Wasn't it scary," I asked, "giving up something definite and practical for something so uncertain?" "Not really," she said. "Mainly, I felt that I was finally doing what I was intended to do."

Over the next few years she worked on a first novel, which went unpublished. "Just as well," she says, "but it got me an agent and some nice rejection letters, which was encouraging." In time she developed a small network of women fiction writers, published two stories in little magazines and then a satire on Watergate in *The New Republic*. "Doris Grumbach, who was then the literary editor, called me up to tell me and asked me who I was, where I'd been all this time. So I realized I might be someone after all."

Now, four books later, Lynne Schwartz looks back at these years and sees mainly herself at work. "I had to learn to write completely alone. There was no help, no other writer to emulate, no one's influence. It was too private for that. Once I got started I wanted the life of a writer so fiercely that nothing could stop me. I wanted the intensity, the sense of aliveness, that came from writing fiction. I'm still that way. My life is worth living when I've completed a good paragraph."

The development of this sense of necessity seems to be the rock-bottom basis for a career as a novelist. Whatever may feed it, whatever may impede it, finally come to be subsidiary to the simple imperative of being at work. At this point, writing fiction has become one's way, in the religious sense of the term. Not that there are any guarantees that it will continue to be for good or that it will make your inner life easier to bear. The life of published fiction writers is most often the exchange of one level of rejection, uncertainty, and disappointment for another, and to go on means to rely upon the same imperilled and durable trust in the process and the self that got them published in the first place.

(1985)

Part Two

Tertz/Sinyavsky: A Secret Agent of the Imagination

During the six years before his arrest in 1965, Andrei Sinyavsky must have led a strange double life. In the literary circles of Moscow, he was known as a leading research scholar at the Gorky Institute for World Literature. He also wrote regularly for *Novy Mir,* a journal that was cautiously attempting to liberalize Soviet letters. Of the essays and reviews that Sinyavsky produced in this period, and to this end, those that have been collected and translated in *For Freedom of Imagination* reveal him to be not only a keen literary critic but also a politic one, who coolly argued for individuality and complexity as being in the best interests of the literature produced by and for a Communist culture.

Meanwhile, he was writing, and publishing in the West, under the pseudonym "Abram Tertz." His electrifying book *On Socialist Realism,* as well as his stories and two novels, were so intensely individual and complex, so firmly ironical about Soviet positivism, and so intrigued by the "dark and magical night of Stalin's dictatorship" and its aftermath, that it is still difficult to relate the sober, circumspect, relatively orthodox scholar to the free, mordant, and occult spirit who wrote under the disreputable name of Abram Tertz, which, I am told, is taken from a song about black markets, ribaldry, Jewishness, and other anti-Soviet activities that recur in his fiction.

This dangerous double life, as a secret agent of the imagination, also became the ground of his fiction, furnishing both material and tone. His two novels, like his stories, are filled with divided men who are ruled by suppression and surveillance, both external and internal, as well as by sudden bursts of psychic energy. Most of them inhabit a narrow fringe of being that is swept by forces of authority, parapsychology, and paranoia. The first Abram Tertz novel, *The Trial Begins,* opens with its putative author being visited by two plainclothesmen, who scoop up the characters and punctuation marks from a page of his writing and then announce: "You are being trusted." A huge fist, visible through the wall of the writer's room, appears in the sky; other walls open so that he can observe the lives led behind them. One man is singled out, and a voice behind the fist tells the narrator that this bureaucrat is "my beloved and faithful servant. Follow him, dog his footsteps, defend him with your life. Exalt him!" The last the writer cannot bring himself to do. The man in question, Prosecutor Globov, is indefatigably fatuous and longs for a sensational public trial of a Jewish doctor to "clear the air." Globov and his fellow officials present a cheerful, friendly face to the world; their politics are "all inside them, hidden in that secret place where other mortals kept their vices." The writer attempts to suppress his account of Globov's circle, but his rough drafts are retrieved by a device installed in the sewer pipe, and he is convicted of slandering his "positive heroes" by not "portraying them in all the fullness of their many-sided working lives."

As elsewhere, life follows art in the Soviet Union. When Sinyavsky was revealed to be the infamous Abram Tertz and was put on trial with the poet Yuli Daniel, who had also published pseudonymously abroad, the proceedings were conducted under the spell, as it were, of the paranoid legalism, distortion, and defamation satirized in *The Trial Begins.* Sinyavsky has X-ray vision of the pretenses and crudities that stuff the shirts of the Soviet authorities, and though enigmatic and jocular, he cannot help but draw blood. His wit is as eccentric and deadly as Gogol's, and seems as much in possession of him as he is of it. Again like Gogol, he loves to play with the supernatural, to see double. "Art is jealous," Sinyavsky writes. "Moving away from inexpressive 'givens,' it—by force of its burning imagination—paints a second universe in which occurrences unfold at a heightened tempo and in a bared form."

So it is in his brilliant second novel, *The Makepeace Experiment,* in which a bicycle mechanic turns mesmerist and leads his backwoods community through a reenactment of the history of Bolshevism, complete with a population that comes to believe anything he tells them and that he isolates from the rest of the world by drawing a psychic curtain around it. The tale is told by an old librarian, who is under the spell of a spirit from the nineteenth century, one Proferansov, a friend of the great eighteenth-century French chemist Lavoisier and of Tolstoy. The novel becomes a beautifully fused mixture of old and new Russian illusions and phantoms, while, prey to the mischances and perversities of power, life draws slowly on to the only freedom that is safe and complete.

The theme of possession by a demonic force that drives men to express themselves, to act out their fantasies (with the result that they usually end up in Siberia or dead), runs through Sinyavsky's *Fantastic Stories.* A young workman goes to the circus and, inspired by the acrobats and a sleight-of-hand artist, "the Manipulator," decides to enliven his dull life by performing similar feats. After picking a pocket, he is off on a series of manic adventures: The world cooperates and even for a time seems to become a circus in which he is the star performer. But eventually Konstantin commits a burglary and shoots "the Manipulator," for which he is sentenced to Siberia. One fine morning, though, as he marches with the work gang, his inspiration returns, and Konstantin goes leaping and hurtling toward freedom until a guard's bullet sends him into a climactic and terminal somersault.

In one form or another, the "extraneous and magnanimous supernatural power" that brings Konstantin to the fulfillment of his destiny visits each of Sinyavsky's heroes. "The Icicle" concerns a man who briefly acquires the gift of clairvoyance, and, with it, visions of the transmigration of his soul and of other souls. Sinyavsky seizes upon this motif with a particular intensity: the previous incarnations that the character helplessly witnesses provide an insight into the nature of the self.

> Men are so made that they never find their appearance quite convincing. When we look in a mirror, we never cease to be amazed. "Is that ghostly reflection really mine?" we ask. "It can't be." . . . I imagine that there is someone inside us who violently objects at every attempt to persuade him that the person he sees in front of him is none other than himself . . . and so we begin to bluster, and make faces as though to express our skepticism about the apparition defiantly stuck there in front of us.

Shortly thereafter, the narrator, having watched several of his past funerals, is horrified by a vision of "himself" being hanged in a later incarnation; it is as if the face of his future torment were staring at him across the desert of time. In the story "You and I"—a chilling study in the dynamics of schizophrenia—there is a similar queasy fluidity and separation of the ego in a parapsychological context, this time carried to pathological lengths by a character who spies on himself.

All of which suggests not only the habitual direction of Sinyavsky's imagination but also the extreme tensions under which he labored in his double life as a writer. Such tensions proved to be very fruitful, since they placed him in immediate touch with the inner, secret life of a society ruled by a literally mesmerizing terror and faith. Sinyavsky's ventures into the occult are seldom more than an irony away from a critique of the monstrous idealism of Stalinist thought control. At the same time, Sinyavsky rightly speaks of himself as an "idealist," and his inspiration, like his peril, lies in his responsiveness to demonic and psychic forces, as well as political ones. In his story "The Graphomaniacs," which Sinyavsky at his trial suggested might contain "certain autobiographical features," one of the legion of Soviet scribblers announces that the only purpose and hope of writing is "self-suppression":

> That's why we labor in the sweat of our brow and cover wagonloads of paper with writing—in the hope of stepping aside, overcoming ourselves, and granting access to thoughts from the air. They arise spontaneously, independently of ourselves. . . . You composed one thing yourself, so that it's worthless, while another thing is not yours and you don't dare, don't have the right to do anything with it. . . . And you retreat . . . in terror at your own nonparticipation at what has taken place.

The sense of being ruled "from the air" is restated near the end of "The Graphomaniacs," when the main character, returning to his family from a writing spree, suddenly feels that his motions are being controlled by "someone's fingers as a pencil is guided over the paper." Like the dark street, the sleeping houses, his whole long unsuccessful life suddenly seems to be part of a relentless literary composition. He raises his fist toward the sky and shouts, "Hey you there—the graphomaniac. Stop work! . . . You're unreadable."

For a writer to maintain himself in this incredibly paradoxical, threatened, and divided mode of existence without going dumb or mad, he must have sources of unity deep in his nature. In Sinyavsky's most recent writing published in the West, "Thought Unaware," he reveals himself to be a secret Christian. The nakedly personal meditations assembled under this title seem, at first glance, a far cry from anything else he has published either as Tertz or as Sinyavsky—so direct and austere are they, so single-mindedly committed to the Christian account of the world and of the moral world within. Sinyavsky's reflections on God, faith, death, sin, prayer, nature, create some of his most luminous and moving writing. And the more one ponders these reflections, the more intimately they seem connected to the affirmative moments in his fiction, as well as being the sustaining ground of his irony and satire. Just as "the graphomaniac" is a negative, comic, covert image of the God to whom Sinyavsky ardently subjects himself and all his values, so the imagery of his other fiction—as well as the framework of his enigmatic essay *On Socialist Realism*—emerges as a sardonic transmutation of the Christian worldview, corresponding to the corruptions and perversions by which its mysticism still manifests itself in politics, art, the occult, sex, etc. Thus "Thought Unaware" not only provides the unifying matrix of Sinyavsky's art but indicates the abiding sanctuary of "selflessness," which, I suspect, has enabled this writer to endure his situation.

It is worth noting that the word "Christian" does not

appear in any of the writing collected in *For Freedom of Imagination,* not even in the long essay on Pasternak's poetry. Here, as elsewhere in the collection, Sinyavsky's point of view is entirely secular and "progressive," and he justifies Pasternak, another secret Christian, as a Soviet poet who fulfilled his primary Marxist obligation to reflect, in a positive way, the history of his age. As an orthodox critic and liberal, in his public guise, Sinyavsky had to be deliberately obtuse in dealing with Pasternak, the Russian writer with whom he is probably in greatest sympathy, if he hoped to rehabilitate the latter's reputation and to champion his methods and values as the basis for the renewal of Soviet poetry. Such, in general, are the narrow ideological boundaries within which Sinyavsky could safely and productively operate as a Soviet critic.

Even so, he manages to impart a great deal of literary education, functioning as both a liberal spokesman and a teacher of the tribe, a role traditional for Russian writers, whom even the Bosheviks honored as "the technicians of souls" before they began to destroy them. Standing where he does, thirty years after the modernist tradition was almost totally wrecked and abandoned, Sinyavsky is like a sophisticated architect who has inherited a spacious but decayed mansion, full of dry rot and violations of the code. Much of his criticism is a kind of basic renovation, laying new foundations, clearing out the debris, replacing warped doors and windows, bringing in power. To impose the rudimentary principles of freshness, concreteness, and individuality, he constantly calls on the assistance of Mayakovsky, who appears to have become the Soviet Homer, and uses his precepts and verse to reproach the official poets for their vague, abstract, repetitious, hackneyed, inaccurate, derivative, depersonalized, feeble, and supremely smug verse. What they most notably lack is what Mayakovsky called "tendency," which Sinyavsky defines as "a living, formative, creative principle in verse, a movement which breaks down dogmas and clichés and does not permit compromises and wishes to live in a new way, an individual way."

Polite but devastating to the literary hacks, unyielding in his insistence that Yevtushenko live up to his claim that he has abandoned his superficiality, Sinyavsky writes with an immediate feeling for the imaginative power of poets like Akhmatova and Frost. His strongest essay deals with the poet and diarist Olga Berggolts, whose ability to seize her experience, to identify—and make the reader identify—her most individual responses with the inner life of her country and people, represents for Sinyavsky the right direction for a truly Soviet art—"the unity of the personal and the general which forms our way of life."

The closest Sinyavsky comes to pointing his criticism toward the nature of his own creative work is in an essay on science fiction. Wishing to free this genre from the encroachments of socialist realism that have made it ludicrous—its timid fantasies often lagging a decade behind the realities of Soviet science—Sinyavsky offers an eloquent redefinition of science fiction as a form for rational hypotheses that envision an "ever more difficult, beautiful, and therefore fantastic goal." Just as the spiritual images of Olga Berggolts are able to reveal the "true existence" that lies behind and illuminates the dull inexpressiveness of everyday life, so Sinyavsky argues for a fiction that uses the imagination of the future to reveal what he terms in *On Socialist Realism* "the grand and implausible sense of our era."

It is just here—in the realm of the visionary—that Sinyavsky and Tertz touch and join. Here, and in an epigram of Gorky's that, as both Tertz and Sinyavsky, he frequently quotes—and that, for the time being, as he serves his seven-year sentence in a forced-labor camp, can stand as the motto of this great writer and man—"the madness of the brave is the wisdom of life."

(1971)

A Soviet Writer and His Censors: A Case Study

In September of 1941 the German armies entered and occupied the city of Kiev, which the Russian high command had abruptly abandoned. Much of the population of this major city of the Ukraine, which had resisted and been devastated by the land reforms of the previous decade, regarded the Germans as heroes and liberators. To Anatole Kuznetsov, a boy of twelve, the rabble of half-starved Russian soldiers, many of whom were pleading for civilian clothes so that they could desert, were a pathetic contrast to the sleek, efficient Germans, who were passing out baskets of bread and who seemed to have stepped out of the films of Russia's invincible new ally that had been shown in school only two years before.

A few days later, the Kreschatik, the main thoroughfare of Kiev, where the Germans had set up their headquarters, was all but destroyed by bombs and fires that were clearly the work of the Soviet secret police. The next day the entire Jewish population was rounded up for deportation—"the Yids" being held responsible for the destruction of the district—and marched through streets lined with visibly pleased and jeering Ukrainians. Even young Kuznetsov, whose best friend was half Jewish, found himself aping his grandfather's delight in this turn of events. Soon it became clear that the Jews were not being taken to trains but to a huge ravine called Babi Yar, on the outskirts of the city, from which the sound of machine gun fire could already be heard. One Jewish boy managed to escape and return to the neighborhood, and, as Kuznetsov looked on, one of the neighbors quickly sent for the police, who recaptured the boy.

Now, almost all of the details in the above paragraphs will not be found in the version of *Babi Yar* that was published in Russia in 1966. They appear in this new version, which Kuznetsov claims is the original uncensored manuscript, along with certain additions, which he smuggled out in microfilm along with his other original manuscripts in the course of his escape to England sixteen months before. In order to demonstrate the nature and extent of Soviet literary censorship, he has had the censored material—about one fifth of the book—set in boldface type; the added material, set within brackets, largely comprises observations and opinions that emphasize his anti-Soviet point of view. There are also three long passages that Kuznetsov claims he initially removed himself on the advice of his editor. The first one directly accuses the NKVD of destroying the Kreschatik in order to bring on the Nazi terror; the second similarly holds the NKVD responsible for the destruction, attributed to the Germans, of the famous Kiev-Percherk monastery; and the third describes the previously suppressed "revenge of Babi Yar" in 1961, when the Soviet effort to fill in the ravine, which it regarded as an embarrassment and a source of philo-Jewish feeling, resulted in a terrific avalanche of mud that killed several thousand more of the people of Kiev.

So this new version of *Babi Yar* is a fascinating document—provided one believes Kuznetsov's claim for it. In his "London Letter" (*Saturday Review,* December 12, 1970),

Herbert R. Mayes suggests that the new version is a fraud, that Kuznetsov added the "censored" material after escaping to England, so as to increase the value of the book as a case study of Soviet literary repression, the first of its kind. It is easy for Mayes to draw the cloud of suspicion that surrounds Kuznetsov's character over his book as well, to say that a man who lied about a conspiracy within a circle of Soviet writers in order to curry enough favor with the authorities to carry out his escape from the Soviet Union is capable of anything, certainly of bearing false witness about a mere book.

Mayes offers other reasons for doubting Kuznetsov's word as well as his claim for the text. But in fairness to Kuznetsov, it must be said that Mayes's reasons are vague, conjectural, or misleading. He is vague when he tells us that he finally met Kuznetsov and, having "asked questions" and been "given answers," he decided to warn the readers of *SR.* He is conjectural when he disputes the story of the microfilm on the ground that Kuznetsov couldn't likely have gotten that much film into the lining of his coat or past the authorities at either end of his trip. He is misleading on a number of matters that bear on Kuznetsov's credibility, such as his frequent escapes from death recorded in *Babi Yar.* (Actually, they are much less frequent than one might expect, considering that young Kuznetsov was daily combing the streets in search of food and disobeying various Nazi edicts, and further considering that one third of the population was killed during the occupation.) Most misleading is Mayes's assertion that the "new uncensored version" is "approximately the same" as the Soviet one, except that Kuznetsov shows that the "Communists were no less ruthless and dreadful than the Nazis." The differences between the two versions are far more extensive and intricate than that.

Until a more cogent argument comes along, I think it is

well to believe Kuznetsov's claim for the text. For one thing, if he were simply the opportunistic liar Mayes makes him out to be, Kuznetsov would be sitting comfortably now in his home in Tula, writing novels of flawless socialist realism. Each of his four books has run into trouble for being anti-Soviet; he appears to have been a barely tolerated spokesman for the young, a kind of safety valve of dissident feeling that could be regulated by editors and government censors to maintain the proper pressure and degree of half-truth and a plausible atmosphere of tolerance. I have not seen his other novels, but, from the various reports, I imagine them to be rather like Yevtushenko's poetry—both outspoken and positive. Kuznetsov's work has appeared mainly in *Yunost,* a youth-oriented journal that is given a bit more latitude by the authorities, in return for which its editors man the boundaries of the permissible against the pressure of writers like Kuznetsov. In a journal he also smuggled out, Kuznetsov describes his fight with Boris Polevoi, the editor of *Yunost,* over the "correcting" of the text of *Babi Yar.* Polevoi, a novelist himself, remarked: "You think you're going to write and I'm going to carry the can? The writing is yours; the backsides are ours."

This rings true; so does Kuznetsov's account of his rage at what was done to *Babi Yar* both in manuscript and in galleys, presumably by the official censors. It is clear from the book itself that he had packed into it the two most terrible and decisive years of his life, that he had struggled to express how his character as well as his view of the human condition had been shaped by the experience, and that much of this material had disappeared along with the anti-Soviet content. Moreover, the cutting that was done is alternately deft and gross: sometimes a matter of excising a few words that alter or tone down the emphasis but allow the point to be made, the narrative to run smoothly; sometimes the amputation of a whole passage, much of it unobjectionable but containing a controversial detail. Some changes are rational and systematic, given the purposes involved, while others seem capricious or inscrutable. Finally, *Babi Yar* in its new version is written in a direct, headlong, earnest, assertive style that seamlessly joins the "censored" material to the rest. In his introduction, Kuznetsov tells us that he initially tried to write the story of Babi Yar according to the rules of socialist realism—"the only guide to writing which I knew"—but that the recollections he had preserved in a notebook turned dead in his hands. Given the nature of these recollections, it is easy to see why he instead wrote the powerful, stumbling, honest book he says he did, and hard to see why he would have written the thinned-out, cagey, self-mutilating book that Mayes believes Kuznetsov originally wrote.

Babi Yar is mainly the story of how he survived the Nazi occupation and was changed by it. At the time the Germans arrived he was a robust, studious boy. His father, who had recently moved elsewhere and remarried, was a former Red Army officer and Party official, who had participated in the murderous agrarian reforms and spoke of them freely. His mother was a schoolteacher, a sensitive but hard-working woman who was seldom at home. Anatole was mostly raised by his grandparents, both former peasants. His grandmother's gentle piety and his grandfather's obdurate hostility to the Bolsheviks were completely at variance with Anatole's indoctrination in school and in the Pioneers, and he tended to play the one set of influences off against the other as a way of keeping his wits about him. Like most active, alert city boys, he received his primary education in the streets, but he was also clearly on his way to a good career in the ever-widening horizons of the Soviet future.

Within a few weeks of the occupation he had become a

half-famished street urchin, selling matches or cigarette paper or whatever he could get his hands on, shining shoes, stealing beets or potatoes from moving trucks, and prowling the city and countryside like "a young wolf." Living near Babi Yar, he could hear the machine guns firing almost every day as, according to Nazi custom, the Jews were succeeded by mental patients, Gypsies, political prisoners, victims of the frequent reprisals, slackers, jokers, thieves, and other "unreliable elements." Along with the terror, famine spread through the city. The price of two pounds of bread was nearly equal to a worker's monthly wages, and in the nearby prisoner-of-war camp the Russian soldiers were eating grass to stay alive, while the surrounding fields were filled with unharvested potatoes. In time, young Kuznetsov, who ultimately came down with tuberculosis, did forced labor on a farm and then in a canning factory. At one point the boy stole into a closed soup kitchen:

> In an effort to find at least a grain of corn I started crawling around examining the cracks in the floor. But everything had been brushed up. . . . I sniffed at a [frying pan] and found it smelt of fried onions. . . . It made me whimper . . . and I started licking the frying pan, either imagining or actually getting the faint taste of onion. I went on whimpering and licking, whimpering and licking.

Eventually he worked for a sausage maker who gave him the bones of the horses he used. (Another "sausage maker" was arrested after a human finger was found in one of his casings.) Meanwhile, Anatole watched as ever-larger segments of the population were rounded up like cattle and shipped to Germany. When the age limit was lowered to fourteen, Anatole was picked up for a transport, but managed to run away and escape the bullets fired at him. Later he says to himself:

> You've got the guns, but I've got my legs. . . . I know now why I am alive, scratch around among the market-stalls, gnaw horse's bones: I am growing up so as to be able to hate you and fight you . . . to fight against the evil ones who are turning the world into a prison and a stone crusher.

As Anatole becomes tough, resourceful, persistent, fearless in his body, he also becomes so in his mind. Learning to see through the Nazi propaganda to the danger and evils it cloaks, he begins to recognize the similarities of the words and deeds of Nazi "socialism" and "humanism" and the Soviet versions. With ample time and reason to brood, he perceives the connection between the forced famine of the 1930s and that of the present, between the cannibalism his father described and the tales of the sausage maker and of the prison camps. When he comes home one day to find his mother desperately burning their books and family records, he thinks back to a similar scene during the Soviet investigations and purges a few years before. He realizes that the dull passivity of a group of peasants about to be deported, accepting their enslavement as a matter of course, is owing to the fact that all their lives they have known nothing but the yoke of privation and terror. He observes that the very same building that housed the Ukrainian secret police has been taken over by the Gestapo, and adds that after the war it would revert to its original tenants. He thinks that someday it may become a museum displaying "the destruction of man in the Ukraine and his transformation back into an ape."

Needless to say, this growing awareness of the world as an extension of Babi Yar was filleted from the original text as the spine from a fish. Not only do the anti-Soviet references go, but so do Kuznetsov's comparisons of himself, his fellow sufferers, and mankind itself to one form or another of animal life. He is not allowed to have murderous impulses, even toward men who have beaten him to get the few beets he has stolen. If he connives to get a second portion of soup at the canteen, that is deleted. If he steals fir trees to sell at the New Year holiday, that is deleted. The development of his survivalist mentality is as much a heresy as his disbelief in progress, compassion, and cooperation. If he insists that true culture requires that men not be murdered and debased, it is stricken from his book. If he even inquires, in good Marxist fashion, about the wretched lives that were necessary to support an Alexander of Macedon or a Napoleon, "not to mention any other of our great benefactors," or for that matter a Hamlet or Anna Karenina, that is stricken from his book. If he asks why young people today are indifferent or hostile to politics, that is stricken from his book.

To the Soviet censors, the data of Kuznetsov's eyes and ears are as unreliable as his behavior or his thoughts. Russian prisoners of war being marched to a camp did not number in the "thousands," did not appear "unfeeling" and "frightened," did not scramble madly after a few raw potatoes that were thrown to them. Kuznetsov did not meet two Russian soldiers serving as scouts for the Germans, or hear that the most sadistic guard in the concentration camp at Babi Yar was Russian. He was not "confused" by a fatherly German soldier, a "very pleasant, smiling character," who regards as "Bolsheviks" the Jews, women, and children he has killed, and who makes Anatole realize that the machine gunners at Babi Yar are probably the same sort of simple, hearty men. The people of Kiev were not thrown into a panic during the German air raids and did not lack bomb shelters; they did not loot the abandoned shops nearly as much as Kuznetsov says they did; did not docilely cooperate and collaborate; did not brutally rob, beat, betray, and kill each other. The presence of the Jews in Kiev is minimized as much as possible, and the concern for withholding sympathy from them goes as far as to cut out the fact that one boy who managed to escape for a while was "a good-looking child with lovely eyes." The word "Palestine" is excised even from the rumors about the Jews' destination.

The inflexibility of Soviet orthodoxy is everywhere evident. One of the Jewish women believes that after they arrive in their new home their baggage will be divided up "equally. Then there won't be rich and poor anymore." The material in quotes was censored. So is all mention of an old woman, once the wife of a manufacturer, who lives in her bourgeois past and who fascinates Anatole as much as if she had come from the moon. Because one of his aunts was a beggar, she too must go. There are frequent deletions of his grandmother's religious practices, her superstitions, and other peasant folkways. The word "miracle" is apparently impermissible in any context. Collective farmers do not go hungry or ragged even in wartime. Stalin is preserved from all accusations of incompetence, deceit, and brutality; the NKVD is either whitewashed or erased. Most of Kuznetsov's veiled attempts to associate the Soviet régime with that of the Nazis, such as his observation that their flags are both red, or that the Germans used the blood-soaked Stalinist phrase "enemy of the people," are deftly ferreted out. But sometimes the association is made by Soviet guilt itself, as when Kuznetsov, speaking generally, refers to such "absolute madness as war, dictatorship, police terror," and the censor strikes the last two examples.

The protocols of Soviet censorship are also incredibly priggish. Soldiers cannot be shown defecating, and the naked corpses in the portable gas chambers enslimed in their feces and urine are cleaned up by the blue pencil. The deaths of two Jewish women vanish from the record because they were raped. A suspected Jew cannot be examined to see if he has been circumcised because in the Soviet Union neither the living nor the dead have sexual organs. Anatole is not permitted to discover some photographs of naked women, nor is a young mother allowed to bare her breasts in desperation to show the guard that she has a nursing child at home. Two pretty Russian girls in the entourage of a German general are removed without a trace, their offenses being both carnal and political.

I shall not try to catalogue others of the fifty-seven varieties of things that cannot be written about, openly or covertly, in the Soviet Union. The final point I want to make is that even if Kuznetsov doctored the Soviet version of his text in order to make this new version, we would still have an appalling account of what it is like to be a writer in the Soviet Union today, for then the incessant distortion and impoverishment of consciousness reflected in the deleted material would have been the work of an internalized censor and the more chilling for that. In one of his entries in the journal I referred to earlier, Kuznetsov speaks of his increasing anxiety and despair about his vocation and of his fear that he is becoming more and more "stupid," is turning into an Ionesco rhinoceros. Partly this is owing, he says, to his lack of contacts with the West and its writers. But it is also owing to the gap between what he knows and feels and what he can say, between his experience and the expression of it. What socialist realism asks the writer to do is not only to lie but to lay waste his experience, to lobotomize himself, and to denature the world.

"When you come to think of it," Anatole remarks after delivering some delicacy to the concentration camp commander at Babi Yar, "the whole world was a prison: restrictions on all sides . . . you can only go here, live only like this, think only like this and speak only like this." The last two phrases were cut.

(1971)

Milan Kundera: Repression East and West

The Book of Laughter and Forgetting begins with a joke about repression and its double meaning. Back in 1948, Party leader Gottwald made a speech to the people of Prague. It was a snowy day, he was speaking from a balcony, and one of his comrades, Clementis, gave him his fur cap. The speech proved to be historic, and a photograph featuring the two men became famous. Four years later, Clementis, now foreign secretary, was hanged as a traitor and his figure was airbrushed from the photograph. Where he had stood was now a blank wall. All that remained of him was the cap on Gottwald's head.

Pure East European humor: a message flashing from Gogol to contemporary Prague—the void under the fact, the commonplace detail with a surrealist twist and a manifold meaning; a hatful of terror and oblivion, and an unruly sense of humor that resists them. The joke is also typical Kundera—a Czech with iron in his irony who has never had to go out of his way to find his material.

A cocky, derisive, antinomian spirit from the start, Milan Kundera was kicked out of the Communist Party in 1950, probably by a tribunal of his young peers—the fate of Ludvik Jahn, the antihero of his first novel, *The Joke*. Kundera describes watching his erstwhile comrades dancing in the streets of Prague, "its cafés full of poets, its jails full of traitors," on the day that Zavis Kalandra, a famous Surrealist, was executed, the smoke from the crematorium rising to "the heavens like a good omen." Excluded from "the magic circle" of the orthodox, Kundera realized that he belonged now with Kalandra, among the outsiders and the fallen. These early years of the "idyll for all," as he puts it—"timid lovers held hands on movie screens, marital infidelity received harsh penalties at citizens' courts of honor, nightingales sang, and the body of Clementis swung back and forth like a bell ringing in the new dawn of mankind"—appear to have confirmed him in his sardonic individualism.

Against a kind of second Soviet takeover, the relentless positivism and dogmatism, Kundera imposed his view of the vanity of human desires, of the crossing of purposes within and between people, of the child that continues to father the dissident and the apparatchik alike. Honoring the cap on Gottwald's head, Kundera placed what faith he had left in the irrational, the accidental, even the perverse, which provide now and then a little space in the interstices of an authoritarian society for life and truth to break through. He wrote a lot about gratuitous acts—particularly of people jumping out of windows, morally speaking, to spite and shame their persecutors—exploring through the private life the defenestration tendencies of his so frequently conquered country, placing the compelling fantasies of his sexual marksmen alongside those of the state and its henchmen. Having ruined his life by his political "joke," Ludvik Jahn then completes his humiliation by trying to seduce the wife of his chief betrayer. In *Life Is Elsewhere*, a Nabokovian account of the short life of a precocious literary and political opportunist which parodies the tradition of Romantic poetry and politics, Jaromil Volker simultaneously achieves the zenith and nadir of his life when he informs on his girlfriend and her brother. The main interest of Kundera's last novel, *The Farewell Party,* leads up to and away from the impulse that prompts a dissident intellectual to allow a young nurse to poison herself accidentally.

Since neither the political nor the cultural commissars of Czech life were tolerant of baleful satire, Kundera went unpublished, except for the period of the Prague Spring, when *The Joke* appeared. It made him immediately famous, and two years later, his country having returned to "the warm loving embrace of the Soviet Union," it made him again a nonperson. The only work he could get was writing horoscopes for a socialist youth magazine under the pseudonym of a nonexistent mathematician; when his identity was uncovered and a young editor fell with him, he decided he was bad news for everyone and managed to leave the country for good.

The Book of Laughter and Forgetting is his first writing from exile. It is made up of seven narratives suspended like bridges from the two themes of its title, as though Kundera were trying to write his way across the gap between East and West, past and present, rejoining what the conditions of the Cold War and of his own life have sundered. Thus the cap from Clementis's head finds a lovely parallel in a section of the final story, which describes the funeral of Victor Passer, a fellow refugee who had continued to believe in his life even in its agonizing terminal stage, much as he had stubbornly clung to his vision of a new and humane politics. The funeral soon turns comic when the grave attendants miss their cue and lower the coffin into the grave, even as the speaker goes on addressing his remarks directly to the deceased. Then a gust of wind blows the hat from the head of Clevis, one of the mourners. A self-conscious, indecisive man, Clevis finally brings himself to chase down the hat, which has become the center of everyone's attention, but it continues to elude his furtive gestures and finally blows into the grave. The mourners are all racked by barely repressed laughter, particularly so when each of them must drop his shovelful of earth onto the coffin, on which sits the hat, "as though the indomitably vital and optimistic Passer were sticking his head out."

Another Czech who insists on being remembered and who illustrates the cruel, homely, perverse, and zany way things happen—the human comedy, Czech style—is a dissenter named Mirek. Mirek still smarts from the realization that many years ago he took as his first mistress an ardent Stalinist who, worse yet, was ugly. It is 1971, the authorities are closing in, he has carefully kept many incriminating documents of his and his friends' activities, believing that "the struggle of man against power is the struggle of memory against oblivion." Instead of hiding his papers, however, he races off in his car to see his Zdena and ask her to return his love letters. Mirek has some revisionism of his own in mind. His trip is full of Proustian slips—the memory of his willingness to bark like a dog so that she wouldn't say he made love like an intellectual, even the memory of a begonia-decked summer house that delivers the astonishing message that he once loved her, big nose and all—but none of this prevents Mirek from airbrushing her out of his life, for "Mirek is as much a rewriter of history as the Communist Party, all political parties, all nations, all men. . . . The only reason people want to be masters of the future is to change the past."

Meanwhile, Mirek's other purpose—to pursue his fate as a soldier of memory—is going forward on its own: that is, when he arrives home the police are already going through his papers. "You don't seem to care much about your friends," one of them says. But though his son and ten of his comrades will go to prison with him, Mirek is fulfilled. "They wanted to erase hundreds of thousands of lives from human memory and leave nothing but a single unblemished idyll. But Mirek is going to stretch out full length over their idyll, like a blemish, like the cap on Gottwald's head."

Mirek's story is clear in its meaning but enigmatic in its tone, somewhere between bemusement and derision. Though he is deeply concerned about the "struggle of memory," Kundera is generally sardonic about the dissidents who carry it on. Politics seems to have set his teeth permanently on edge. Elsewhere he distinguishes between the "demons" and the "angels"—and their respective modes of laughter, the former being generated by the irrational, incongruous, disorderly principle, the latter by the rational, harmonious, dogmatic one. He tells us that both principles are needed, but since the angels of dogma are in control everywhere he looks ("they [have] taken over the left and the right, Arab and Jew, Russian general and Russian dissident"), he sides with the demons of heresy. Which is hardly a choice for him: a subversive conservative, he identifies the demonic with the burdens of history, adulthood, memory, remorse, and love; the angelic with the innocence, indifference, present-mindedness, sensuality, and conformity of childhood.

This distinction runs through and animates most of the other stories. Its principal embodiment is a beautiful Czech refugee named Tamina, who seems to be a surrogate for Kundera's soul and its situation. Tamina supports herself as a waitress but sustains herself with the memories of her happy marriage, her husband having died soon after they escaped to the West. Immured in the inward silences of her devotion to their shared past (Kundera calls it a small green plot on which a single rose grows), Tamina listens patiently to the childish chatter of her customers—mostly political and literary blowhards, orgasm freaks, and other victims of Western inanity—waiting for the hours when she can resume the litany and reconstruction of the vacations, holidays, and other time-marks of her marriage, as well as the daily re-creation of her husband's face. This is her joy; her despair is the blank spaces in her chronology, the dimming of her husband's features and expressions in her imagination. Meanwhile, her diary and letters remain in Prague. Eventually she gives herself to a fatuous young intellectual who has promised to pick up her papers in Prague. Able to seduce her but unable to enlist her in his "universe of blood and thoughts," Hugo succumbs to *litost* (the Czech term for Kundera's master human emotion—an angry mixture of humiliation and vindictiveness) and tells her he cannot go to Prague because his one published article, on the demystification of power, has made him a marked man there.

In Tamina's encounters with her customers as well as her glimpses of the contemporary culture, Kundera is not only placing an adult in a world of children but also placing what one might call the way of gravity next to the way of vacuity. This is not a matter of East versus West, for as the companion story makes clear, what gives weight to one's existence is mainly a fealty to the past, which is everywhere under attack.

Tamina in her vigils is looking not for nostalgia but for reality; "she is not compelled by a desire for beauty, she is compelled by a desire for life." But with her access to the past stymied, she enters a realm of fantasy or dream or parable, in which a young man named Gabriel advises her to "forget her forgetting," and escorts her to an island of children, a place where "things have no weight," where there is no remorse. There Tamina abandons her memories, then her modesty, then her adult sexuality along with its "hellish" context of love—the tensions, fear, and anguish that went into the drama and responsibility of her passionate marriage. As she plays around in the bathroom and then in bed with the nude children, her own early eroticism is released, and, like another of Kundera's characters, who is wildly turned on by a girl who resembles his mother's sexy friend from his youth, Tamina finds it delicious. "Sexuality freed from its diabolical ties with love had become a joy of angelic simplicity."

Into this grave lyric of Tamina's progress toward death, Kundera weaves a far-reaching accompaniment of commentary. It begins with reflections on Kafka's treatment of Prague as a city without memory, of a humanity that has lost all connection with humanity. As such, his novel *The Trial* has become a looming prophecy of the present regime, which has dismissed many of its historians from the universities and sent most of its practicing humanists into prison or exile—an organized campaign of forgetting aimed at the extinction of the national identity. In time, Husak, "the Premier of Forgetting," appears in the story: Kundera and his father hear him making a speech nearby to an audience of Pioneers: "Children! You are the future. Children! Never look back."

As Husak speaks for a childlike future, the life of Kundera's father is drawing near its end. A famous pianist, a scholar, a man of the past, he has spent his final years writing about the Beethoven sonatas, particularly the variations of the profoundly introspective No. 111. "Now I understand," he tells Kundera, shortly before he closes his eyes and begins his strenuous journey toward death, imparting to his son a hint of why Beethoven used this mode of composition to explore his inner universe, a hint that has inspired the technique of this book of themes and variations. Kundera compares the way of his father's life to the dying tradition of music itself and the nature of Husak's state to the standard harmonies, banal melodies, the demagogic rhythms of pop.

Back on the island, Tamina's erotic adventures soon come to a predictable end in boredom, rivalry, and then animosity. In time, she adjusts to the politics of a fun-and-games world, but amid the transistorized music, the writhing of the children's bodies, she realizes that the previously pleasant buoyancy of her new life has become terrifying, an "unbearable absence of weight"; she tries to swim away from the island, struggles all night in the water, and goes under where she began, much like the long ride on horseback to hide his body that Kundera imagines his father making.

"The Angels" is not the most effective story in this book of often amazing variations. There is too much content in it to control, possibly too much personal grief. But it is the most deeply meant and the key to the book as a whole. It is an intricate parabolic meditation, I think, on Kundera's situation as a renegade East European writer who must now make his way through the much "lighter" atmosphere of the West, where everything is permitted but very little matters, precisely the opposite of the atmosphere that has formed him. It also carries a tutelary message to a longtime sensualist who has reached the other side of middle age, where desire is harder to come by than gratification and the lure of the "angels" is as hard to resist as it is to be nourished by. Several of the stories I have not touched on carry out Kundera's exploration of the inner world he brought with him to the West in lieu of his notebooks and files. I have not done justice to their range and cohesiveness, to Kundera's ability to keep the most disparate material working together in a story mostly by means of the power of his images to startle and radiate and connect. But less a storyteller than an image maker, he sometimes allows his fiction to be victimized by his virtuosity, an impatience at having to test his convictions by dramatizing them instead of just stylizing them. More's the pity, since these convictions about the way of gravity and the way of vacuity are diamond-hard, formed under the pressures of a life and its changes that beggar a Western reviewer's experience but still can instruct his moral imagination.

(1980)

George Konrád's Burden

Some years ago, when I was traveling in the Soviet Union, I was taken to the studio of a Georgian artist. Much of his work had a strong erotic or religious feeling, sometimes both together. We became friendly and I asked him whether all of these sensuous curves and devout figures and symbols might not get him in trouble. He replied that he was a Georgian artist, that he painted the culture of his people: his female forms expressed their regard for the generative principle, his saints were the bearers of their history of oppression and resistance. At one point he showed me a painting of a kneeling male figure shackled to a post by a collar and chain: it was titled "Self-Portrait." What about that? I asked. Couldn't it be taken as a protest against the restrictions of the artist in Soviet society? "People can think what they want," he snapped. "The chain and collar is my art. I cannot escape from it, but it is what holds me to my place in the world. It is an obsession but it also tells me who I am, why I live. I painted it just after I recovered from a dangerous illness." When I returned to Moscow I related the incident to a writer who knew the artist. "I couldn't tell whether he was serious or ingenuous or evasive or cynical." "All of them," the writer replied. "Like most of us."

I sometimes think of that story when I read the work of

the East European dissident writers: Sinyavsky, Aksyonov, Konrád, Kís, Kundera, Hrabal, et al. There is an apparent simplicity about them—a direct relation to the creaturely life of their people. On the other hand, they are subtle, devious, unexpectedly brutal, macabre—a kind of theatrical trafficking in the forbidden feelings as well as subjects, an easy recourse to the inhuman. There is also the obsessiveness that haunts their pages, a stylistic equivalent of the fatedness that presses down on their characters, both confining them and weighting them, giving them a dimension beyond themselves, the sense of having a destiny, however wretched or absurd it may be.

All of which, along with the political risks, goes into the perception of an inner necessity that we admire in these writers and for lack of which so much Western writing seems to be dying on its feet. Each of George Konrád's three novels is essentially the monologue of a Hungarian intellectual who can't stop talking because he feels so constrained by his experience, so burdened by the weight of the life around him, and so needled by his conscience that he must keep trying to deliver himself or at least exhaust himself into silence. One of his speakers is a case-hardened social worker; the second is a community planner in a treacherous bureaucracy; the speaker in *The Loser,* Konrád's new novel, is a scarred and callous dissenter. Each of them is shackled to a situation that is unyielding and highly equivocal but from which he draws his saturnine vigor and lucidity, his "solitary invective," as one of them puts it. Though they are distinct individuals with their own voices, they are brothers under the skin, a family of deep-sea divers, existentially speaking, weighted down by their fateful positions, encased in inner concerns that enable them to resist the external pressures of the state that would otherwise disable them. Because they continue to choose the role that entraps them, the tone of their voices runs the full register of irony—baleful, mordant, sardonic, sarcastic, chagrined, wry. Written from what seems to be the same ongoing crisis of belief, these three fictional memoirs are psychologically signed by the same hand, provoked by the tensions of a fallen humanism.

Yet they differ considerably in literary texture and emotional impact. Konrád's first novel, *The Case Worker,* is the most artistic—a short work of formidable pathos. It is a tour through the lower depths of Budapest, conducted by a welfare worker who is resigned to "the faulty nature of things," who merely "steers the suffering this way and that," but who soon begins to succumb to the guilt of his dreams, the curiosity of his reveries: Gorky meets Kafka. One of his cases is a five-year-old idiot whose father has never recovered from being unjustly denounced and imprisoned as a Nazi collaborator. Old Bandula begs in the cafés, cannot hold a job even as an orderly in a morgue, but insists on keeping the boy, against the protests of his neighbors. Lying on the bare springs of his bed, while the naked child, tied into his crib, plays with scraps of food and his wastes, the former minor official tells the caseworker, T.:

> Remember all those principles, rules, and punishments? If I may say so, you're still a slave to all that. You rarely think of yourself—only, let's say, when you have a toothache. None of that applies to me. I'm no more human than my son. Let's have a cigarette. I'm a freak. Of course, that, too, is a human word.

T. is fascinated by this fringe of being, this last-ditch moral space the broken man and his permanently dazed wife insist on defending against the authorities. Then one day they abruptly abandon it, pass into the "terrible inviolable freedom" of suicide, and T. finds himself sitting on Bandula's bedsprings and watching the child, as hairy, healthy, and reeking as a bear cub, gnawing on his vanished mother's brassiere. Another life, not much more lurid and phantomlike than the one T. is leading, begins to stalk his mind: He can give up his job and family and settle in here, keeping the child from the horrors of the children's asylum, taking in piecework for a living.

The experience of replacing Bandula is no less compelling for being a reverie—indeed, so intense and graphic is it that many readers mistake it for the fact. Moreover, by the end of his long day of imagining his new life T. finds that the wound of his own despair has somehow closed. He places the child for the time being and goes back to his other cases. "Let all those come who want to; one of us will talk, the other will listen; at least we shall be together."

Like Dostoevsky, Konrád is both a psychological terrorist and a compassionate witness; and in exercising these talents with the Bandulas and the other inhabitants of their woeful slum, along with the teenage suicides, battered wives, crippled workers, and other examples of nature's and society's derelictions that T. broods about, Konrád is carrying on the great theme of nineteenth-century Russian fiction—the forging of the human bond between the privileged consciousness of the writer and the mute despair of people.

He has also carried it forward to stand over against the actual mentality of state socialism. Though *The Case Worker* does not deal with politics as such, Konrád is intent on pouring back into Hungarian consciousness the personal, the disruptive, the irremediable elements in life that Communist culture tries to leach out by its relentlessly collectivist, nationalistic, and positivist ethos. In a historical analysis, *The Intellectuals on the Road to Class Power,* that Konrád wrote with Ivan Szelényi, the authors describe the "marginal" writers who have taken the risk of distancing themselves from the official state culture because "in speaking of the human condition they could not derive from socialism optimistic solutions for the problems of illness, loss, death or even disappointment in love." *The Case Worker* is this wry comment armed and barbed and delivered with shattering force.

The City Builder lacks this clarity, concentration, and fierce intentionality. In the main, Konrád is an intellectual who writes novels rather than the other way around. The point of view of each of his novels is a closely held first-person one, and given Konrád's penchant for commentary and self-scrutiny, we are almost always listening to the teller rather than to the tale: Consciousness is all. This is one reason why the reverie in *The Case Worker* is such an appropriate and effective device. But in *The City Builder* there is little to alter and complicate the speaker's awareness, to take him where he hasn't been. Konrád runs an intermittent narrative thread through the speaker's successive states of mind, opaque with metaphor and paradox, within which he struggles to explain and justify, lament and revile his situation as a guilty ex-husband and father and as a technocrat in a regime that has betrayed him and his ideals. The book aims to evoke and personalize the class consciousness of the intellectuals who participated in and still serve the revolution, but it does so in such a generalizing, introspective, and cryptic way that one suspects Konrád may have written it in spite of himself, haunted by the image of the Hungarian thought police looking over his shoulder.

What saves *The City Builder* from the kind of rhetoric with which French radicals preen and torment themselves ("Assuming reality—even if only in name—is humiliating. Opening the window of my cramped and constant world to let in time, I try to figure out who is scratching and whining in this dark room . . ." and so on), what gives the book Konrád's stamp, is the intense nagging that is going on behind the screen of his language between the speaker's sardonic resignation and his restless conscience: a couple that can't get along and can't stay away from each other; a perverse dialectic that generates the remarkable energy of his sensibility even when it falls into a manner. In the clear stretches of the speaking, that is, when the force of events—the war, the Holocaust, the 1948 revolution—provide expressive scenes to go with the sound track, the planner's monologue suggests the genuine testament it might have been.

The Loser is Konrád's effort to write that testament. It is nothing if not specific and outspoken: the direct experience and evolving attitudes of a veteran Hungarian radical. Bearing the same identifying initial, T., as the speaker in *The Case Worker,* he too has been through it and through it. Even more so: his horrors being political ones—battlefields, torture chambers, prison cells, and Central Committee meetings. Committed to the concrete, which in this case weighs a ton, Konrád makes himself shoulder the burden of T.'s history—from his entry early in World War II as a student anti-Fascist to his exit in the mid-1970s as a prominent dissident who ends up in a mental hospital, where he finally can free himself of politics and can stop lying.

The grandson of a prominent Jewish merchant, scholar, and seer, and the son of an emancipated, even somewhat decadent land developer, T. loves the former but imitates the latter, his early life being highlighted by his precocious seductions. Even as an anti-Fascist courier he remains something of a *flâneur,* though less so than his younger brother Dani, who becomes his accomplice and betrayer, a man whom the politics of terror will deprave rather than merely corrupt. T.'s heady apprenticeship abruptly ends when he is caught, badly beaten, and forced to watch his girlfriend hang by her arms while he continues to withhold information. During the war he serves in a brutalized

is becoming a facile existentialist, formulating a studied response to a moral crisis he has stripped of its anguish.

So it will go through most of his moments of crisis. Whether he bravely refuses to betray his colleague and friend during the purges, or refuses to falsify his past under torture, or agrees to deliver the opposition government's foolhardy order to the Soviet minister in 1956, thereby ensuring himself another prison sentence at the very least—T.'s consciousness of what he is doing and why has much the same lack of affect that characterizes his acts of compliance with brutality. Here he is speaking of his state of mind as a Communist official:

> Oppression is simply an educational tool; let the people learn that they can wish only for what we wish for. First they'll be beaten into submission; then, through us, they will regain their self-respect. . . . What else could I become but a Communist? The war was over, but the fighting went on between old and new, good and evil. The bourgeois hoards, the Communist fights. He considers more and more of the hoarders his enemies; he provokes them, hurts them, and this makes him proud of himself. This part is fairly easy; what's more difficult is to fall in love with the party.

No doubt such thoughts were thought. The point is that T. merely takes them in the stride of his sardonic equanimity. "Today I cannot argue with the man I was then: I look at him as though he were my son, though I am not moved by him." To be sure. But we are also to believe that the T. who begins speaking in this book from a mental hospital in a whirl of frightened and guilty images is a man worthy of our sympathy; just as he is at the end, when, in his final encounter with the inhuman, he assists his demonic brother in hanging himself but refuses to join him in death. From first to last, though, the immense destructiveness that T. has witnessed and immersed himself in has done little more than reinforce his essential aloofness—the ground tone of his voice, the bottom line of his experience.

Such aloofness may well overtake a Hungarian intellectual who chose the road, even only part of the way, to class power. As T. tells himself at one point: "Here's your chance to spill the beans about your class, to blurt out its unconscious secrets, write its collective memoirs." But what this comes down to are such "beans" as:

> It was quite a lark; a historical sleight-of-hand: with your pals you laid the foundation of intellectual class power, which was pretty nasty at first but which will in time become more pleasant and it will never be supplanted by another kind of power.

Whatever such aloofness may gain for the book as a document it loses as art. Aloofness is never a basis for art, because the way to the depths is closed to it; it lacks the will to struggle, being secretly preoccupied with the wounds of the ego. Hence T.'s conflict between awareness and conscience is often weak and equivocal and, unlike his counterpart's in *The Case Worker,* unable to be resolved: one reason why Konrád has to bring in the tangential issue of the brother's murder of his girlfriend and his suicide to end *The Loser.* Except that the ending does remind us of what T. actually is: He is less a loser, since he has never had much, morally speaking, to lose; he is mostly an accomplice.

And yet there are many moments when he is more, when he does not make light of the crushing weight of his experience, when the writing sheds its fitful, ambivalent ironies and becomes closely knit by strong feeling. These moments often have to do with T.'s pious grandfather and with his moral legacy, which now and then enters T.'s mind to strengthen or enlighten him. "Like drunkards we live in a fog of self-love," he remembers his grandfather saying, "and, confusing good and evil, we grope our way in the darkness and laugh when our neighbor falls"—words that prophesy the political nightmares to come. At one point, T. comes upon a pile of fresh corpses in a forest, victims of a Nazi killer squad:

> The naked bodies are sexless; I can see they shielded the backs of their heads like infants as they were toppled over by a round of machine-gun fire. . . . A bearded man's head rests on a young girl's whitened thighs; the cold groins are as indistinct as a frozen indentation in a dirt road. Now you know how perishable is he who is so very like the earth, how little he differs from the clay he was fashioned from—he who was created by God in His image. . . .

And T. goes on to speak of the good and evil in this creature, of the one who "slipped a piece of bread to those hiding in the henhouse," and of the one who "pulled an old man in a hat from a woodshed." Another voice seems to be speaking to us at such moments of deep creaturely feeling than the garrulous T., alternating between his world- and self-weariness and his glibness. It is a voice buried deep in his nature, a source of energy and direction for the struggle his author might have made to provide a more engaged and deeper account than this one of the nightmare of history that continues to obsess him. There is enough material in *The Loser* for five novels. I hope that the next time, Konrád chooses, as he did in *The Case Worker,* to employ the extraordinary strength of his consciousness and the passion of his concern to bear the full weight of one of them.

(1983)

Jacobo Timerman as Prophet

Jacobo Timerman is like the surprise witness at a trial whose revelations throw the whole case into a new perspective. The burden of his startling and reverberating book, *Prisoner Without a Name, Cell Without a Number,* is that the violence and terror that have reigned in Argentina for the past decade have culminated in a regime not merely and reliably "authoritarian," as our own authorities would have us believe. Instead it is a neototalitarian state devoted to the ideology and practices of Nazi fascism. Further, in the paralyzed accommodation and passivity of Argentina's Jews, and in the indifference of the rest of the world, Timerman sees the inexorably meshing conditions for another Holocaust.

Jewish paranoia and alarmism? What Timerman writes about he saw with his own eyes, heard with his own ears, felt on his own body, perceived with his own clarity and anguish. As the publisher of Argentina's principal liberal newspaper and a leader of the perilous moderate position, he knew the officials and henchmen as well as those who became victims before he did. In the police stations and prisons, in the secret holding places where he was interrogated and tortured, in the military courtroom where he was tried as a Zionist conspirator, he saw the evil and the madness cooking together and was forced to swallow the mixture.

The authority with which he speaks is in his tone as well as his details, in his character as well as his experience. He is, quite simply, an extraordinary man: reflective, humane, righteous, and withal extremely brave, resourceful, and hardheaded. His prose, at least in translation, is now the rough-hewn argumentative language of an old-time political journalist of the left, now the terse, concrete images dictated by his passion and pain—a natural eloquence. Page after page reflects a rock-solid integrity, psychological and moral, which brought him to his long ordeal, one that began well before his imprisonment and carried him through it. Timerman appears destined to bear this witness, so strong is the sense of unfolding connections between who he was and who he became, what he did and suffered and what he now must tell us: the destiny, that is to say, of a prophet.

The axial lines of Timerman's life can be pieced together from the sparse autobiographical details and passages that crop up here and there in these reflections. He tells us at the outset that he came from an influential family with a tradition of fighting for Jewish rights in their town in the Ukraine ("I bear within me still a vague longing for those tall, bearded unsmiling men"). His parents emigrated to Buenos Aires when he was a small boy; his father soon died, leaving his wife and two sons penniless. They lived in a single room in a tenement in the Jewish quarter; Timerman worked as a messenger and cleaned the halls and lavatories in lieu of paying rent, while his mother sold clothes for their living. His closeness to this strong woman is one of the ground tones of his character and, I imagine, is the source of the striking interweave of caring and ambition in his life.

Her dream of a Jewish homeland became his Zionism,

and the movement's youth groups brought him out of the ghetto and into intellectual and political consciousness. As an adolescent in the late 1930s, he was imbued with the various idealisms of that heady age of Zionist socialism, the Spanish Civil War, the Popular Front, and the cause of the Allies, "that miraculous co-existence of world suffering and Jewish suffering." He grappled as well with their various contradictions. He tried to find a way to fight in World War II, but had to content himself with leading demonstrations against Juan Perón when he came to power in the early 1940s.

Like most Jewish families in Argentina, as elsewhere, the Timermans were addicted to the news, the Jews' early-warning defense system; young Jacobo carried out this fascination and became a political journalist and eventually a well-known television commentator. He is silent about this period of his life, but appears to have had something of the *macher* in him: he started two weekly news magazines in the 1960s and founded *La Opinión* in 1971. Often compared to *Le Monde,* his newspaper made him an influential figure; his circle included prominent moderates from the government, the military, the business world, and the media. Writing of the famous restaurant where they all congregated, Timerman tells us, "In 1946 I had been brought here as the guest of a politician; now, as head of a newspaper, I was the one who did the inviting."

He was to be given plenty of scope for his prestige, his contacts, his liberal convictions, and his sense of responsibility. As early as 1966, Cuban-trained guerrillas had appeared in Argentina. Five years later, Peronist provocateurs, kidnappers, and killers who covered most of the political spectrum were creating the public fear and disorder that would bring the former dictator back to power. The rampant factionalism of Argentine politics combined with "the eroticism of violence"—Timerman's term for

Latin America's contribution to the lethal psychic forces of the century—to make the middle 1970s into a kind of Hobbesian state of nature:

> Co-existing in Argentina were: rural and urban Trotskyist guerrillas; right-wing Peronist death squads; armed terrorist groups of the large labor unions . . . ; para-police groups of both the Left and the Right; and terrorist groups of Catholic rightists. . . . Hundreds of other organizations . . . existed, small units that found ideological justification for armed struggle in a poem by Neruda or an essay by Marcuse.

As one Peronist regime followed another, the situation became so desperate that Timerman tried to persuade his moderate cronies in the military and the legislature to take over the government; he saw this as the only way to suppress the kidnappings and extortions, the murders and disappearances, on all sides. At the same time, he called for reinstituting civil rights. A senator said the risks of a military alliance were too great; a general merely laughed at the idea. Timerman was more successful in organizing a group of labor and political journalists who tried to marshal public opinion by boldly attacking the extremists, and thereby end the terrified silence in which they swam. It is clear that, at least in part, Timerman was seizing the opportunity to redeem his absence from World War II. "We're lucky at least to be here, with a newspaper at hand, at a time when the country is being besieged by fascism of the Left and Right," he exhorted his colleagues.

Though he was to remember this speech with irony, Timerman continued to aim his pen and press at the perpetrators of violence and the authorities who had abolished civil rights. He also took strong, clear pro-Israel positions, which made him more hated by the left and more suspect by the right. He supported Salvador Allende in Chile and attacked Fidel Castro's exporting of revolution and his treatment of prisoners. But he also opposed his own government's decision to terminate relations with Cuba. These and other complexities of liberal doctrines and positions, so taken for granted in North America, offended the simple verities of the militants and the military. Both sides dispatched death threats; when one of each arrived on the same day, Timerman took the occasion to reaffirm his principles in a signed article that wondered which side would wind up with his corpse. Sixty-five journalists had by then died or disappeared.

Timerman had passed now into a realm where he was virtually alone—except for an English-language newspaper and some members of the Roman Catholic Church. When the military finally seized power in 1977, his peril was complete—and soon his despair. The assassinations and disappearances continued, but they were now mostly perpetrated by the clandestine agents of the government itself. By insisting on *habeas corpus,* Timerman found himself in a double bind. He was told by the junta that it would let him alone if he ceased publishing these pleas, along with the names of the missing that gave them substance. He was also responding to the pleas of the missing victims' families, although he knew that victims thus named tended to be executed summarily. Trapped by this assertion of principle and sympathy that was also an exercise in futility and danger, he put his convictions through the fire: "How to explain to myself those scores and hundreds of articles appealing for mercy for a kidnapped soldier, a missing terrorist, pleading for the lives of the very individuals who wanted to put an end to my own." Was this the prompting "of a kind of omnipotence in being the victim or . . . some vague guilt hidden behind my principles, my intrusive honesty, my inexplicable humanitarian mission"? On the other hand, there were "the faces of relatives that appeared at *La*

Opinión, plus the absurd conviction that it was possible to recover a human being, plus the need to believe that a newspaper constitutes a powerful institution." The easy resolution of the dilemma was to abandon it, to follow advice and emigrate to Israel. But from the crucible of his situation emerged a simple and final truth: "the one thing that was impossible was to close your eyes."

His character was now annealed, the weaker material of the entrepreneur burned away. When he was arrested, he did not break under the torture, under the misery of inhabiting a cell little better than an open grave with a board over it, under the relentless interrogation to make him admit that he was the agent of a worldwide Zionist conspiracy to seize Patagonia and thereby open the way to Antarctica. Absurd? Doubly so, when it emerged that his interrogators wanted him to admit that the conspiracy's centers were in New York, Moscow, Tel Aviv, and Buenos Aires, and that Menachem Begin was advising the leftist terrorists. As Timerman came to realize, however, "such questions were less absurd when you're being tortured to extract an answer." You begin to see the patterns behind the questions.

In the months that followed, culminating in his trial, Timerman sought to understand the combination of hatred, fear, and fantasy that a consistent logic wove in the minds of the Argentine officers. Their controlling premise is that World War III has already begun; the enemy is left-wing terrorism, and the first battleground is Argentina. This terrorism was created by Marx, Trotsky, the founders of the state of Israel, and many other Jewish revolutionaries. At the same time, the foundation of the Christian worldview, on which society should stand, has been undermined by Einstein, just as the Christian family has been undermined by Freud. Their work continues to be carried on by the natural and social sciences, the arts, the media, and the legal profession, which are all permeated by Jews;

and by the principal leftist powers, which are also controlled or heavily influenced by Jews. So if Begin's book, *Revolt in the Holy Land*, is found in the possession of Argentine guerrillas, it follows. If the publisher of *La Opinión* is a declared Zionist who interferes with the stamping out of leftist terrorism and subversion and refuses to be driven out of the country, it also follows.

Pursuing this logic—as well as the compulsive need for the simple, orderly, hermetic world of the army barracks, the cruiser, and the flight squadron—the Argentine military instituted strict moral codes in the arts, eliminated majors in sociology, philosophy, and psychology, forbid the use of Freudian psychiatry, and imposed a Catholic education on all public schools. And to ensure that the subversive doctrines would be destroyed root and branch, the junta also eliminated "thousands of individuals in Argentina who had no relation with subversion but who . . . represented that world which they found intolerable and incomprehensible and who hence constituted the enemy."

Understanding this murderous juggernaut of neo-Nazi fantasy did not arm Timerman against the forces of hatred that propelled it. He found he could hold on to his sanity, could even resist the temptation of suicide—the one sensuous image his brutalized psyche could rise to—by deliberately obliterating all tenderness, all hope, all thought and memory that was not impersonal. What he could not obliterate, because it was continually shocked, beaten, and cursed to life by his accusers and guards alike, was his Jewish identity. And what he found he could not cease thinking about and remembering was the silent complicity of the Jewish leaders:

> My incarceration and torture were a personal tragedy, but nothing more, for in view of the sort of journalism I practiced, the possibility of my arrest and assassina-

> tion fit into the rules of the game. Whereas the panic of Argentine Jewish leaders constituted a nightmare within the tragedy. And it was the nightmare that agonized me and kept me awake.

The final sections of *Prisoner Without a Name* are filled with passionate arguments against and denunciation of the Argentine Jews' "gilded ghetto" mentality—one that quietly complies and accommodates, refuses to make trouble, guides and consoles itself with the idea that the magnitude of anti-Semitic actions is still far from Holocaust proportions. To Timerman, no idea could be more misleading and ominous. In his attack on it, the exhausted, tormented man revives, and one sees the fearless activist, the humanitarian, and the Jewish spokesman—the "powerful Timerman" who had made the Jewish community feel proud and protected. The whole man, whose integrity we have seen so acted out and acted upon, stands up near the end and delivers these scorching words:

> The Holocaust will be understood not so much for the number of the victims as for the magnitude of the silence. . . . Using my newspaper as a base, [I] fought so that not even the slightest anti-Semitic trace should be left in silence, for the silence of the Jews is the sole indicator of the current presence of the Holocaust in the Jewish historical condition.

The whole Timerman and perhaps something more. In his study of the Jewish prophets, Abraham Heschel suggests the process of impersonalization by which the prophet, through struggle, loneliness, and concern, leaves behind the normal, trimming self that maintains equanimity by not seeing or feeling or saying too much. In Heschel's words, "Our eyes are witness to the callousness and cruelty of man, but our heart tries to obliterate the memories, to calm the nerves, and to silence our conscience."

Timerman is not an observant Jew; his faith is in the Zionist way of strengthening Jewish identity and understanding. "Being," as he puts it, "is more important than remembering." Still, this critic of the gilded ghetto of survivalism is to me a secular version of the early prophets. At the end, Timerman the entrepreneur and political pundit gave way once and for all to the man who could not close his eyes to suffering or refuse "to print what had to be printed." In prison he discovered that his Jewishness was the one irreducible element of his personhood, and his rage against the obtuseness and timidity of the Jewish leaders became his source of strength as well as the object of the need to intensify responsibility that has wrung this book out of him. Let us listen again to Heschel:

> The prophet is the man who feels fiercely. God has thrust a burden upon his soul, and he is bowed and stunned at man's fierce greed. . . . Prophecy is the voice that God has lent to the silent agony, a voice to the plundered poor, to the profaned riches of the world.

(1981)

A Witness of Vietnam

In April 1969 I was invited to Honolulu as one of the guest speakers of the Young President's Organization. The honorarium was the opportunity to live like the head of a multimillion-dollar corporation for five days. Just down the way from the Waikiki Hilton was the Army's R & R center, whose beach was filled with young men on their five-day furlough from Vietnam. Though I found myself wandering down there a lot, there wasn't much to feel about these soldiers. Sunbathing, playing touch football, chatting up girls, or lying quietly with their wives, they seemed more like the college crowd at Jones Beach than the temporary survivors of a vicious war. On the final evening, I skipped the banquet and went for a walk. It was around midnight and the road took me past the Army center. A line of green buses was drawn up there, and they soon were filled with soldiers and drove off, leaving behind a small group of young women. One of them walked away ahead of me, and I watched as her shoulders began to shake.

Though we were then four years into the war this was the first time its effect on the lives of the other America had come home to me. It was not only that weeping girl but those buses returning their passengers as surreptitiously as possible to the carnage, while six hundred yards away another group of Americans lived it up, some of them no doubt on profits from the war, and remained as oblivious of the human costs as the Army authorities meant them to be. As the government meant the rest of the country to be.

Though this little epiphany stayed with me, I wasn't much changed by it. I quickly went back to viewing the war through the abstracting lens of my politics, which easily converted the soldiers, marines, and pilots I saw on TV into the sacrificial dupes or violent zealots of Nixon and Kissinger. The only servicemen who were real to me were the veterans who opposed the war; they and, of course, Calley, who confirmed the worst. Then the war ended and, like most Americans, I put it out of mind, except when the Watergate revelations provided an oblique sense of retributive justice.

Which brings me to *A Rumor of War,* whose title expresses the remoteness I have been trying to characterize but whose pages steadily obliterate it. The author, Philip Caputo, achieves this by the relentless immediacy of his descriptions of this "war of endless dying" (quite equal to the World War II writing of Mailer and Jones and very little since); by the acuity of his comments on the psychological and moral devastation of fighting a "people's war"; and, most to the point, by placing himself as a marine lieutenant directly before the reader and giving the American involvement a sincere, manly, increasingly harrowed American face.

If you've had much contact with the upper reaches of blue-collar America, you'll know Caputo right away. Though he went on to become a foreign correspondent for the *Chicago Tribune,* he is still closely in touch with the earthy, hot-blooded, ambitious, adventurous kid who grew up with a fly rod or a .22 in his hands in a tract-house development out on the prairie west of Chicago. He doesn't tell us much about his background, but it's easy to imagine him as the hard-nosed player who wants the ball in the closing minutes; also as the English major from a working-class family who now and then asks a question that cuts through the literary cant. In short, to use David Halberstam's phrase, Caputo was among "the best and the brightest" of the social class that fought the war. As such he is an excellent witness and interpreter of men, much like himself, who came from the "ragged fringes of the Great American dream," who embodied its "virtues as well as flaws: idealistic, insolent, generous, direct, violent, and provincial." And from being their articulate and troubled spokesman he draws much of his fierce will to make you listen and much of his authority.

His career in the Marines was no less representative and expressive. In the early 1960s he signed up with the Marine ROTC because he was sated with "security, comfort, and peace" and "hungered for danger, challenges, and violence" that would test his manhood. Hence the Marines. At the same time he was full of the altruism that went along with the truculence of the Kennedy years and he was eager to respond to the ringing exhortation of the Inaugural Address. Hence his thrill in March 1965 to be an officer in the first combat unit sent to Vietnam. After about a year, most of it spent in the field, Caputo was charged with ordering the murder of two Vietnamese civilians, of which he was ambiguously, understandably, and, by then, almost inevitably guilty.

A Rumor of War is thus the true story of the transformation of one of the "knights of Camelot," whose "crusade" was Vietnam and whose cause could only be "noble and good," into a vindictive, desperate, and chronically schizoid killer in a war that he had come to realize was futile and evil. As Emerson put it, "the lengthened shadow of a man is history": Caputo would no doubt agree, for the course and character and damage of America's involvement was registered on his altered body, mind, nerves, and spirit.

The causes and stages of his transformation form the spine of his narrative. It begins with Caputo's account of his summers at Quantico, where reserve officer training differed little from the fabled sadism of marine boot camp. Along with the physical ordeals and mental abuse, there was the brainwashing in the classrooms and mess halls: the voices chanting in unison "Ambushes are murder and murder is fun," or a litany about the Marine Corps' invincibility, ending with "Gung Ho! Gung Ho! Gung Ho! Pray for War!" All of which, as Caputo observes, was "designed to destroy each man's sense of self-worth . . . until he proved himself equal to the Corps' exacting standards." Though he saw through much of this cult of "machismo bordering on masochism," he was also driven to embrace it by his overwhelming desire to succeed as a marine officer. His most significant experience was being chewed out for smoking during a maneuver, which he believes lastingly reinforced his fear of criticism and yearning for praise. "By the time the battalion left for Vietnam, I was ready to die . . . for a few favorable remarks in a fitness report."

Though lean and mean, his head filled with the jargon and tactics of "counter-insurgency," adapted from the British success in Malaysia, Caputo was not prepared for Vietnam—not for its climate or terrain or its lethal, determined, phantomlike enemy. As soon as his company moved away from guarding the airfield near Danang and began to practice its "spirit of aggressiveness," what had been "a splendid little war" became miserable, terrifying, and absurd. Their search-and-destroy missions were mostly in the Annanese Cordillera, mountainous rain forests which "the Vietnamese themselves regarded with dread." There the heat was awesome, "a thing malevolent and alive," capable of inflicting a stroke by raising a marching man's body temperature to 109 degrees. The jungle was all but impenetrable: elephant grass that cut through field uniforms; bamboo thickets and vines that had to be hacked through with machetes; barricades that were likely to be mined; trails made deadly by almost invisible trip lines, sniper fire, ambushes. Into this nightmare green world where, as Caputo remarks, the whole NVA could easily have been concealed, the helicopters would fly in a couple of rifle companies. Moving at the torturous rate of three or four miles a day, they might, if successful, flush out and kill a handful of Viet Cong and have only that many marines hit or blown apart. The mental strain, if possible, was worse than the physical: a file of men desperately bunching up, despite the danger of an ambush, because "even the illusion of being alone in that haunted dangerous wilderness was unbearable."

It took only one such mission for Caputo and his company to revert to the primal fears and lusts that Hobbes described as the "state of nature." At the outset, when a platoon of VC, heavily outnumbered, is spotted and shelled, Caputo feels sorry for them: "I [still] tended to look upon war as an outdoor sport and the shelling seemed, well, unfair." But once they attack the ridge, one man shoots a wounded VC in the face, another slices off ears, and Caputo himself, having picked up a VC's bloody spoor, suddenly realizes that he doesn't really want to take him prisoner. "All I wanted to do was kill him—waste the little bastard and get out of that dank, heat-rotted ravine." Afterward, he remarks, "we felt like ghouls."

Murderous rages followed by guilt and remorse and the sense of degradation continue to stalk Caputo. On staff duty for a few months, he finds himself mainly keeping track of the casualties on the American side, the "kill ratios" and "body counts" on the VCs. Identifying the shattered bodies of men he served with, receiving a report on the fatal wounds of his best friend, he begins to dream of leading a platoon of resurrected corpses and suffers hallucinations in which a man's dead face peeks through the living one. His mind begins to split under the pressure of his obsessive fury, grief, guilt, as the casualties and atrocities steadily mount during the NVA offensive. Finally, he manages to return to line duty, but the monsoon season has begun and the torments of the summer campaign are but a prologue to those that follow.

With each month he appears to have more fury to burn, more moral numbness to account for in needlessly destroyed villages and hamlets. He wrestles with the mockeries of the "rules" of engagement: "it was wrong for an infantryman to destroy a village with phosphorus grenades but right for a fighter pilot to drop napalm on it." He concludes that military ethics seemed to be a matter of killing people at long range with sophisticated weapons. But the actuality was the official American strategy of "organized butchery." In his final month of duty, the commander of his half-decimated company is offering a can of beer "and the time to drink it" for any enemy casualty.

Caputo's book is not as relentless as I am making it appear to be. It is not meant to be one long damning indictment of a war that demoralized and brutalized him. There is the humane as well as the sadistic, sometimes together: two grunts rubbing salve on a baby's jungle sores while their officer threatens to pistol whip the uncooperative mother. There are the frequent accounts of the loyalty and concern of American troops bonding together not only for survival but to preserve their humanity. There are Caputo's close, brilliant accounts of the exhilaration and tension of combat: the heightening of the senses and mind to a pitch of acuity. There is his almost "orgasmic" pleasure of leadership when his company responds perfectly under the stress of battle. There is the transcendent moment when Caputo's fear of death disappears: "I would die as casually as a beetle is crushed under a boot heel. . . . My death would not alter a thing. I had never felt an emotion more sublime or liberating."

But this moment also marks a further stage of numbing. Indifferent to his own death, he is still ravaged by anxieties and deliriums of violence about his steadily dwindling company. When a village boy reports that he knows of two VC in an adjacent hut and when nothing is done about it, Caputo frantically decides to capture them. He sends in a team of his most reliable sharpshooters: "If they give you any problems, kill 'em." As he then admits, "In my heart I hoped Allen would find some excuse for killing them and Allen had read my heart." When the two bodies are duly brought in, one of them is the boy who gave the information.

What was Caputo's degree of guilt? By the time one reaches this culminating incident, one believes him when he says, "Something evil had been in me that night." One also believes him when he says, "The war in general and U.S. military policy in particular were ultimately to blame for the death of Le Du and Le Dung." One wants to see Caputo exonerated, which he was. For the ultimate effect of this book is to make the personal and the public responsibility merge into a degreeless nightmare of horror and waste, experienced by the former, assented to and concealed inhumanly by the policy makers and the generals. Out of the force of his obsession with the Vietnam war and his role in it, Caputo has revealed the broken idealism and suppressed guilt of America's involvement. And listening to his honest voice, one's own conscience begins to stir again though more complexly than it did ten years ago.

(1977)

Teaching the Bomb

The following comments on "The Fundamental Project of Technology," by Galway Kinnell, were written for an anthology, *Singular Voices,* in which a poet chooses one of his poems and talks about how he came to write it. Since Kinnell did not wish to do so, the editor of the anthology, Stephen Berg, asked me to fill in. Being neither a poet nor a critic of poetry, I was reluctant, but when I read the poem I was so struck and moved by it that I wanted to say why.

The Fundamental Project of Technology

"A flash! A white flash sparkled!"
—Tatsuichiro Akizuki
Concentric Circles of Death

Under glass, glass dishes which changed
in color; pieces of transformed beer bottles;
a household iron; bundles of wire become solid
lumps of iron; a pair of pliers; a ring of skullbone fused to the inside of a helmet; a pair of
eyeglasses

taken off the eyes of an eyewitness, without glass,
which vanished, when a white flash sparkled.

An old man, possibly a soldier back then,
now reduced down to one who soon will die,
sucks at the cigaret dangling from his lip, peers
at the uniform, scorched, of some tiniest schoolboy,
sighs out bluish mists of his own ashes over
a pressed tin lunch box well crushed back then
when
the word *future* first learned, in a white flash, to
jerk tears.

On the bridge outside, in navy black, a group
of schoolchildren line up, hold it, grin at a
flash-pop,
swoop in a flock across grass, see a stranger, cry,
hello! hello! hello! and soon, *goodbye! goodbye! goodbye!*
having pecked up the greetings that fell half
unspoken
and the going-sayings that those who went the day
it happened a white flash sparkled did not get to
say.

If all a city's faces were to shrink back all at once
from their skulls, would a new sound come
into existence,
audible above moans eaves extract from wind
that smoothes
the grass on graves; or raspings heart's-blood
greases still;
or wails babies trill born already skillful at the
grandpa's rattle;
or infra-screams bitter-knowledge's speechlessness
memorized, at that white flash, inside closed-forever
mouths?

To de-animalize human mentality, to purge it of obsolete
evolutionary characteristics, in particular of death,
which foreknowledge terrorizes the contents of skulls with,
is the fundamental project of technology; however,
the mechanisms of *pseudologica fantastica* require,
if you would establish deathlessness you must first eliminate
those who die; a task attempted, when a white flash sparkled.

Unlike the trees of home, which continually evaporate
along the skyline, the trees here have been enticed down
toward world-eternity. No one knows which gods they enshrine.
Does it matter? Awareness of ignorance is as devout
as knowledge of knowledge. Or more so. Even though not knowing,
sometimes we weep, from surplus of gratitude, even though knowing,
twice already on earth sparkled a flash, a white flash.

The children go away. By nature they do. And by memory—
in scorched uniforms, holding tiny crushed lunch tins.
All the ecstasy-groans of each night call them back, satori
their ghostliness back into the ashes, in the momentary shrines,
the thankfulness of arms, from which they will go

again and again, until the day flashes and no one
 lives
to look back and say, a flash, a white flash sparkled.

I know nothing about how Galway Kinnell wrote this poem, but I imagine that he came to it in the common way, drawing upon an image and a feeling that the nuclear age fosters in most of us. The image is that of the white light that I sometimes envision when I walk to work in the morning in Manhattan, the last thing I've been told I'll see before all these buildings and people and I disappear. The feeling is the one I have sometimes when I see one of my sons in full relief and think of the awful precariousness of his future. These items of shared experience recur through the poem's patterns of observation, vision, and prophecy: the homing devices, as it were, by which Kinnell stays on his course through the dark imponderables of his subject.

The poem opens with a series of objects that one of the two atom bombs we exploded in Japan has turned into images and omens. By these we can begin to imagine and foresee. The poet begins pretty much where the reader is, standing before some material objects, taking them in. The objects have certain things in common: (1) They are in a display case in a museum; they are relics: i.e., pieces of history as well as of matter. (2) They are human relics, most of them household items, or otherwise—like the eyeglasses or the skullbone inside the helmet—made for human use. (3) They are more or less global in nature; there is nothing particularly Japanese about these relics, nothing that trips the little protective device in our minds that distinguishes between them and us. (4) They are, with one exception, objects that are made by one or another heat process—cooking, forging, smelting—and hence have a high degree of heat resistance. This is also true of the exception, the relic of the once-animate object, the person whose skullbone was one of his most heat-resistant parts. Thus, if we are fully heeding the opening stanza, we must begin to imagine for ourselves a heat that transforms, melts, or otherwise alters glass, wire, helmet metal, human bone. (5) The items are unified in their meaning, semantically fused, as it were. The skullbone and the eyeglass frame are of no more or less significance than the wires become iron lumps. In this glass case lies a small world of objects with only one common meaning which levels the distinctions between them—between glass, metal, and bone; between a thing and a person. Not even the relics of Pompeii are so tenaciously held in the grip of their event, so implacably signed by it.

The poet's voice in the first stanza is as neutral a medium as the glass through which one sees these objects, as impassive as the objects themselves. Just as they require our imagination to turn into deep images of an instant holocaust, so the tone is emotionally uninflected until we begin to read the lines with our own fear and pity. In these ways Kinnell counteracts the banality of another poem about the Bomb and also the underlying wariness, evasiveness, and dimness most of us bring to it. The objects speak for themselves; the poet appears at our side rather than on a platform. Part of the poem's power to move is in its sense of sharing rather than telling.

The material of the first stanza, like that of the poem as a whole, is subtly wired and timed. It moves not only from the inanimate to the human images, that is from a lesser to a greater degree of identification (in both senses of the word), but also from a lesser to a greater degree of emotional implosion. For example, note the sequence of verbs, which grow more expressive as significances begin to hit home. This is accompanied by the slowly rising rhythm that thrusts aloft the final three verbs—"taken off," "vanished," and "sparkled"—leaving them to brood over the latent desolation and terror of what has come before and to anticipate what is to follow. That is to say, the wholeness of the poetry creates a rising movement from objectivity through pathos and into mystery. This is a traditional movement of prophecy, which the rest of the poem will follow.

The figures of the next two stanzas, the old man in the museum, the schoolchildren outside, carry the pathos forward, connected as they are by the scorched school uniform, the crushed lunch box. But the poem is also moving quietly toward prophecy, and these figures are placed in an unfolding visionary field that distinguishes between them. In his recent book, *The Gift,* Lewis Hyde develops the distinction between the two Greek words for life—*bios* and *zöe.* The former "is limited life, characterized life, life that dies." The latter is "the life that endures; it is the thread that runs through bios-life and is not broken when the particular perishes." The old man is seen mainly under the aspect of bios-life: Subject to its accidents, he was elsewhere when the white flash sparkled; subject to its fate, he will soon die. However, as a human being he bears the imprint of generic, possibly genetic, feeling: as naturally as he might gaze into a fire, he sighs over the memento of a schoolchild who died that day. The schoolchildren of stanza 3 are seen mainly under the aspect of zöe-life: They are as animated and collectivized as a flock of birds, they evoke the ongoing revitalization of life from generation to generation; vivid creatures of the here and now, they also fade into their counterparts in the preceding generation, those of the scorched school uniforms and crushed lunch boxes. With them and, to some extent, with the old man, Kinnell's sight is turned into vision, passes into the zöe-life and its eternal present—or rather what used to be before "the word *future* first learned, in a white flash, to jerk tears."

The zöe-life is often invoked in Kinnell's poetry—the perdurable moment that resonates through time, the incandescent image that illuminates a universal: a boy sighting a pond for the first time from a high tree from which he is about to fall; four older men struggling to keep their doubles game going as night and winter settle over the court. By such images we are led to the mysterious context of our lives, can move outside the "small ego," as Hyde calls it, into the collective consciousness and experience, the solidarity we share as human beings. Such images also function decisively in the circuitry of the poem. The images of stanzas 2 and 3 work like a relay network, gathering up the meaning and feeling previously fused in stanza 1 and shunting it on ahead to the vision of unprecedented horror that unfolds. The relics are omens from the white flash, flashing from past to future as the poet's eye and imagination, seeing together, begin to foresee and envision, his consciousness to join the collective one of the race itself in its terrible new disjunctions. Or, more concretely, the life in the old man about to pass into the unknown and the schoolboy relics lead to the sudden appearance of the schoolchildren—creatures of renewal, who are associated instead with the dead schoolchildren of Hiroshima. From this disjunction of the zöe-life in the poet's mind is engendered the prophetic question about an unprecedented sound on earth.

In the deep circuitry of the collective mind into which the poet has now tapped and through which the sense of the white flash obsessively flows, the brain-impacted helmet presages a whole city's population of faceless skulls; the earthly sounds of the old man's sigh, the children's goodbyes, presage the sound of an ultimate final lamentation beyond any previous obsequies of the wind or of the human voice, even the "infra-screams" made at Hiroshima and Nagasaki. Thus stanza 4 mingles the bios- and zöe-life at the split moment of extinction of the human mentality. From this expanded and intensified network of images, layer upon layer, comes its prophetic meaning: the elimination of the creaturely terror of death by means of technology, the answer "*pseudologica fantastica*" offers to religion, humankind's previous way of coping with this foreknowledge and fear.

I noted earlier that one of the other conduits of the poem's manifold power is the movement of its tone from objectivity to pathos; in stanza 5, the irony that has delicately limned the tone—the old man smoking his way to death, the animation of the schoolchildren in *their* black uniforms, the "flash-pop" of the camera—now moves front and center to present the berserk rationalism of the nuclear weaponry. Objectivity, pathos, and irony, playing effectively off each other, have particularly potent synergy: the eyes, the heart, and the wit working together under difficult circumstance, harnessing oppositions, modulating incongruities, making them resonate in the mind in a complete way. What is happening in the poet's consciousness he makes happen in ours, passes on the impact of his vision as well as its burden. The tone of the poem is again finely tuned from moment to moment; its development is cunningly timed to deliver the abstract proposition of stanza 5 as an appalling vision, on the one hand, and to dramatically contrast with and test the emotionality of what has gone before on the other. Or to put it another way, objectivity and pathos are fused and triggered by wit, producing that laconic/tragic note of which Shakespeare was the master and his Hamlet the ultimate spokesman, particularly when he is most aware of outrageous fortune.

A third source of the poem's power lies in the development of its thought, the progressive widening of the consciousness in which its core image and feeling are held. Among the Herman Kahns and Albert Wohlstetters who think about the unthinkable, the trick is to narrow and reify the subject of nuclear war until writer and reader alike are sedated by statistics and terminology, not to mention ideology. Before we can blow up most of the earth and the human race, we must first shrink and numb our consciousness, beginning with that of death.

The tone of stanza 6 modulates out most of the previous irony to expand the context into a religious one, the broadest one there is for contemplating the earth and mankind and our relation to them. Like the Japanese trees, the reader is "enticed down toward world-eternity" by the quiet contemplativeness in the language of this stanza, built by its sounds and slow cadences to produce a hush, as it were, in its mood. At the same time, the movement of consciousness is very rapid: the *pseudologica fantastica* of technology is whisked away and replaced by the ancient pantheism of Shinto and by Zen's paradoxical ways of enlightenment, of knowing and not knowing, into which the poem's concerns are gathered.

Or so it seems to me. I know little about Japanese religion, but the poem instructs me well enough to grasp how Zen Buddhism, too, is a repository of the eternal present, invoked like a wise and ancient sage to minister to our disjunctions and apprehensions. Like the other world religions, Zen is a repository of the zöe-life from which we come and into which we return. Following the course of its cycle, the two generations of schoolchildren, the one killed, the other imperiled, merge as they go away by nature and by memory, ghostly surrogates of the children we hold gratefully in our arms and release helplessly to the future of the white flash and the end of both the bios- and the zöe-life.

It is very difficult to write about Hiroshima and about the ten thousand Hiroshimas that are poised to happen. The subject is at once banal, incommensurable, and heavily defended against. We know and do not want to know. But the pathos and terror of this poem make the awareness of our situation permanently more difficult to evade or dismiss.

(1984)

Part Three

The Telling Story

I

Walter Benjamin, in his magisterial essay "The Storyteller," argued that the art of storytelling was dying out, that it was being superseded by the modern media of information and by the story's younger and more topical relative, the novel. There are reasons to believe that, writing in 1935, Benjamin was gloomily prophetic, but there are other reasons, embodied in this collection,* to believe his prognosis was premature. Or even wrong.

In an interview a few years back (*American Review* 15), the novelist John Barth speculates that it may be the novel, as we know it, that is passing out of literary history, but this "doesn't mean the end of narrative literature, certainly. It certainly doesn't mean the end of storytelling." Arguing against that article of the modernist literary faith which holds that plot—the constitutive element of storytelling—is a retrograde device, Barth says that there are "ways to be quite contemporary and yet go at the art in a fashion that would allow you to tell complicated stories simply for the aesthetic pleasure of complexity, of complication and un-

***Best American Short Stories of 1978* ed. Ted Solotaroff and Sharon Ravenel (Boston: Houghton Mifflin, 1978; New York: Bantam Books, 1979).

ravelment, suspense, and the rest." One can add that beyond the writer's pleasure, there still lies the reader's, however sophisticated he may be, in the well-told story—a pleasure that may have become distracted, displaced, and undernourished, but one that is programmed into his nature as surely as gazing meditatively into a log fire (and not unrelated to it), a pleasure that can be so quickly and powerfully revived by a true storyteller like García Márquez. And no less basic in the human creature is the pleasure of telling stories. Indeed, the need to do so, as any bartender will tell you.

Benjamin's use of the term "story" corresponds more closely to what we would call a "tale": i.e., it has its roots in the oral tradition, its favorite domicile was the hearth or the workroom, its archetypal artists were the peasant, the seafarer, the artisan; for "it combined the lore of far-away places, such as a much-traveled man brings home, with the lore of the past, as it best reveals itself to natives of a place." Thus its favorite province was not the here and now but the more philosophical there and then. For its principal distinguishing feature, in Benjamin's view, was its heuristic value. It dramatized a moral, practical instruction, or illustrated a proverb or maxim. In other words, the tale was spun into a useful fabric, one that provided counsel for its audience, "counsel" being understood, as Benjamin puts it, less as "an answer to a question than a proposal concerning the continuation [and significance] of a story which is just unfolding." And because such stories were typically drawn from the ways of the world, from shared or readily communicable experience, their counsel becomes "the epic side of truth," namely wisdom, which, like storytelling itself, Benjamin believes is dying out.

As I understand Benjamin, then, the story is less an evolving art form than a continuing if fading cultural resource: a vehicle for communicating and passing on the wisdom of the race by evoking "astonishment and thoughtfulness." Though open to individual embellishment, its nature is to be repeatable; hence the narrative line is clear and coherent: it introduces a situation, complicates it, and then resolves it. Like, say, Gogol's "The Overcoat" it does not depend upon psychological explanation for its coherence, its psychology is characteristically simple, uninflected, and it withholds explanation, part of its art, to allow the listener or reader to grasp its import by means of his own imagination and insight. Further, it is the lack of dependency on psychological nuance that contributes to, in Benjamin's lovely phrase, the "chaste compactness" of the story and enables it to be remembered and retold.

This "chaste compactness" is achieved by the craft with which a storyteller like Hawthorne hews to the main lines of a person's character, tracing them through situations that test and illuminate them, thereby casting a glow on the manners, mores, and attitudes of the tribe, animated by a man's life process flowing through them. Benjamin frequently relates the story to "natural history," the disparate, variable, mutable ingredients and events of the world which nonetheless draw ineluctably if fortuitously on to a predetermined end, which is, of course, death.

The storyteller is conversant most of all with fate and mortality. His art—layer upon layer of transparent incidents moving both indeterminately (suspense) and inexorably toward a fixed ending—is derived from his feeling for natural history. Indeed the older the storyteller, whether historically or personally, the more likely he is to identify his vision of life with nature and the "great inscrutable course of the world," and hence the more conversant he will be in communion with the transitory and mortal. But whether he is as early as Herodotus or as late as Nikolai Leskov, the nineteenth-century Russian writer whom Benjamin uses as his principal touchstone and source of examples, the signature of the true storyteller is found in the movement of his tale toward *completeness,* the sense it leaves of an earned definitiveness of experience, however open its meaning to speculation and mystery. In a remarkable passage, Benjamin associates death and storytelling as follows:

> It is characteristic that not only a man's knowledge or wisdom, but above all his real life—and this is the stuff that stories are made of—first assumes transmissible form at the moment of his death. Just as a sequence of images is set in motion inside a man as his life comes to an end—unfolding the views of himself under which he has encountered himself without being aware of it—suddenly in his expressions and looks the unforgettable emerges and imparts to everything that concerned him that authority which even the poorest wretch in dying possesses for the living around him. This authority is at the very source of the story.

Part of Benjamin's explanation for the decline of storytelling is that death and its revelations have been pushed from the realm of domestic, lived fact to the periphery of our awareness by the ways in which we isolate ourselves from the dying and the dead. The point is typical of Benjamin's approach to the problem of the story. He does not concern himself with the arguments, familiar by 1935, that the conventions of plot are falsified by the random, provisional, indeterminate aspects of reality, that the freestanding, solid, explicable characters, more or less bereft of an unconscious, are belied by psychology as well as by our own inner life, that fiction with a moral in tow or designed to illustrate a maxim is immediately suspect of simplifying experience and subverting art. Since virtually all didactic fiction today is a form of propaganda for authoritarian systems, the form is doubly dubious. Of course, Benjamin would say he is talking about "counsel," not thought control. And he would attribute the decline of counsel and wisdom to the fallen value of experience itself, whether of the person or the community or the race, its supersession by the bewilderment of man in the face of his incessantly changing society, of a world that has gotten out of hand and has passed beyond the human scale of understanding and judgment. Hence the story is dying because of the incommunicability and incommensurability of being-in-the-world. He points out that the men returning from the First World War were silent rather than full of stories, and the novels that were later produced were "anything but experience that goes from mouth to mouth." What they communicated instead was mostly the enormity of modern warfare, the overwhelmment of the person. As he puts it,

> A generation that had gone to school on a horse-drawn street car now stood under the open sky in a countryside in which nothing remained unchanged but the clouds, and beneath these clouds, in a field of force of destructive torrents and explosions, was the tiny, fragile, human body.

What are we to say fifty years further along in the acceleration of history, which hardly requires war to reduce persons to random social particles? The mass society does that very readily, while its culture further undermines the communicability of experience by its various modes of pseudo communication, the more pseudo the better, as the TV ratings testify. Benjamin, who died in 1940, did not live to see his military image expand across the social spectrum, but he was already well aware of the media of information as a conquering adversary of the story. The product of the up-and-doing middle class with its preference for the factual and the explicable, the daily flood of information, works directly against the function and value of the traditional story. Though drawing upon the ways of the world,

Benjamin's storyteller is indifferent to the verifiability of his account and offers no explanations for life in the there and then. Like man himself, the imaginative interest on which his story does depend has diminished to the meagerness of the "news story."

One can see how the primacy of information over genuine narrative has penetrated and altered our reading habits by comparing the child's to the adult's way of taking in a story. Still relatively innocent of the penchant for news, the child's request to "tell me a story" is qualitatively different from his parents' "Let's see what's in *The New Yorker* or *Ms.* this week." Like Benjamin's weavers at their looms, in which the rhythm of the work induces a receptivity to narrative—Benjamin calls it "self-forgetfulness"—the child, relaxed in his bed, creates a special state of attentiveness in which the story provides a passage from the day's activities through contact with otherness, preferably with a touch of the rich and the strange. The imagination takes over and leads the self toward contentment and rest. The process is perhaps similar to the much more abbreviated, out-of-the-blue imaginings in an adult that presage that he is about to drop off.

But though adults also typically use bedside reading to put the day behind them and prepare for sleep, they do not open themselves to story in the way the child does. If an adult is reading a magazine and comes to a story, his mindset does not alter and prepare to receive the rich and strange, but rather slightly adjusts itself to assimilate a more indirect kind of information, presented in a more personal but often no more imaginative form than the articles: the way we live now, etc. Most magazines most of the time reinforce this tendency by providing stories that do not come from afar, whether in time or place, but are rather news from the private sector, usually in keeping with the magazine's characteristic interests and tone, and the class imagery of its editors and readers. A few popular magazines, such as *Esquire* and *The New Yorker,* which are responsive to literature, will sometimes publish stories that have little or nothing to do with the rest of the content, but the fictions of Barthelme, Borges, or Bashevis Singer no doubt seem esoteric to most of the readers and have the air of distant relatives or odd guests of the family.

The media are not the only lethal impediments and adversaries to Benjamin's notion of the story. There is also the novel. It departs from the story at its very outset, its roots being not in the oral tradition but in the printed word. The effect of this medium is, typically, to distance the writer from his audience: Instead of a man among men, who "takes what he tells from experience—his own or that reported by others . . . and in turn makes it the experience of those who are listening to the tale," the novelist keeps his narrative to himself and has to be his own audience until he is finished. Anyone who has successfully told a story to a circle of people and then, encouraged by his performance and their responsiveness, has tried to write it is aware of how the spontaneity and intimacy of the oral turns into the self-consciousness and loneliness of the written. It is partly this difference that Benjamin has in mind when he goes on to write about the novelist in what seems to be a rather arbitrary and extreme way:

> The novelist has isolated himself. The birthplace of the novel is the solitary individual, who is no longer able to express himself by giving examples of his most important concerns, is himself uncounseled, and cannot counsel others. To write a novel means to carry the incommensurable to extremes in the representa-

> tion of human life. In the midst of life's fullness, and through the representation of this fullness, the novel gives evidence of the profound perplexity of the living.

Defoe? Fielding? Or, even more notably, Dickens?—the writer whose novels took their place at the hearthside of countless Victorian households, who was so much the counselor of his society, whose fullness of presented life was so securely organized and intuitively understood that it provided his readers with intelligence rather than bewilderment: Benjamin's storyteller with endless staying power.

But if one thinks about it, the further Dickens traveled in his career, the more his figure begins to take on the lineaments of Benjamin's novelist. In the later novels like *Little Dorrit, Great Expectations,* and *Our Mutual Friend,* the fullness of life burdens rather than elates, as it did the younger Dickens, while his faith in its center—the enterprising middle class—collapses and turns into despair and contempt. His later protagonists and spokesmen, such as Arthur Clennam, Pip, Bradley Headstone, far from being counseled, are respectively stifled, bewildered, consumed by hate. Instead of the élan of curiosity, wit, and broad imagination, the relish in oddity, the confidence in the natural, the decent, the just, whose figures by and large win out, the later novels are driven by darker energies, a welling up of the destabilizing, destructive, and perverse elements of society and character which lead toward the study of the demonic that was beginning to take form in the unfinished *Mystery of Edwin Drood.* Instead of the sense of intimacy between Dickens and his characters, in the later novels he seems to stand alone, brooding over individual conditions and social forces that denature his people, isolate them, imprison them. Once his faith in progress, nurtured by the course of his own life as well as by the age, declined and turned mordant, he increasingly found life to be, in Benjamin's term, "incommensurable"—and his main recourse if he was to go on writing was precisely in developing an increasingly complex and centrally placed psychology. It is also interesting that as this development was carrying him beyond and against the expectations of his audience, Dickens developed a need that became obsessive to appear before them in public readings, as though sensing that while he was losing his hold on them through his published words, he might still regain it through his actual voice, reinvoking the mutual spell of intimacy through recourse to the oral.

And yet, and yet . . . Dickens continued to write stories to the end, short ones as well as the elaborately plotted late novels, which remained his only way to organize and to some extent comprehend life's fullness and perplexity.

For Benjamin the "short story"—a term he uses only once—is less a development of the traditional story than another example of the various abbreviations of the forms and processes of the past by the modern means of productivity. Rather than carrying on the craft of the tale, the short story is, to his mind, an abbreviated novel. In any case, he writes about the story as though Chekhov, Mann, Kafka did not exist, though he also wrote perhaps the best single essay on Kafka and was, I suspect, haunted by him. He even begins his essay with a story about Potemkin, who was once undergoing one of his paralyzing depressions and paralyzing the state as well. A petty clerk, Shuvalkin, deciding to attack the problem directly, entered Potemkin's room with a sheaf of documents, and emerged triumphantly with them signed, only to discover they had been signed "Shulvalkin . . . Shuvalkin . . . Shuvalkin." The story, Benjamin writes, "is like a herald racing two hundred years ahead of Kafka's work. The enigma which beclouds it is Kafka's enigma." He uses several other stories to illustrate the range of the doomed transactions of Kafka's cosmically burdened characters with the world and its authorities, but he deals with Kafka as not so much a storyteller as the creator of a theater in which, like the classical Chinese, happenings are reduced to gestures, though in Kafka's case generally incongruous, enigmatic, confused, or futile ones.

But certainly Kafka was a storyteller of the there and then, and there is probably no better illustration of Benjamin's favorite kind of story, in which the elements of myth and fairy tale interpenetrate the natural, than "Metamorphosis." To be sure, Kafka is without counsel and there is no more perfect witness than his protagonists to the profound perplexity of the living in the midst of life's fullness, no author who has carried the incommensurable to a further extreme. And yet Kafka was full of stories, and even parables, myths, and fables.

I agree with Benjamin about the human usefulness he finds to be the story's defining ingredient, but I believe that it can be conveyed by other means than the counsels of the there and then. The contemporary short story is typically concerned with the here and now, particularly in cultures like ours, in which the new, the perplexing, the ominous, the random constitute our central universal. It is no accident that the storytellers of the there and then are today largely found in Latin America, where the past still flows through and shapes the present, often tragically so. I believe that the usefulness of the contemporary American story lies precisely in its fight in behalf of the human scale of experience and its communication against the forces that seek to diminish and trivialize it. I find that most stories that interest me accept the incommensurability of experience and struggle against it to make sense of the otherwise senseless, to locate the possibilities of coherence (in both senses of the term) in the otherwise incoherent flux of a society whose members are dazed by its mutability and by the babbling of its media about this "event," that "trend," which flatters our knowingness while impoverishing our understanding.

II

In the middle of life's fullness and perplexity, I come upon the first story in last year's Pushcart Prize anthology—"Lawns," by a young writer named Mona Simpson. It begins as follows:

> I steal. I've stolen books and money and even letters. Letters are great. I can't tell you the feeling, walking down the street with twenty dollars in my purse, stolen earrings in my pocket. I don't get caught. That's the amazing thing. You're out on the sidewalk, other people all around, shopping, walking, and you've got it. You're out of the store, you've done this thing you're not supposed to do, but no one stops you. At first it's a rush. Like you're even for everything you didn't get before. But then you're alone, no one even notices you. Nothing changes.

Unlike Benjamin's archetypal story and like the standard contemporary one, this story has a narrator whose character is complex, full of psychological nuances. She is both brazen and reflective, devious and forthright, without compunctions but troubled as though she were bereft of them, both empowered and emptied by her secret vice. It's not easy to make up one's mind about her, mainly because her compulsive stealing comes across less as a pathology than as, say, an orphan's behavior, though we learn early on that she is not an orphan, that her father drove her to school and left weeping. She is a freshman at Berkeley, a top student, who works Saturday mornings in the mailroom of her dormitory, where she commits most of her thefts. She steals money, packages of clothes and cookies, and letters, but only letters addressed to three of her former high school classmates, who had belonged to the elite group:

> And now I know. Everything I thought those three years, worst years of my life, turns out to be true. The ones here get letters. . . . And like from families, their letters talk about problems. They're each other's main lives. You always knew, looking at them in high school, they weren't just kids who had fun. They cared. They cared about things.

This widening view of a poignant kleptomaniac takes into account her otherwise "normal" behavior. She falls in love and begins to sleep with a fellow student, a handsome boy who cuts the campus lawns. Glenn was once subject to trances but is now healthy; both of these aspects draw her to him. "I'm bad in bed," she blurts out at one point but thrives on his reassurance and her own gratitude. Her performance in school also fortifies her. When she is questioned about the missing packages and mail, she easily wards off the threat:

> Four-point-oh average and I'm going to let them kick me out of school? They're sitting there telling us it's a felony. A Federal crime. No way, I'm gonna go to medical school.

The complex aura of the narrator's account of herself proves to be a foreshadowing of the proposal the story now makes, in Benjamin's terms, "concerning its continuation," from which its "counsel" is derived. The narrator's father, who appeared briefly and enigmatically in her thoughts, now turns up for a surprise weekend visit. The proposal is daring, less from the fact that they sleep together than from the matter-of-factness that they will do so:

> So he's here for the weekend. He's just sitting in my dorm room and I have to figure out what to do with him. He's not going to do anything. He'd just sit here. And Lauren's coming back soon so I've got to get him out. It's Friday afternoon and the weekend's shot. OK, so I'll go with him. I'll go with him and get it over with.

During her account of their behavior, both in his hotel room and in the preceding five years, since he initiated it, the reader experiences the "astonishment and thoughtfulness" that Benjamin designates to be the final cause of the storyteller's art, that which clears and deepens the space in our minds the story will henceforth occupy. What is most remarkable about the relationship is her tone of unremarkableness. The narrator speaks of the present state of affairs much as she did of her thefts:

> So next day, Saturday . . . we go downtown and I got him to buy me this suit. Three hundred dollars from Saks. Oh, and I got shoes. So I stayed later with him because of the clothes, and I was a little happy because I thought at least now I'd have something good to wear with Glenn. My dad and I got brownie sundaes at Sweet Dreams and I got home by five. He was crying when he dropped me off.

The sexual fire and brimstone we associate with incest is notably absent. She speaks of her father's attentions as she would those of any unwelcome older man, a high school teacher or a family doctor, say, who had seduced her and whom she continues to indulge. The conventional scenario of domination has been displaced by the perversely conventional one of exploitation. She hates her father less because he is her father than because he is so sheepish and jealous: "Jesus, how can you not hate someone who is always begging from you."

In a passage quoted earlier, Benjamin speaks of the emergence of "the unforgettable" in the face of the dying man as conferring an "authority [that] is at the very source of the story." The force of this statement has a particular pertinence to "Lawns":

> He waited till I was twelve to really do it. I don't know if you can call it rape. I was a good sport. The creepy thing is I know how it felt for him. I could see it on his face when he did it. He thought he was getting away with something.

It is just here that the story calmly places its finger on the heart of the matter and becomes unforgettable. As the passage goes on, describing the rape, or whatever, in its understated way, the father's expression presides over it with the authority of sin, which proves to be what the counsel of the story is about. Its wages quickly prove to be his moral undoing as a father and a man and her guilt-free ability to take whatever she wants:

> My dad thought he was getting away with something but he didn't. He was the one that fell in love, not me. And after that day, when we were back in the car, I was the one giving orders. From then on I got what I wanted.

This, of course, she has learned to do from him, in his principal act as a role model, which has the authority of the expression on his face of "getting away with something," at the most impressionable moment, to put it mildly, of her life.

The proposal of an unmanned, lovesick father and an adaptively perverse daughter enables what has come before in the story to cohere with what follows. She is frightened now by her father's importunity because she now has something important to lose, namely her newfound stability and hope, her place with Glenn at life's feast. She calls her mother, a self-absorbed lawyer she has heretofore despised, and asks her for help. Here the story enters the realm of the topical but resists settling there, guarding itself against the topical's superficial counsel of information and knowingness:

> She found this group. She says, just in San Jose, there's hundreds of families like ours, yeah, great, that's what I said. But there's groups. She's going to a group of thick-o mothers like her, those wives who didn't catch on. She wanted me to go into a group of girls, yeah, molested girls, that's what they call them, but I said no, I have friends here already, she can do what she wants.

She tells Glenn, who quickly drops her. Desolate again, she turns to her roommate, Lauren, who at one point takes her for a ride. They stop in front of an elementary school in a mixed neighborhood and watch the children playing at recess. Lauren then speaks to her, in a way that redeems the topical by placing it in the human scale:

> Eight years old. Look at them. They're eight years old. One of their fathers is sleeping with one of those girls. Look at her. Do you blame her? Can you blame her? Because if you can forgive her, you can forgive yourself.

The "thoughtfulness" of the reader is fostered in two ways by the story. The first, as I've been suggesting, is by Mona Simpson's making her own proposal about an incestuous relationship and keeping it free of the current fashions of reductiveness that surround it as a social problem, a hot media topic, and a feminist cause. In the clear space she has come to in her mind, the narrator thinks about her past and tries to take into account her father's view of the good times they've had together. She finds that her memories are no worse than equivocal. Then she goes on:

> But that's over. I don't know if I'm sorry it happened. I mean I am, but it happened, that's all. It's just one of those things that happened to me in my life. But I would never go back, never.

Her acceptance may seem shallow or perverse to the knowing and the militant. But it is no more so than her determination is and indeed grounds it. She wants to be what the story proposes her to be—an individual rather than a generic victim, someone who has a life rather than a case history or a legal brief or a gender grievance. The story is painful precisely because the narrator presents herself less as the victim than as the daughter of her father, whose attachment has kept her vulnerable even as her contempt has enabled her to exploit the situation. At one point earlier in the story, still a bit squeamish about being in bed with Glenn, she reflects:

> It's so easy to hurt people. They just lie there and let you have them. I could reach out and choke Glenn to death, he'd be so shocked, he wouldn't stop me. You can just take what you want.

The exaggeration of people's vulnerability here is itself telling—an outcropping of the psychopathology of her everyday life. But it is also a perception of the human condition that the dominated share with the dominating, and, in this instance, that one side of her mind shares with the other. Part of the psychological authority of the story comes from its easy intercourse between the normal and abnormal, the natural and unnatural: It tacitly counsels us that this is also true of its subject, which is why incest is such a deeply implanted taboo and sin. It is normal for a daughter to do her father's bidding, to want to please him and be admired by him, just as it is for a father both to exercise authority and to fondle and dote on his daughter. Moreover, it is in the context of the natural that the unnatural asserts itself most clearly and forcefully in our minds, because it becomes both sharply focused and commensurable in the human scale. For example, the most unforgettable moment in Terrence DesPres's *The Survivor* is not in his full account of the terror and privation of the death camps but in his brief passage on what it must have been like to wake up each morning at Auschwitz. The forming of this kind of insight, this sudden flare of light in the dark which naturalizes the unnatural and restores it to the human scale, is what we look to in the literary imagination as a resource of thoughtfulness.

The second way that "Lawns" conduces the reader to reflect is by its movement toward healing, which in the story also takes on a kind of natural aura. Sometime after he rejects her, the narrator meets Glenn on campus:

> I felt the same as I always used to, that I love him and all that, but he might just be one of the things you can't have. Like I should have been for my father, and look at him now. Oh, I think he's better, they're all better, but I'm gone, he'll never have me again.

Her words here and elsewhere convey a sense of time's changes and attenuations, of her progress being an aspect of what Benjamin calls "the great inscrutable course of the world." There is no one "reason" offered by the story as to why her wound is healing over. The good she initially received from Glenn, her confessions, the counsel of Lauren, her mother's belated support, and so forth have all contributed, but the number and variety and mixed effects of these agents indicate that they have no common denominator except the way one good thing can lead to another, just as one bad thing in her life has led to others. The connections are left to our thoughtfulness to establish. Again, this is not to imply that the story is complacent about incest, that it is proposing that time heals all wounds, so what's all the fuss about, the hot lines and support groups and alarming statistics? Such a reading induces thoughtlessness by stripping the narrator of her individuality, the story of its psychological nuances and grasp of natural history, and by countering its proposal with a position. That is, it turns a telling story about human nature into an antifeminist document, which flatters our knowingness while impoverishing our understanding.

Toward the very end of the story, the narrator tells us that she has begun to steal mail again—"not packages and people I know" and only one letter every Saturday ("I'm really being stern"), because she feels desolate and in need of excitement. Then, on the last Saturday of the story, she receives a letter addressed to herself, the first she's gotten. There is no return name and address on the envelope; it comes from Benjamin's great inscrutable course of the world. But since she knows it is not from Glenn, who has another girlfriend now, she throws it away and finishes her work for the day:

> And then I thought, I don't have to keep looking at the garbage can, I'm allowed to take it back, that's my letter. And I fished it out . . . and I held it a few min-

> utes, wondering who it was from. Then I put it in my mailbox so I can go like everybody else and get mail.

And so ends Mona Simpson's "Lawns," a story that takes on the fullness and perplexity of contemporary life and provides the kind of counsel that Benjamin regards to be "the epic side of truth," namely wisdom.

(1978, 1987)

Radical Realism: The Art of John Fowles

It is strange that a novelist as superbly imaginative as John Fowles should be content to write within the canons of conventional textbook realism. Of the four stories in *The Ebony Tower,* three are simple, linear structures—situation, complication, resolution—the incidents rationally linked through the probable interactions of credible characters, the action and theme neatly illustrating each other. The fourth story is somewhat more open-ended and covert: a picnic in the country that ends in a disappearance and, by implication, a suicide. One has to draw the connections for oneself and see the sudden gathering storm at the end as an epiphany. But this is a technique that Joyce was practicing in "Dubliners" at the turn of the century and that is still being practiced, from week to week, in the pages of *The New Yorker* and elsewhere.

Yet each of these stories is anything but obvious or thin. However conventionally they begin and proceed, there comes a point when their issues dramatically engage and take on complexity and power—it's as though one had picked up a simple, familiar object, casually examined it, and suddenly found it shaking in one's hands. By the same token, Fowles's seemingly typecast characters—a lascivious old artist meets his decorous young critic, a timid literary scholar is ripped off by an aggressive hippie—have a way of slipping out of their mold, surprising us first as individuals and then as the strange faces that our most intense experiences tend to take on.

The popular writer turns life into clichés, the artist of realism turns clichés back into life. But why start with clichés in the first place and why tie yourself down to the restrictions and reductions of a plot? Why all this outmoded literary law and order? It's as though a brilliant playwright came upon the scene, a master of illusion, who insists upon practicing the three unities.

One may believe Fowles enjoys being so clever and also the rewards it has brought him as a writer of highly intelligent books that manage to be very popular. But judging from *The Aristos,* his "intellectual self-portrait," Fowles has more ambitious goals in view: in his quiet, detached way, just as much as Mailer does in his very different way, Fowles wants to create a revolution in the consciousness of his time. Still, if this is so, surely he must suspect that his fiction is going about it in the wrong way. Tidy narrative structures, well-rounded characters, consistent point of view, lucid prose, accurate descriptions of times and places —aren't these the techniques, at our late stage of modernism, that confirm the most retrograde bourgeois tastes, that are valuable only so that they can then be superseded or, better yet, destroyed by the writer's innovations? Learn the rules so that you know what you're doing when you break them—so the young writer is told. Learn the craft so that you can then practice the art: craft being what all writers are supposed to be able to do, art being what only the individual writer can do because true art is the creation of new *forms* of consciousness, which only the individualist can achieve. Right?

Wrong. Partly wrong in theory and increasingly wrong

in practice. New consciousness does not necessarily require new forms in literature any more than it does in any other field of writing. When Shakespeare wrote the "Dark Lady" sonnets, he was doing something original in love poetry, and hence for love itself, though he left the sonnet form undisturbed. And while it is true that new literary forms can provoke new consciousness, it tends more often to work the other way around. In any case, modernism, which has tended to identify originality and individuality with formal innovation exclusively, has left the writers who still subscribe to it increasingly high and dry: i.e., rarefied and empty. Or as Fowles himself put it in *The Aristos:* "There is the desperate search for the unique style, and only too often this search is conducted at the expense of content. This accounts for the enormous proliferation in styles and techniques . . . and for that only too characteristic coupling of exoticism of presentation and banality of theme." If you don't think he's right, pick up an anthology of current "experimental" fiction or poetry and see how much genuine new consciousness you find and how much of the same surreal solipsism, forlorn or abrasive. Talk about conventionality.

In one of Fowles's new stories, "The Enigma," John Marcus Fielding, a wealthy Conservative M.P., a model of respectability and responsibility, mysteriously disappears. An astute young detective is assigned to the case, who after weeks of checking and interviewing comes up empty-handed. Finally, he goes to see the girlfriend of Fielding's son, another of those grave, bright, smashing young women whom Fowles likes to write about, who are, as in Henry James, the sunlight and moral agents of his world. "Sergeant Mike Jennings," he says to the girl, who is somewhat puzzled by this spruce public-school graduate on her doorstep. "The fuzz."

They hit it off very quickly and she tells Jennings several somewhat compromising things she has kept from the other investigators: that Fielding, though he could barely manage to indicate it, had seemed to admire her independence of spirit and that, the evening before he disappeared, she had mentioned she would be going to the British Museum the next day, the last place Fielding was traced to. After some charming fencing with Jennings (few writers bring the sexes together as happily and subtly as Fowles does), Isobel reconstructs Fielding's disappearance by putting him in a story in which the author, who believes in giving his characters and hence himself the perils of freedom (there is a fascinating discussion of this question in Chapter 13 of *The French Lieutenant's Woman*), finds himself with a character who has decided to vanish without a trace.

What has eluded Jennings through his scientific police work comes in buckets to the literary Isobel as she draws out the implications of her own two meager clues and produces so shrewd a scenario that it eventually convinces the smitten but all the more skeptical Jennings. For several related reasons, Fielding has chosen to play the "God game"—by absconding (the theme that wells up so powerfully at the end of *The Magus*). But the underlying point of the story is that there is a wisdom that passes scientific understanding embedded in the narrative process itself, one that can weave intuition, imagination and the generative logic of storytelling into deep but lucid inquiries into human conduct and destiny.

Hence for fiction to abandon narrative is rather like having science abandon the scientific method because some phenomena are too elusive or enigmatic or distortable to be fully understood by its methods. Fowles's practice of providing or suggesting alternative endings to his previous two major novels is not just cleverness but an acknowledgment that narrative art, like science, like reality itself, terminates in paradox and mystery: the double ending being a kind of fictional equivalent of Bohr's principle of complementarity.

An awareness of what the loss of narrative has meant seems to be rapidly growing these days: Reynolds Price spoke of it in his review of Graham Greene's latest novel in the *Times Book Review,* so has John Barth in *New American Review 15;* it is also evident in the growing influence of Nabokov, Borges, and García Márquez, who are, first and foremost, storytellers, revitalizers of the art, surprise witnesses at the useless inquest of the absconded novel.

Fowles's contribution has been twofold. In *The Magus,* he creates what might be called an existential narrative, using realism itself to mock and alter its assumptions. The novel is made up of a huge mesh of incidents, most of which are as convincing as they are duplicitous. A sensible and evasive young Englishman takes a job teaching on a Greek island, becomes a habitué of a rich man's estate, and soon finds his credulity being successively flattered and betrayed. His relationship with a demonic millionaire and his entourage becomes a treacherous terrain of psychological traps and moral land mines which eventually branch out into the rest of his life, until daily reality appears to crumble and human existence resembles the behavior of subatomic particles: probability contending with chaos, the knowable with the unknowable. This plot (in both senses) in which Nicholas Urff finds himself (in both senses) is an extraordinary if exasperating creation that employs all the nuances of verisimilitude, not to confirm our worldliness but to undermine it, so that the world's randomness, contingency, and hazard can be revealed in their full truth and power as the price we pay for our freedom.

This is Fowles's master theme and objective: to restate the terms of human freedom. In *The French Lieutenant's*

Woman, Fowles uses the conventions of nineteenth-century romantic fiction not only to write a brilliant study of Victorian manners, morals, and morale but also to do something no less interesting and more difficult—to portray the light wind from the future blowing into "the age of steam and cant," sowing the seeds of what we call modern consciousness in three young people—a stifled governess, a bored gentleman and amateur scientist, and his ignorant but fashion-minded servant—each pursuing her or his own image of independence to ends they would never have dreamed of.

None of the four long stories in *The Ebony Tower* has the originality of those two novels or even the tour-de-force quality of Fowles's *The Collector,* a shocking parable of contemporary class warfare confined to two characters in two rooms. Fowles tells us that these new stories were written as variations on some of the themes of his novels, and they do tend to have a kind of relaxed, mopping-up feeling about them. But if you haven't been reading Fowles, you'll find them magical enough and a good way to get your feet wet; if you have been reading him, you'll have the pleasure of making connections.

The richest and most expressive one is the title story, about two days that shake the life of a successful young "color painter" and critic. David Williams's abstract canvases are as attractive, rational and low-keyed as his character, his marriage, his existence. The gifted son of two architects, he has had his way paved into the art world and he has sensibly made the most of it. In the course of writing an essay on Henry Breasley, an eclectic painter whose work has gone through many changes while his life in France has remained consistently scandalous, Williams travels to Brittany to interview him.

In his late seventies, Breasley is still going strong, indeed painting the major pictures of his career—a series of "dreams" in a forest setting—and living with two English girls, whom Williams finds sunbathing in the nude when he arrives. He is surprised to find that Breasley still has the dress, manners, and affable inarticulateness of the English upper class he fled so long ago; but once he is in his cups, the angry old lion in him stirs and begins to claw at Williams and his tradition of "obstructs." "Triumph of the bloody eunuch. . . . Spunk. Any spunk. Even Hitler's spunk or nothing. . . . Not fundamentals. Fundaments. . . . All that goes with them. That's reality. Not your piddling little theorems and pansy colors. . . . Mess of scientific pottage. Sold the whole bloody shoot down the river. . . ." Or as "the Mouse," the more sophisticated and fetching of the two girls, puts it for him: "Art is a form of speech. Speech must be based on human needs, not abstract theories of grammar. Or anything but the spoken word. The real word."

By the end of the next day, Breasley's words and new work, the pagan atmosphere of the household, the adjacent forest and the coolly alluring Mouse, have cast their spell and Williams has succumbed. He has come, he feels, to the end of his careful way; Breasley's way is just a step across and the Mouse (Breasley's nickname has nothing to do with her temperament: it stands for Muse with the female *0* added) is holding out her hand. But at the crisis point, Williams's habits of dutifulness reassert themselves, he hesitates, and is lost. Driving back to Paris, he realizes that he has been defeated all along his front, or rather, that a long-standing ramifying defeat has finally been exposed:

> One killed all risk, one refused all challenge, and so one became an artificial man. The old man's secret [was] not letting anything stand between self and expression; which wasn't a question of outward artistic aims, merely styles, and techniques, and themes. But how you did it; how wholly, how bravely you faced up to the constant recasting of yourself.

Hence vanity, prejudice, and amorality are as essential to a Breasley as paint and canvas. And terrified of them, the tolerant, diffident, considerate, self-evasive Williams has not the wherewithal to change. His experience "remorselessly demonstrated what he was born, still was, and always would be: a decent man and eternal also-ran."

In seeing through himself, Williams also sees into the prison where his painting has led him. Breasley was right there too. "Turning away from nature and reality had atrociously distorted the relationship between painter and audience: now one painted for intellects and theories. Not for people; and worst of all, not for oneself." The result has become an art of outer space—daring, quickly banal, frozen—in which only the artist and the critic in their special space suits exist and have value.

The closing pages of *The Ebony Tower* are, of course, an assertion of Fowles's own guiding values, and they go a long way to explain and justify his practice of writing about live men, women, and issues in a direct, accessible way. In the unfashionable conventions of realism, he finds his mode of opposition and his medium for recasting himself. At one point, Williams asks the question that haunts most contemporary artists, composers, and writers alike—are they living in the sterile aftermath of modernism, in one of the dead spots of cultural history:

"Art had always gone in waves. Who knew if the late 20th century might not be one of its most cavernous troughs? He knew the old man's answer: it was. Or it was unless you fought bloody tooth and . . . nail against some of its most cherished values and victories."

(1974)

Baring the Breast: Philip Roth

The English psychiatrist Joan Riviere once conjectured that "all artists work largely through the feminine side of their personalities." The idea is worth thinking about. The male fiction writer stays home with his feelings and waking dreams, while the other men go off each morning to hammer away at their piece of the practical world, one that doesn't much depend on or care about their feelings toward it. What the fiction writer creates and nurtures is within himself, his work being a slow process of developing a "germ," as Henry James liked to put it, of consciousness—of mothering it, as it were, into life. He even experiences the creative process in much the same way that a woman speaks of being delivered after pregnancy, and one could trace a suggestive set of parallels from the initial planting of the seed to the final stages of labor, including analogous feelings of elation, uncertainty, nausea, touchiness, dreaminess, fierce oral cravings, and, in the later stages, burdensomeness, possessiveness, anticipation, mounting pressure, anguish, transportedness, peace, emptiness, depression.

The male fiction writer is perforce drawn into the world of feelings, of manners, of relationships that are traditionally woman's domain. He must learn to be attentive to the social and psychological nuances of furnishings, of dress, of speech and gesture—cultivating a savvy that is virtually second nature to the female writer. Also he must come to live on easier terms with the imaginal, the intuitive, the irrational, than males are customarily trained to do.

This involvement with producing something of value in one's innards and with attending to the soft as well as the hard facts of life can have a threatening effect on the male writer's masculinity. This seems to have been particularly true of American writers: American men generally tend to be less comfortable with "the feminine side of the personality" than are European men, the latter having been more exposed to a civilizing wisdom that relates sensitivity and virility rather than holding them anxiously apart (a wisdom that the younger generation here have been learning from the feminist revolution.)

This uneasiness may partly explain why a cult of masculinity has flourished so abundantly in American fiction as a kind of defensive reaction to the nature of the work itself. The prototype in this respect is Hemingway, with his heavily self-publicized macho activities, his penchant for depicting soldiers, boxers, hunters, fishermen, and their simple codes, his hard-boiled attitude toward experience, his spare, emotionally uninflected style, and his mystique of writing itself as a form of honest manual labor and of grace under pressure, as though a novelist were something of a cross between a carpenter and a bullfighter. All this overlay of virility, and yet the one novel by Hemingway that seems now to have been psychologically signed by him is *The Sun Also Rises,* whose hero's superior sensibility is not unrelated to his sexual wound.

The young American male who was starting out to write fiction thirty-five years ago would likely have fallen under the influence not only of Hemingway but of a general pattern of literary conditioning that identified fiction with masculine aggression and tough-mindedness. Dreiser, Dos Passos, Faulkner, Farrell, Wright, Steinbeck, Wolfe, Henry Miller were all writers who radiated a strong masculine force, bent as each was on mining large veins of native experience and developing the heavy-duty style that could swing their ore up into the light. The power of their influence is immediately apparent on the next generation of writers, such as Mailer, Jones, Bourjaily, Algren, Styron, who picked up the tradition of muscular realism and a good deal of the stoical Hemingway stance.

These generalizations suggest why the solid masculine talent became the model it did for the professional fiction writer in America. I can think of some other reasons as well—the frontier spirit, the influence of American journalism—but I want to get on to my point that this model has been breaking down pretty rapidly in recent years, along with the taboos that helped to support it. The example at hand is Philip Roth, whose transformation from the cool, steady realist of his first three books to the blue comedian of *Portnoy's Complaint* and *Our Gang* has led him now to write a short and devastating book about a literature professor who turns into a female breast—*The Breast* being, among other things, a fable of bisexual recognition in all its strangeness, torment, and possible use.

Actually, Roth has been stealing up on this theme, or it on him, since *Goodbye, Columbus.* Both *Letting Go* and *When She Was Good* bear an undercurrent of despair that grows out of Roth's preoccupation with the power of women to control their men's lives by a kind of moral one-upmanship that attaches his virtue, indeed his humanity, to his willingness to satisfy her needs, however unending or perverse these may be. But this mechanism needs a socket in the man to plug into, a complicated set of vulnerabilities to the woman's demands and desires. In *Letting Go,* Roth focuses on the moral opening and in *When She Was Good* on the

he reality of strangeness. Like Kepesh, Roth loves
eme in literature . . . [is] fascinated by its imagery
er and suggestiveness." By turning his hero into a
d then by maintaining an exact attention to the
tails of the metamorphosis and by exercising a
le control of a tone that keeps humor married to
on (black humor has produced one of its few clas-
h creates a high-tension portrait of the imperiled
. Exploring its responses of adaptation, rebellion,
tance, he draws close to the core of human being
ll its mystery.
doing, Roth virtually provokes comparison with
amous story of another radical form of male anxi-
f the self's heroic and absurd struggle to conserve
ty even as a dung beetle—a mode of existence that
ross the border of "reality" from the one Gregor
s left as a traveling salesman. Kafka's "Metamor-
one of the toughest acts in all literature to follow,
earns his own, and much more unwieldy, inven-
y step of the way, so that the shade of Gregor
on falls astern of one's attention as it becomes
David Kepesh's transformation. It begins as the
f nightmares, from which Kepesh must surely
So poor Kepesh himself continues to believe and
r along with him, the latter's suspension of dis-
coming increasingly a burden he wants to have
by Roth's admission that Kepesh has been dream-
pping or going insane. "Okay, enough is enough.
n up or bring him down," I began to say to the
its final stages. To which the story implacably
No, more, and even more than that." Because the
the imagery of Kepesh's situation are so bold and
, Roth can allow himself to understate, to work by
n, and to slowly build up the credibility of the

cultural one. With *Portnoy* the inquiry becomes more basic and desperate, Portnoy's humor being both a way of getting into the nitty-gritty and a manic defense against the depressive position of finding himself tied, in all the ways that matter, to Sophie Portnoy's apron strings, some of which have been double knotted by her husband. Hence Portnoy's compulsive masturbation, which he performs in about the same way with a woman as he does with his fist or with several substances in between, is his way of maintaining the original Oedipal fund of excitement and guilt, each supplementing the other. So, too, are his other emotional habits, his sense of his worth, his work as a noble public servant, even his identity as a Jew—all tied up with his mother. Add them up and you get a pretty heavily feminized side of his character, which is another reason or two why he clings so much to his penis.

Given this view of Roth's intentions, it's only a short distance, though a long brave leap, from the Portnoy whom we leave squirming in his impotency on Spielvogel's couch to David Alan Kepesh, who regains consciousness one day in a hospital to discover that he has been transformed into a female breast. There are strongly marked similarities between Kepesh and Portnoy. Kepesh is another high achiever from a strenuous and somewhat hysterical Jewish family who has cultivated, reasoned, and gentled himself into the professional class and its classiness. He has had his various sexual flings, his stormy marriage, but now he has chosen proportion and dignity once and for all, and he has his life pretty well under control: the orderly satisfactions of teaching—along with the chance to safely indulge his taste for the "extreme" in the writings of Kafka, Gogol, Swift, and the other metaphysical comedians—and of a sensible relationship with a luscious and stable girl. Still, certain problems have cropped up: a marked decline of his sexual interest in Claire, and then a strange red blush at the base of his penis, which is soon accompanied by an exquisite erotic sensitivity; his potency is more than restored, though he notices that in the moanings and clutchings of his ecstasy he seems to himself more like a woman than a man. But having been confirmed by his recently completed analysis in his life strategy of "putting one foot after the other after the other," he tries to take these strange turns of event in stride. In sum, Kapesh might be Portnoy five years later: Dr. Spielvogel's work has been finished; the inner tumult reduced to a manageable nervousness, the vanity to a certain finickiness; the wild joking replaced by a cool wit; the depressive ties to Jewishness, family, and especially to women all loosened and made manageable by a little gap that has been opened between impulse and act, known as reason; and the swamps of the id, at least the more malarial of them, reclaimed by a solidified ego. The terms of the reality principle having been clarified, accepted, and internalized, Kepesh is all set for the well-adjusted life, and then reality turns him into the grandiose image of his deepest fear (and desire): six feet and one hundred fifty-five pounds of blind, immobile, and maddeningly tactile flesh in which all his newly found "strength of character" and "will to live," to quote his analyst, are buried intact and put to this ultimate test.

It's no idle stroke that Kepesh's large and all-important nipple—through its milk ducts he is able to maintain communication of sorts with the world—has been made from his penile tissue, which shortly leads him to discover, as he is being washed, the one physical activity and pleasure that is left to him. Indeed, his first stage of life as a breast is marked by a frenzy each time his nipple is touched by his nurse and then, more purposefully, by Claire, and this soon escalates into a consuming desire to arrange intercourse with both women. What now passes for his "head" has become one libidinal powerhouse which his superego strug-

gles to contain, and a crisis ensu
version of Portnoy's perpetual
he wants sexually and, after all,
little he can afford himself. As
chiatrist, Dr. Klinger, who has
to help him adjust:

> Why shouldn't I be rubbed
> and sucked and licked and fu
> why shouldn't I have anythin
> think of *every single minute of t*
> port me from this miserable
> prevent me from having wha
> here being sensible! There's
> *being sensible!*

And as Kepesh eventually comes

> . . . what alarmed me so about
> tesque yearning was that by doi
> ing myself irreparably from my
> kind. . . . my appetites would
> sively strange, until at last I reac
> tation from which I would fal
> void. I would go mad . . . and ev
> as a result, what would I have b
> flesh and no more?

And so, with the aid of a light ane
to wash him, this conflict is resolv
to another and even worse crisis.

I don't want to create the impres
hyped-up spin-off of *Portnoy's Comp*
it's a more radical, complex, and m
picks up where *Portnoy* left off and
to an imaginal extreme that turns o
certain human realities, including so

such as
"the ex
and po
breast
inner
remar
desper
sics),
male e
and ac
itself

In
Kafka
ety an
its ide
is jus
Sams
phosi
but
tion
Sams
rivet
crazi
awa
the
belie
rem
ing
Wa
stor
rep
ide
we
im

incredible, while sealing it against any simple, reassuring interpretations.

Thus *The Breast* grows in power and complexity as Kepesh continues his fight to put one foot after the other after the other, even though, as he shrieks at one point, "I have no feet." The full measure of his absurdity comes home to him when he invites his most unflappable friend to visit him, and the mordant, suave Schonbrunn immediately breaks out in a fit of giggling and rushes away. Trying to recover from this shock, Kepesh tries to prove once and for all to himself that he is dreaming, and when that becomes untenable, to prove that he has gone mad, locked into a schizophrenic delusion from which, having finally recognized it, he can now begin to emerge.

So begins the final and most harrowing struggle (for him and for the reader), in which he pits "the little wavering flame of memory, intelligence and hope that still claimed to be David Alan Kepesh" against Dr. Klinger's immovable insistence that Kepesh is indeed both a breast and sane and that he will truly go mad if he persists in believing otherwise. They resume their analytic relationship, in which Kepesh draws upon all his eloquence, cunning, and desperation to persuade Klinger that what he is saying to him about his sanity is the very opposite of what Kepesh hears and that his delusion will dissolve if only he can reach the secret of its primal causes. This reprise of the experience of analysis is Roth's most brilliant move in the book, and the most affecting. Here is Kepesh, trying to remember being nursed: "It is all too far back, back where I am. I claw the slime at the sea bottom but by the time I rise to the surface there is not even silt beneath my fingernails. . . . How I talk! Anything! Everything! I'll hit upon it yet! I will not be silent until I am sane!"

But this strategy fails too, a new stage of acquiescence

arrives, and Kepesh moves on to other ways of coping with his new identity. He listens to Shakespeare on records, "Making the effort—always the effort—to be as serious about myself as I can." His bitterness still wells up, his morale still breaks down—and that, too, he tries to accept: "Permit my dignity a rest, won't you? This is not tragedy any more than it is farce. It is only life and, like it or not, I am only human." At the end, he is entertaining the idea of exploiting his condition, of making money and getting women and other satisfactions from it, enlisting the help of a hip young colleague. "If the Beatles can fill Shea Stadium, so can I. . . . If the Rolling Stones can find girls, if Charles Manson can find them, we can find them too. I will live by my own lights." So he writes his story as the first step of his liberation, such as it will be, and concludes, in his former professorial fashion, with a poem—Rilke's great "Archaic Torso of Apollo"—to make his final point and final stand: the enduring power of consciousness to work its ways and will through matter, however deformed and incomplete that matter may be, the torso standing for the imperatives of human being by which all of us are searched out:

> for there is no place
> that does not see you. You must change your life.

With these lines a great deal of meaning and feeling come together, and *The Breast* takes on some of the final cryptic gleam of the poem. For me, the point within the final point is to mark the power of the artist, if he is imaginative and brave and steady enough, to make his or her bisexuality into a secret strength. In its movement from male panic at to acceptance of the female part of the psyche, *The Breast* is a bizarre, radical reenvisioning of the dark side of creativity: what Edmund Wilson formulates as "the wound and the bow" from the myth of Philoctetes, or James Hillman calls "the pathologizing process," by which soul manifests itself and makes itself available to male domestic novelists and other strange sports of human nature.

(1972)

The Genius of Stanislaw Lem

Stanislaw Lem is a Polish writer of science fiction in both traditional and original modes. Seven of his books have been published here since 1970, mostly by The Seabury Press, in small printings, and his reputation has been slow in developing. Elsewhere in the world his books sell in the millions, and he is regarded as a giant not only of science fiction but also of Eastern European literature. As well he should be. Lem is both a polymath and a virtuoso storyteller and stylist. Put them together and they add up to genius.

Lem's marriage of imagination and science creates various intricate worlds. Some are just around an indeterminate corner from our everyday one; some are just beyond the horizons of our own space age; some are far distant, parabolic extrapolations of the folklore of the past into a legendary future of statistical dragons and microminiature kingdoms, of psychedelic utopias that mask universal suffering, of autobionic mortals who persecute monotheistic robots—as though the tutelary spirit of Lem's imagination were a composite of Jonathan Swift and Norbert Wiener.

Although he has been highly praised by Leslie Fiedler, Theodore Sturgeon, Ursula K. Le Guin and other writers, not much is generally known about Lem here. He was born in Lvov in 1921, went through the Nazi occupation as a garage mechanic, and afterward studied medicine. In a valuable afterword to Lem's novel *Solaris,* Darko Suvin describes Lem as a "cultural phenomenon unto himself," who has written numerous articles on a range of scientific, technological, and literary subjects—past, present, and future—and produced several major speculative works: *Summa Technologiae,* which deals with the "Man-Nature game, sociocybernetics, and prospects of cosmic and biological engineering"; *The Philosophy of Chance;* and *Getting into Orbit*—studies of Dostoevsky, Camus, and futurology—among other books. Meanwhile, he has been steadily producing fiction that follows the arcs and depths of his learning and his bewildering labyrinth of moods and attitudes. Like his protagonists, loners virtually to a man, his fiction seems at a distance from the daily cares and passions, and conveys the sense of a mind hovering above the boundaries of the human condition: now mordant, now droll; now arcane, now folksy; now skeptical, now haunted—and always paradoxical. Yet his imagination is so powerful and coherent that no matter what world he creates, it is immediately convincing because of the concreteness and plenitude with which it is inhabited and the intimacy and authority with which it is governed.

If there is any dominant emotional tone in Lem's vision, it is the dark fusion of the ordinary and the macabre that has flourished in this century in Eastern Europe, the principal charnel house and social laboratory of the modern age. (Indeed modern Eastern European history seems like a scenario for science fiction in which a peaceable pastoral planet with centers of high culture is repeatedly invaded by lethal, authoritarian robots.) What gives Lem's writing its regional signature is its easy way with the grotesque—what one might call its domestication. This is the sensibility that creates the corpse with a rose behind his ear, the stone-faced bureaucratic chief with a winklike tic, the rural community that is inanely proud of the cement factory that is destroying its environment and its people's lungs, and so on throughout the postwar literature and films of Poland, Hungary, and Czechoslovakia.

The difficulty with writing about Lem is that any bare-bones account of his narratives makes them seem a bit corny or banal. In *The Invincible*, for example, a mammoth space cruiser with its impregnable force field and its antimatter artillery is defeated by hordes of flylike mechanisms on a planet where evolution has proceeded for some five hundred thousand years from the robots that colonized it. In *Solaris*, the "adversary" is a colloid-like sea that functions as a homeostatic regulator of the gravitational fields exerted by the planet's two suns; it passes its eons creating huge protean, mimetic, or binary structures from its waves: "extravagant theoretical cogitations about the nature of the universe . . . exploiting the implications of the Einstein-Boevian theory." After almost a century of research into its mysteries, various Earth scientists have been led off on so many tangents that they have lost touch with each other, and a final group of four men, in their frustrations, have bombarded the "sea" with X-rays. Possibly in retaliation, each of the four scientists is visited by an exact and alive model, "read" from his memory traces, of the one person in his past about whom he feels most guilty.

Well, that's right off the sf rack, you might say—except these situations come across with a rigor and complexity of description and conjecture that make them seem as if they were developed at Princeton's Institute for Advanced Studies. Here, for example, is one of the electronic "flies" from *The Invincible:*

> [Their] strictly symmetrical trapartite structures resembled the letter Y. . . . The smaller section, forming the arms . . ., constituted a steering system. . . . The micro-crystalline structure of the arms provided a type of universal accumulator and at the same time an energy transformer. Depending on the manner in which the micro-crystals were compressed, they either produced an electrical or magnetic field, or else produced changeable force fields that could raise the midsection's temperature to a relatively high degree, thus causing the stored heat to flow in an outward direction. The resultant thrust of the air enabled the 'insects' to ascend.

And so on for several pages that explain their aerodynamic properties, their apparent communications devices, their behavior patterns. But, as usual in Lem, the control system of the horde itself, its "mind," is baffling and remains so, even as its power increases.

This clarity and richness of detail pervades Lem's accounts of both these farfetched worlds, so that they become in time just as credible and coherent in their strangeness as, say, Thomas Mann's Biblical Egypt or Nabokov's Terra. Further, the behavior of the beleaguered earthmen is so finely attuned to their characters, particularly in *Solaris*, and so powerfully dramatized, that we believe in their experience because of the depth at which it is perceived and suffered. These narratives are not just told, they are imposed—minutely, completely, inarguably.

The Investigation is a novel closer to home, though no less bizarre and even more intricate. It takes place in London and some outlying suburbs, where a series of corpses have changed their position in their coffins, or else have disappeared. Been moved or moved themselves? The last one is found in the snow outside a mortuary, but the constable guarding it runs head-on into a passing car, and what he saw is locked away in his coma. Meanwhile, Lieutenant Gregory, a coldly determined detective from Scotland Yard, struggles with the findings of a creepy but brilliant statistician named Sciss, who has determined that the incidents form a regular pattern: The distance between the incidents, the time elapsed, and the temperature of the given night form a constant, while the extent of the corpse's movement correlates with its distance from the center of the area where the incidents have all occurred. Moreover, this area has an exceptionally low incidence of death by cancer.

What is Gregory to make of this esoteric data? Or of the dead animal that is found near each site? Or of Sciss's lies about his own movements? Or of the derelict on a subway who looks so much like a photo of one of the missing corpses? Or of the ghoulish photos and artifacts in his chief's flat? Or of the pattern of sinister sounds that emanate from his landlord's bedroom each night? Or of his own horribly cogent nightmares? The atmosphere of the novel becomes as macabre as the corpse in the snow, as spectrally placed on the fringe of being between the definite and the indefinite. At the center of Lem's heuristic puzzles are black existential holes. The tense cat-and-mouse game between Gregory and Sciss continues, the former being bent on finding a perpetrator, the latter on demonstrating the indeterminacy of what we call "reality," except by statistical methods.

Lem, in his characteristic way, works out the situation by carrying it to a deeper level of enigma than the one on which it began. His science fiction and mystery novels are renovations of genres, much like Fowles's *The French Lieutenant's Woman,* that exploit their conventions to uncover what they conceal: the problematic universe that underlies their assurances and any others.

Including those of cybernetics—Lem's pet field. At one point Sciss predicts that the arms race will eventually proceed by other means: competition between the computer technologies. "Human control over the [electronic] brains' decisions will decrease in proportion to the increase of its accumulated knowledge." Eventually, the world will be a chessboard and men "will be pawns manipulated in an eternal game between two mechanical players."

Memoir Found in a Bathtub is a comic, pathetic, and gruesome evocation of such a future. It is set in a vast espionage center called Pentagon III, buried in the Rocky Mountains, sometime after the collapse of capitalist society. The center is controlled by a supremely complicated "brain," but one whose conduits of control—orders, tactics, codes, chains of command, etc.—are riddled with paranoid subterfuges to guard its secrets from an enemy that may, in fact, no longer exist. To add to the madness, the flow of information is so torrential by now that the system appears to have decided to operate in a totally random way: Every document will arrive at the right desk . . . eventually.

So, too, the nameless narrator—who spends his time scurrying from office to office trying to find out what his orders are—is caught up in a maze of incidents that seems now entirely fortuitous and now part of an inscrutable scheme. To test him? To entrap and reveal him? To drive him out of his mind? To kill him? All the officials are like walking codes—their true purposes lurking behind their simulated advice, cajolery, or threats, behind their cunning disguises, even behind their occasional murders or suicides: all creatures of the "brain," which dissimulates its own simulations, and hence spawns its own double, triple . . . sextuple agents. At the center of the maze is an empty bathroom with a razor to which the narrator returns for sanctuary and, finally, for surcease when he finds that his principal ally (or decoy?) has killed himself.

One can read *Memoir Found in a Bathtub* as a spy novel that takes its conventional involutions to absurdity, as a Cold War satire, or as another Lemian experiment with his Möbius strip of randomness and design. But in its dizzying depths, which I have barely suggested above, lurks the dark side of Lem's paradoxical attitude toward the man-machine relationship, which dominates his fiction. Is Pentagon III a perversion of humanity produced by the further evolution of computer technology? Or is this evolution being perverted by the uses to which human folly puts it? And beyond this lies the further problem that humanity and technology are locked into a symbiotic relationship that progressively amplifies its consequences of good and evil.

In *The Futurological Congress,* for example, the mounting violence and terrorism of 1990 is mainly held in check by "benignimizers," which turn a revolt in Costa Rica into a love-in. Some fifty years later, a wretchedly overpopulated reality is made habitable and even happy by "mascons" and a host of other drugs that completely falsify the world. Lem has great fun inventing a vocabulary for his "psychem" society—"opinionates" and "algebrines," "absolventina" and "brahmax" and "zoroaspics," not to mention "yogart" and "mishnameal," and on through "obliterine" and "authentium," and a hundred other terms for this permanently stoned world ruled by a handful of "chemocrats." In time, the horrors behind the euphoria are revealed to the narrator and he awakens from what is finally a nightmare, greatly relieved to find himself back in a sewer in Costa Rica.

Still, Lem's queasiness is not simply that of an old-fashioned humanist. Some of his most inspired and charming writing is produced by his feeling for the interchanges and interfaces of humanity and technology. This writing comes mainly in an original form that Lem has been developing for the past twenty years, best described as the futurist folktale, two volumes of which have appeared here—*The Cyberiad* and most recently *The Star Diaries.* Michael Kandel, who has turned four of Lem's books into marvelously readable and resourceful English (he was nominated for a National Book Award in translation in 1975), quotes a passage from an autobiographical sketch in which Lem remarks on his special feeling as a boy for all sorts of broken bells, alarm clocks, old spark plugs and "in general for things derailed . . . used up, homeless, discarded. . . . I would turn some crank or other to give it pleasure, then put it away again with solicitude."

This sense of play, of delight in gadgets, of imagining a life for them, informs *The Cyberiad,* whose two heroes, Trurl and Klapaucius, are "constructor" robots who perform miracles with odds and ends. For example, there is Trurl's electronic bard—programmed with much of the history of the world—which first produces a lecture on "sub-molecular magnetic anomalies," then goes through other malfunctions, and only begins to function effectively when Trurl throws out all the logical circuits and replaces them with "self-regulatory, egocentripetal narcissistors." Or there is Trurl's kingdom in a box: with its towns and rivers, armies and castles and marketplaces, "days of backbreaking labor, nights full of dancing . . . and the gay clatter of swordplay." And with plots, conspirators, false witnesses, "a necessary handful of heroes, a pinch of prophets and seers, and one messiah and one great poet." Trurl hands the kingdom over to a deposed tyrant as a consolation and he immediately begins to tyrannize it.

Trurl moves on through space and, returning to his own planet, tells his rival, Klapaucius, about his feat, but Klapaucius is horrified: "Are we not as well . . . nothing but the minuscule capering of electron clouds . . .? Is our existence not the result of . . . the interplay of particles, though we ourselves perceive those molecular cartwheels as fear, longing, meditation?" So they return to the kingdom to find it covered with all manner of microminiaturized intelligent life, including a tiny mushroom cloud; the box has become a shrine and the tyrant has been dispatched into space.

A few of the stories at the beginning of *The Cyberiad* are a bit coy, but the later stories grow in power and implication and culminate in an extraordinary series, "The Tale of Three Story Telling Machines," including the Beckett-like story of "Mymosh the Self-Begotten," who comes together by pure accident on a cosmic junk pile of tin cans, wire, mica, and "a hunk of rusty iron which happened to be a magnet." Mymosh is immobilized by further accidents, and since his only reality is his thoughts, he uses them to create a "Gozmos . . . a place of caprice and miracles."

In much the same spirit, *The Star Diaries* relates the adventures of Ijon Tichy, who in his one-man spaceship goes whizzing around a universe that seems about the size of Poland. By and large, Lem seems to use these stories to satirize and parody the interests and themes of his darker books; thus there is a lot of horseplay about pseudoscientific space and time travel, about the folly of an anthropocentric view of the universe, about the habitual tendency of mankind to abuse its technology. In Tichy's cosmos, as he reports, robots have a "natural decency" and "only man can be a bastard." Also, perhaps because he is writing in a comic way, Lem feels freer to play with Iron Curtain satire, as in Tichy's encounter with a planet that coerces all its citizens to believe that water is their natural element and to behave accordingly. When an editor makes the mistake of writing that water is wet, he is purged. "You have to look at it from the fish's point of view," he confesses to Tichy. "Fish do not find water wet—ergo, it isn't."

The major story in *The Star Diaries* deals with robot theologians who are forced to live in catacombs because they insist on maintaining a religious faith that their mortal masters have long since abandoned in their delight in changing into whatever forms science enables them to assume. The theology of the monks proceeds from the paradox that "faith is, at one and the same time, absolutely necessary and altogether impossible." In the pages of explication and argument that follow, as subtle and precise as Lem's account in *Solaris* of the history of "Solaristics" (which also terminates in a purely religious conception of the "sea"), there is plenty of reason to believe that Lem is enunciating the grounds of his own faith. It is a faith that proceeds and returns to the indeterminacy of all that surrounds and retreats from the structure of human consciousness. This indeterminacy is God. Without it there is only a treacherous eschatology of freedom, of which the autobionic mortals are grisly examples. God is the mind's necessary constraint.

In these pages, among the most fascinating that Lem has written, lies his resolution of the central paradox of cybernetic man and his future. So it seems to me. But read Lem for yourself and by your own lights. He is a major writer and one of the deep spirits of our age.

(1976)

American Review Fiction

The fiction published in *New American* (later *American*) *Review* was a function partly of the magazine's strange identity and partly of its principal editor's groping taste. As essentially a little magazine published for the mass market—with all the opportunities, problems, paradoxes, and risks such a venture entails—*NAR/AR* tried to attract a community of readers who were culturally literate rather than elitist. Hence the editor and his staff looked for material that was broadly interesting—catholic, lively, topical, venturesome. We published a fair amount of experimental as well as more traditional types of fiction; took chances with various stories that tested the barriers of erotic description and language, which were only beginning to weaken; gave a certain advantage to manuscripts that were telling of the political, social, and cultural upheavals of the 1960s and 1970s; and in general tried to keep our fiction conversant with our essays, many of them bearing the imagination of alternatives that was abroad in the land.

All of which was not simply a matter of marketing calculation. *NAR* tried to establish a footing between the traditional culture and the counterculture; our purpose, as it evolved in the late 1960s, was to try to apply the critical standards of the former to the ideology and sensibility of the latter, and occasionally vice versa. In fiction~~, this mainly~~

meant publishing work that was articulate and whose point of view and effects were earned by craft rather than asserted by rhetoric, while at the same time recognizing that new modes of expressiveness test and alter one's notions of the articulate and the earned.

This is to put these matters, though, in a more schematic and balanced way than the actual process of editorial judgment allows. It assumes that your taste is sufficiently sure and flexible and objective to be equal to every manuscript that comes your way. Sometimes you think it is: at least, you know that you have to publish this narrative, however unconventional—or conventional—it may seem, if you're to go on making sense of what you're doing; you know you won't publish that one for the same reason, no matter how fashionable—or unfashionable—the author or the writing may be. Those are the easy ones. The hard ones are those that drive you to your fence and sit you down on it. The author may simply have a more subtle imagination than yours—and one that doesn't leave tracks. Or he may take you, however resistantly, into a place so sordid or depraved that your respect for narrative power tells you one thing and your disgust another. Or you may think a story is terrific up to the end but that its end is too obvious or obscure, though its author stubbornly doesn't. These are only a few of the cases where your decision-making process falters into doubt. It may be that the bottom line of how you really function as an editor is to what you give the benefit of your doubts. That may also be the bottom line of what makes your magazine continue to be interesting, because benefits of doubt are where the risks are, and as our poetry editor, Richard Howard, liked to remind me, "only the risky is truly interesting."

During the years I was editing *NAR/AR,* the benefit of my own doubts tended to go to the less known, the topical, and the innovative. This was in keeping with its claim to being a "magazine of new writing," but it was also consonant with a stage of my own journey. Like many intellectuals of my generation, I was reevaluating a good many of my values, and trying to create some space for growth in a mind that had been overly influenced by careerism and a faith in authority. With respect to literature, I came off some of my graduate-student elitism and tried to develop the idea that literature was too important a democratic resource to be left to the literati. By the same token, I felt that the heavy hand of the modernist tradition which academicism had laid on the norms of literary value needed to be resisted and that, in Auden's words, "new styles of architecture, a change of heart" should be encouraged. This made me open to the plain-speech style and democratic vistas of the new generation as well as to its cultural eclecticism, its expansion of consciousness, its relaxation of forms and categories to free up energy, and so forth.

Well, the counterculture has been over for a decade or more, and I'm fifty-three now and growing conscious of the selectivities that come with aging. As in other matters, my literary interests have less to do with inquisitiveness and more with sustenance. The fictions I find I want most to include in this selection from *NAR/AR* are not especially topical or innovative, or else these qualities are subsumed in more general and less easily defined ones. Perhaps the closest I can come is to say that their consciousness of life and their artistry are seasoned—not as a salad is but as wood is, as character is. They have a genuine subject—a complex situation or course of events taken at the full. This sense of plenitude, of having much to say and tell, comes from a subject that is deeply held, steeped in feeling, rich in implication. Hence the pressure of the narrative seems to come naturally to it, a function of the inwardness, of the dream energy pressing for expression, and of the narrative art that concentrates and empowers this energy as a magnifying glass does the sunlight.

Sometimes the resulting intensity is immediately evident, as in Gilbert Sorrentino's "The Moon in Its Flight"—a *cri de coeur,* sounding down the corridors of memory, of an unconsummated and still unresolved summer romance between a Catholic street kid from Brooklyn and a Jewish princess from Mosholu Parkway: "I don't even know where CCNY is! Who is Conrad Aiken? What is Bronx Science? Who is Berlioz? What is a Stravinsky? How do you play Mah-Jongg? What is schmooz, schlepp, Purim, Moo Goo Gai Pan? Help me." The strength of the narrator's experience, its erotic tenderness, longing, and pain, are witnessed by the extraordinary vividness of details with which the girl, himself, the setting, the time—everything—is remembered. The truth of the ache is in the tone of the writing—nostalgia mixed with chagrin, wonder with anger: this complexity being further evidence of the force and depth with which the emotion of the story is held. This is the voice of a man who is writing for his life, in the sense that his life has been diminished so far by his failure to fathom the experience.

A number of the other stories have a similar declarative intensity: Robert Stone's "Aquarius Obscured," Leonard Michaels's "Getting Lucky," Harold Brodkey's "Innocence"—another remembrance of young love, which has "the authority," in Brodkey's words, "of being on one's knees in front of the event." But there are other registers of the narrative voice that bespeak the same generative attachment to the subject, the same sense of necessity that this much, at least, must be said. William Gass's "In the Heart of the Heart of the Country" is written in spare, objective vignettes of dailiness in a small town in Indiana that is slowly failing even as its life goes on, just as the narrator's mind goes on observing even as his spirit sinks in longing and grief. In this case, the emotional burden of a broken relationship, one between the middle-aged narrator and a young woman, is not front and center; it is rather like an ache in the back of his descriptions of the town's neighbors and landscapes, commerce and socializing, education and religion. The urgency of the narrative, parodoxically enough, lies in its control—the slow-breathing control of a man trying to hold himself together, not an actor but a patient in whom little is going on save pain and the slow influx of the world. What is so remarkable is the poise with which Gass holds the narrative on the interface between the personal and the phenomenological in a kind of attenuated curiosity, the grief and the observation validating and deepening each other.

Grace Paley's "Faith: In a Tree" is another example of a distinctive voice narrating a social scene, specifically the Greenwich Village scene of young mothers without husbands. Comic rather than elegiac, Faith's voice is indefatigably gregarious and subtly lonely. With her savvy eye and impetuous heart, she provides the minutes, as it were, of the Saturday-afternoon conclave at the Washington Square sandbox. At the center of the action are needs that none of the stray men who come by are likely to fill, just as Faith's consciousness circles around and around the hole left by her transient husband.

A writer seized by his or her subject in the ways I have been trying to suggest is likely to make a move against or beyond the conventions of narrative—a bold adaptation of the form to the pressure and reach of the content. In Grace Paley's story, the first-person point of view is summarily stripped of its limitations, and lines of telepathy are set up to handle the incessant flow of information and communication that animates the scene. Along with its charm, the device expresses the helpless intimacies of this circle of Village women and children, where everything hangs out. In Gass's story the innovative stroke is the deliberate elimination of any overt narrative development, to accord with the patient-like passivity of the speaker and the sense of entropy at work in the community, and by extension, in the heart of the country. Toward the end of Sorrentino's "The Moon in Its Flight," the narrator abruptly invents—or is it an invention?—a scene of consummation ten years later, when he and Rebecca accidentally meet again. He speaks of this scene as "the literary part of this story," the implication being that fiction will now provide what life has withheld. On the other hand, he speaks of Rebecca's having "gone out of the reality of narrative," the implication being that what follows did happen but is too melodramatic to be believed. I don't think that Sorrentino means the ambiguity to be resolved one way or the other, for the story is not only about desire but also about art: the transactions that imagination carries out in both realms, if indeed they are finally separate realms in this case.

To my mind, this is the true province of innovation and experiment—not for its own sake but for the subject's sake, provided the subject is a genuine one. A sign of a genuine subject, as I've suggested, is the strength, vibrancy, and resilience of feeling it releases into the prose itself; another sign is the complexity it sustains—the doubleness of vision that literary art mediates and resolves into a rich fusion of incident and context, living and meaning. In García Márquez's story of a senile angel who is found lying moribund in a villager's chicken yard, where he is successively marveled over, exploited, and then ignored, the natural and the supernatural keep touching down in each other's realm in droll, surreal, and indomitably innocent ways. "His only supernatural virtue seemed to be patience. Especially during the first days, when the hens pecked at him, searching for the stellar parasites that proliferated in his wing, and the cripples pulled out feathers to touch their defective parts with, and even the most merciful threw stones at him, trying to get him to rise so they could see him standing." In García Márquez's hands, the material turns into myth before one's eyes and finally into a parable of the soul's bedraggled journey through the world.

Philip Roth's " 'I Always Wanted You to Admire My Fasting' " begins with an essay that presents two views of Kafka—the familiar crippled refugee from the threat of his own desires and the "writer, father, and Jew" who came out of hiding in the final months of Kafka's life, when the force of his terminal illness liberated him. Then, in his own masterstroke of daring, Roth gives his subject twenty-five more years of life and turns Kafka into one of those refugees who peopled the Hebrew schools and Friday-night tables of America in the 1930s and 1940s. Another turn of the screw of Kafkaesque irony produces this figure of forlorn dignity who briefly courts Roth's spinster aunt, to an inevitable outcome, and dies eventually in a sanitarium in New Jersey, as totally obscure as he had wished.

Roth's piece is first a biographical study and then a story, or, rather, it comes together finally as a hybrid form perfectly adapted to the subject at hand—a life so patterned by irony, so strange in its outcomes, that it beggars any fictional version of it: that is, other than Kafka's own. *NAR/AR* published many other transactions between the modes of fact and those of fiction. A few years ago, when the "new journalism" was all the vogue, its practitioners, led by Tom Wolfe, were applauding themselves for their acquisition of the techniques of the novelists, whom they aimed to supplant as the principal chroniclers of the age. Meanwhile, without much publicity, fiction writers were making their own raids across the dwindling frontier between the realms of factuality and fiction, including what alleges to be one or the other. In an age given over to various channels of public disinformation, ranging from presidential press conferences and State Department white papers, to the institutional ad and the product commercial, the novelist finds a particular opportunity and even a necessity for the kinds of lies he tells, his "false documents" being in the interest of freeing inquiry from the "factual" lies and blandishments of the political and economic regime. As E. L. Doctorow wrote in *AR* 26, "The novelist deals with his isolation by splitting himself in two, creator and documentarian, teller and listener, conspiring to pass on the collective wisdom in its own enlightened bias, that of the factual world."

The pages of *NAR/AR*, issue after issue, contained experiments with tellingly "false documents." Donald Barthelme's study of Robert Kennedy is a kind of synthetic journalism, a collage of real and invented newspaper clips designed to portray Kennedy as a contemporary "representative man," in Emerson's term, the complete media figure: "a pastless futureless man, born anew at every instant. . . . Nothing follows from what has gone before. He is constantly surprised. He cannot predict his own reaction to events. He is constantly being *overtaken* by events. A condition of breathlessness and dazzlement surrounds him." Kennedy himself is speaking, paraphrasing the French critic Georges Poulet. Why not? All sources of imagery are available to the man who is making his self completely dissoluble in his image. Another kind of false document is Max Apple's wholly imaginary account of the career of Howard Johnson in "The Oranging of America"—a genial condensation of the American dream in its capitalist phase. The religion of consumerism finds its quintessential figure in Apple's pseudobiographical account of this visionary of mobility and prophet of profits, who carries out his mission in a customized Lincoln equipped with an ice cream freezer for testing his product, a map for charting his ministry, an office for his helpmate, and eventually a cryonics freezer in tow for prospective resurrection.

There were more seemingly traditional stories, such as William Mathes's "Swan Feast," Dinah Brooke's "Some of the Rewards and Pleasures of Love," Vassily Aksyonov's "Little Whale, a Varnisher of Reality." But they remain no less powerful for that, and being fully imagined and boldly executed, no less new. Originality in fiction is less a matter of the subject or the means than of the distinctive aura of the experience. There have been many stories of violent hunters and amorous cripples and politically terrorized writers. But such is the energy of vision in these respective stories and such the focusing power of their incidents and images that whatever banality we may feel is quickly burned away and the imagination again comes into its own. "Wash Far Away," John Berryman's story of a man teaching *Lycidas* in the midst of World War II, is obviously written close to the bone of an actual experience. George Dennison's story of a prodigious high jumper who takes up ornithology seems as purely imagined as a dream. Yet both writers are pursuing the same mystery—the nature of genius—and from their different directions, both manage to touch her hem.

Henry James said that "the house of fiction has many windows." Yes, and there are many more today than in James's time. It's now more like a high-rise apartment complex, so many are in residence there, so numerous are the points of vantage and view. Most of the accommodations, though, are smaller, and skimpier, more provisional and transient, than in James's time. So it seemed to me during the years I edited *NAR/AR,* when I continued to be struck by the number of gifted new writers who came, as it were, from out of the blue and who, after a story or two, perhaps a novel, often disappeared back into it. The same might be said of *NAR/AR* itself: It came out of the vast realm of American possibilities with various questions on its mind, hung in there for a decade or so, and then went the way of much of the writing and spirit it tried to welcome and give a home to. In an age whose universal is change, virtually everything becomes ephemeral and mutable or at least begins to seem so. Reading through the files of *NAR/AR*, I was surprised to feel as often remote as nostalgic. But then I would come upon another story that was still leading its complex and forceful life, and I put it into the collection, *Many Windows*, to commemorate the magazine's place in contemporary fiction.

(1982)

Part Four

Irving Howe's World of Ourselves

The first generation tries to retain, the second to forget, the third to remember. American-Jewish writing of the past thirty years is, for the most part, a literature of memory, a harking back to family, neighborhood, school, and other formative experience to recover the trail of Jewish identity before it faded out in the shady streets of suburbia and the bright corridors of the professions. Why this interest, though? Why not "stick to the present"? as my father would say. "The farther back you go, the more miserable it gets."

The main reason, I think, is that the third-generation Jew intermittently experiences himself as a case of cultural amnesia, the ancestral promptings and demurrers vaguely pulsing away. But the context of these intuitions of Jewish being, these moral slants and emotional tilts in the way he does his work, relates to his children, votes, justifies his life, chases his desires, remains elusive, full of blank spots, awkward sentiments, impatient questions. Why should it matter so much? asks the lapsed Jew, otherwise comfortable in his acculturation. So much influence from so little content. This is one reason Philip Roth's fiction rings bells so sharply. The stories in *Goodbye, Columbus* turn upon the possessiveness of the Jewish ethos—a theme that develops into the aching comedy of *Portnoy's Complaint,* where Jewish conditioning and the Oedipal complex meet on the psychiatric couch to explain and explain the constrained desires of a model young lawyer with a lust for fashion models. But Roth's keen sense of the entailments of Portnoy's heritage is hardly the whole story of it, and so one reads Bellow and Malamud, Leonard Michaels and Grace Paley, Cynthia Ozick and I. B. Singer, et al., looking for fellow experience and perspective. Or one can study Judaism, even learn Hebrew, hoping to find the way back to the shaping significance that is hardly accounted for by the perfunctory bar mitzvah lessons and seders of one's childhood. Contemporary fiction, though, tends to be too . . . well, contemporary and idiosyncratic to supply much of the missing link, while Judaism, as one soon learns, is not in the business of providing self-revelation. Like all religions, it remains remote unless one meets it more than halfway. The fiction of Chaim Potok would seem to fill the bill, being plugged securely into the ethos of normative Judaism, but in the end a book like *The Chosen* remains parochial in its subject and tone, and reading it is like going to synagogue only once a year, a way of revisiting the gap between the religious Jew and the rest of us.

Jewishness, then, is like a language in which one knows only a few words and phrases and yet is strangely responsive to its intonations and rhythms, its lights and darks of feeling. Like Russian, as I found out on a recent visit. Or more to the point, like Yiddish—that mysterious language in which our parents kept their secrets from us. What remain are a few expressions; a coarseness to the ear which once had a stigma attached, like slurping soup; also a certain singsong rhythm that makes it seem a little dizzying; also a reverberant tonality whose middle register seems devoted to various shades of resignation. So one puts his bits and drops of Yiddish and its intonations into his English, particularly with other Jews, to provide some fellow feeling, an acknowledgment of roots. Imitating Yiddish seems to confirm something basic in one's nature, a kind of free area of expressiveness as well as a contact with one's earlier self. The same is true of telling Jewish jokes in dialect.

And so, like Poe's purloined letter, the missing link to the past has been there all along, right before one's eyes or, rather, on his tongue. For much of the secret source of one's "Jewish" ways, as one recognizes and recognizes in reading Irving Howe's *World of Our Fathers,* turns out to be *Yiddishkeit,* the culture of the immigrant generations.

Howe has written a splendid book, a richly detailed and interpreted narrative of two generations of "bedraggled and inspired" Jewish immigrants on the Lower East Side and beyond, in its manifold political, economic, social, and cultural bearings. A work of history and of art, *World of Our Fathers* is brilliantly organized and paced by brisk, pithy chapters that make up large perspectives: the detonations of new hopes and renewed fear that drove the immigrants out of the Russian Pale after the assassination of Alexander II and the pogroms that followed; the wretchedness and culture shock of the first two decades in New York; the daily family and work life in the filthy, noisy, flaring streets off East Broadway; the dynamic rise of the Jewish labor movement and the emergence of the remarkable Yiddish theater and press, as well as modern poetry and fiction movements; and finally, the rapid, fated dispersion into middle-class America. All of which is exhaustively researched and documented, often in the words of the people themselves. *World of Our Fathers* is also a complex story of fulfillment and incompleteness, a work of sage meditation and ironic vision. Finally, it is lucidly and warmly written, and fleshed in with choice photographs, which touch and bemuse. A richness everywhere.

If you are Jewish, you will find that Howe has written a

necessary book, particularly if you need its blow on the head to deliver you from your amnesia or, better, to help you begin to rescue yourself. Not that Howe's pages are ever particularly startling. Their effect is cumulative—the slow, dawning realization that this world is as familiar to your intuitions as it is fresh to your eyes. You will discover, for example, that the Yiddish word for excommunication, *heren*, became the word for boycott, and a little crease of consciousness becomes activated and gets in touch with your sense of identity. Similarly, Howe's image of Jacob Adler, the matinee idol of the Yiddish theater, lying in state, as he instructed, in English morning coat, Windsor cravat, and *talit.* Or, at the other extreme of *Yiddishkeit*, a sketch by Z. Libin—a writer from the terrible first years, the era of the *farloyrene menschen*, the "lost souls"—about a worker who fears that because a wall blocking his window has been torn down he will have to pay more rent. My favorite trip into the dream life that joins the Jewish generations is provided by an unpublished memoir by David Goldenbloom, one of the self-educated garment workers who become the composite hero of Howe's narrative:

> [When I was about seventeen] I began to take an interest in books. Since I had also gone a little to the Russian school, I began to swallow—I mean, really swallow—Russian books. . . . Turgenev was my favorite, perhaps because there is such a sweetness to his voice. And then Tolstoy and Dostoevsky. I read, of course, Sholom Aleichem, who made the ugliest things in life seem beautiful, and Peretz, who, in his own way, taught me not to lose respect for myself.

In order to perceive the force of the attitudes and values that *Yiddishkeit* pumped through the generational conduits, one often has to recover the conditions that charged and shaped them. It is a platitude, for example, that Jews are mercenary because our forefathers were desperately poor, or that Jewish mothers dote on and stuff and worry about their children because of the immigrants' experience of hunger, illness, self-sacrifice, and hope. How banal, one says, until one reads Howe's harrowing account of the poverty of the Lower East Side during the 1880s and '90s.

"Have you ever seen a hungry child cry?" asks the social worker Lillian Wald, explaining the dedication of her life. By 1885 the crying was everywhere. Wages in the garment industry—the main source of jobs—were cut in half. The population density of the Lower East Side was soon greater than in the worst sections of Bombay, the mortality rate was double that of the rest of the city. Project these figures into conditions and you get men working seventy hours a week in the unspeakable sweatshops and then taking piecework home in order to scrape by, of people sleeping five or six to a room with their boarders, of near epidemics of dysentery, typhoid fever, and of course tuberculosis, the "tailors' disease." For twenty years or so, it was as though the fabled wretchedness of the steerage passage never ended, that those dark packed ships simply came up on land and turned into factory lofts and tenements.

What was most traumatic was the inner darkness. Totally uprooted and alien, driven by a tempo they had never known before, their austere, decorous spirits assaulted and derided by the brutal dog-eat-dog conditions of their existence, their religious institutions in disarray, the immigrants seemed to lose their main possession, the culture that had preserved so many generations of the Pale despite poverty and other oppressions. The collapse of its center, rabbinical authority, is brought home by the anecdote Howe tells of the attempt to establish a chief rabbi to restore order. Soon there were three—a Lithuanian and a Galician (traditional antagonists) and a newcomer from Moscow. When asked who had made him the chief rabbi, the Russian replied, "The sign painter."

"They were Jews without Jewish memories or traditions," reports one Yiddish writer. "With every day that passed," recalls another, "I became more and more overwhelmed by the degeneration of my fellow-countrymen." And in the words of the poet Moshe Lieb Halpern: "If a wolf stumbled in here/He'd lose his wits/He'd tear his own flesh apart." In a radical newspaper of the day, Howe tells us, "the word *finsternish,* darkness, recurs again and again. . . . their lives are overcome by *finsternish* and it is to escape from *finsternish* that men must learn to act." So they listened meekly to their flamboyant agitators, went on bitter and usually doomed strikes, saved their pennies for the Yiddish theater, but mainly lived on their last hope that they might yet see their sons and daughters move on to something better.

Finsternish didn't begin in the New York ghetto. It came in the immigrants' luggage and dreams, the darkness of being cooped up for centuries in their decaying villages and prayer houses and in their sustaining but hapless messianism. But in the Russian Pale it was already lifting, thanks in good part to the Bund, the nascent Jewish socialists from the cities. Here is David Goldenbloom again:

> . . . just a few years before I came [from Russia] people of my generation became very restless. We heard of the Bund, which had recently been started, and to us it meant not only socialism but the whole idea of stepping into the outside world. When a speaker from the Bund came to our town, we saw him . . . as a new kind of Jew, someone with combativeness in his blood and a taste for culture on his tongue. . . . He was our lifeline to the outside world, and that was enough.

In America, it was the distinctively Jewish socialism developed by the Bund that largely rebuilt the community and morale the immigrants had lost. Indeed socialism, mostly through the organizing of the garment trades, provided a collective enterprise, not only as a consequence of despair but also as a movement toward the vision of a "normal life" at last, not merely as a response to privation but also as a recycled moral yearning. Jewish socialism derived, as Howe shows, from Jewish messianism, in which the worldly and otherworldly were aspects of the same destiny, a tradition that was quick to produce political and social movements that had a strong utopian, universalist cast and fervor.

The radicals of the early Lower East Side had been mostly Russian-style anarchists to whom the benighted workers were the shock troops of revolution, good for strikes but hardly worth organizing. The socialists from Warsaw and Vilna who came in droves after 1905 brought organization. They also brought the idea that the Jewish trade unions should reorganize the Jewish community and bring it into the twentieth century by replacing the religious framework with more adaptive and effective social and cultural institutions. The Bund leaders saw their opening in the great strike of the shirtwaist makers in 1909, many of them, like their leader, teenage girls, and of the cloak makers in 1910, in which, as the writer Abraham Liessen declared, "the 70,000 zeroes became 70,000 fighters." From these strikes rose the intense feeling that the Jews had once again fought their way out of captivity and darkness; this élan, along with the moral and psychic restlessness of believers who were rapidly discarding the religious worldview, was rapidly channeled into the ILGWU and the Amalgamated Clothing Workers. The socialists produced the major Yiddish newspaper and set up organizations such as the Workmen's Circle, which provided health and life insurance, hospitals and sanitariums, schools that offered a secular Jewish education, as well as all manner of lectures, courses, and other cultural activities, mostly in Yiddish. From this example, all of Jewish unionism would take its cue: Thus the communists would challenge the socialists with their own children's camps and schools, cooperative housing projects, theater, dance, and choral groups, mandolin ensembles and literary panels, as well as an excellent newspaper. In short, in trying to revolutionize the world that ground them down, the immigrant Jews revolutionized themselves both to resist it and to help their children rise in it.

Reading Howe's pages on Jewish socialism and the labor movements—meticulously fair and even-tempered, though patently written by the editor of *Dissent,* one of the remaining few to whom socialism was a belief "to which they would pledge their lives"—one can see the powerful strains of Jewish idealism and skepticism working away like yeast in bread. Also, in Howe's descriptions of the intricate, shifting, but always bitter struggle between the left and right, of the slow giving way of radical aspirations to practical ambitions in the rank and file, one can find an evolving paradigm of the political behavior of Jews in America as well, perhaps, of the ideological tensions that mark one's own politics. This comes home in Howe's argument with the revisionist view that the Jewish socialist movement was mainly a mode of acculturation instead of a force dedicated to a new society, which was the way it mostly saw itself and the way it actually transformed the consciousness of masses of Jews.

The other powerful force that brought the immigrant community together and enabled it even to flourish was *Yiddishkeit,* also originally an East European movement of the late nineteenth century. Its marrow was the vernacular of the Jews, "a language crackling with cleverness and turmoil, ironic to its bones." Its substance was the Jewish way of life, through thick and thin, the "shared experience, which goes beyond opinion and ideology." Its function was to hold together a people who were undergoing one challenge after another, including, after 1881, dispersion and acculturation in a totally strange secular society. Its spirit was an ironic acceptance of its role of straddling two worldviews—the religious and the secular—which were slowly moving apart and one of which was crumbling.

Even so, *Yiddishkeit* performed wonders while it lasted. It carried the fragmented, rivalrous East European Jews into the modern world. It provided an essential network of communications between the Pale and New York that reached into their respective theaters, union halls, newspaper offices, poetry movements, political cells, life-styles, schools of fiction. It also negotiated the uneven and fateful transactions between tradition and modernity, between communal and individual expression, between its own survival and its people's acculturation. In its very premises that the Jews could remain Jews and yet regain their worldly bearings and lead a "normal life" in Russia and America lay the sources of its enormous energies and contradictions, its startling full life, and its inexorable self-destruction.

In his chapters on the *Daily Forward,* Howe describes how this leading newspaper functioned as a teacher of the tribe—a kindergarten that taught new manners and a university that explained the intellectuals to the masses (and vice versa); a counselor in all manner of family, work, and personal problems; an organ for high socialist essays and lurid crime stories, for Yiddish soap opera on one page and the fiction of I. B. Singer on the next. In sum, as Howe puts it, "a large enclosing mirror that reflected the whole of the world of Yiddish—its best, its worst, its most ingrown, its most outgoing its soaring idealism, its crass materialism, everything." It was all held together by its editor, the remarkable Abraham Cahan, who wrote the one distinguished novel in English about the immigrant experience, *The Rise of David Levinsky,* whose theme is the melancholy wages of success. Cahan knew from the start that the more the *Forward* built a bridge to America, the more of its readers would cross it. At the same time, his newspaper held up the idea of the underlying unity of a culture that would strongly mark the work of American Jews, from the movies of Hollywood to the pages of *Commentary.*

Yiddish theater began as the one refuge in the years of darkness, serving up lofty sententiousness, flooded emotionality, and low pageantry: Moshe Lieb Halpern called it a cross between a synagogue and a brothel. In the fifty years that followed, it tried to inch its way toward modern realism and theatrical art, especially the Russian model. But its audience continued to clamor for the war-horses of historical spectacle or family *schmaltz,* preferably a touch of both, such as *Mirele Efros,* first called "The Jewish Queen Lear," in which ungrateful, worldly sons eventually return to confirm their mother's wisdom. Such plays provided the audience with what they wanted: the brilliant genre acting of Adler, Thomashefsky, Maurice Schwartz, in the higher and lower registers (the best acting in New York, according to Stark Young), and a plot that confirmed the old wisdom that a persecuted minority requires strict family discipline—i.e., Mama knows best. Yet it was just this function that enabled Yiddish theater to flourish, creating something akin to Italian opera, in Howe's view, by the expressiveness and vigor of its uncomplicated theatricality. Perhaps in time, with the development of more sophisticated Yiddish audiences, the theater would have caught up with the aspirations and abilities of its Jacob Ben-Amis and H. Leivicks. But there was no time: "a wink of history and it was over."

There is also Howe's luminous chapter on Yiddish poetry—the soul of *Yiddishkeit* and the most highly developed of its literary arts, leading the charmed and bitter life, as poetry usually does, of public neglect. But then all of the Yiddish arts began to lose their public as America beckoned in English to the next generation. With the rapid development of a middle class in the 1920s, *Yiddishkeit* developed a kind of fugitive second life as an infiltrator of American culture. This insight provides a subtle undercurrent to Howe's treatment of the dispersion of the immigrant ethos, through the comedians from Eddie Cantor to Lenny Bruce, the artists such as Jacob Epstein and the Soyer brothers, and the American novelists from Henry to Philip Roth. Here Howe bears down on the point I began with—the legacy of Yiddish culture in the deeper levels of consciousness and moral will. For example, the abiding commitment to the aesthetic of Judaism itself: "beauty is a quality, not a form; a content, not an arrangement"—the moral and aesthetic belong to the same realm. Even in recent fiction one sees the creation of a new American prose with a Yiddish flavor, and a carrying out of the strategy of the great Yiddish actors—"realism with a little extra," as Harold Clurman put it. At the same time, Howe observes the waning of the Yiddish influence under the same paradox that governed its rapid development and attenuation.

The sense of this rich and terrible brevity provides the tone of *World of Our Fathers*—the note of up-and-doing, striving, even frenzy, mingling with the note of frustration, sacrifice, incompleteness. This tone, now brisk, now elegiac, also arises from Howe's feeling for the tragic dialectic of his story—that the "normal life" that these self-educated workers and their tribunes strove to create proved to be but a staging area for their children's escape from the family, community, and culture. Perhaps the last word fittingly belongs to David Goldenbloom, whom Howe, like the world he lived in, has rescued from near oblivion to tutor us in our obliviousness.

> What else can I tell you. My children went their own way. I am proud of them, but there are things we can't talk about. Still, I have no complaints. My circumstances were what they were. My family has been a whole world to me. I still take pleasure in Sholom Aleichem, and to me Bazarov and Raskolnikov are like friends of my youth. But to think of them is to be reminded that there was a door which, for me, never opened.

(1976)

A Latter-Day Joseph

David Toback was a kosher butcher on the Lower East Side, one of the masses of immigrants from the Russian-Polish Pale on whose bent backs the next generation rose into the middle class. To relieve the strain of his eighteen-hour days in his shop, he liked to scribble—"housewives went home with whole speeches written on paper in which their chickens were wrapped." After he retired in 1933, he decided to write about his early life, beginning his memoir on the first anniversary of the suicide of his oldest daughter, the beautiful sad-eyed Tzerl: "Tzerl, did you think you were an angel? One day you had to climb up to the edge of the roof and fly away." This act of *yizchor*, remembrance, eventually extended to earlier members of his family, as he wrote his way back to them, those who died in the pogroms of the first years of the century and those who managed to live on until the Nazis arrived. In telling his story, David Toback was also saying kaddish for all that life he had once been part of, both honoring the dead and refastening the ties between the generations.

Eventually his notebooks—which he wrote in a stately Yiddish script and, judging from a sample page, without revision, as though he were taking dictation—passed into the hands of his granddaughter, a young writer living in Berkeley. She did not know Yiddish or her grandfather, but she knew a storyteller when she saw one and apparently fell in love with him. Working from a translation of the notebooks, as well as from her reading in the literature of the Pale and from her travels there, retracing the journeys David Toback had made, she wound her way back to this mute inglorious Sholom Aleichem and his lost world. In time, she found herself inhabiting these notebooks and vice versa. She revised and supplemented them, filling in the gaps here, eliminating material there, creating a more coherent tale—indeed one that reads like a picaresque novel.

Some readers may feel uneasy with her procedure and wish to have Toback entirely in his own words. Also one can't be sure that Carole Malkin's transitions conform to her grandfather's sense of the unfolding of his life. My initial response was mistrustful—I felt she was taking over a rich and possibly important document as if it were a writing workshop project—but as the narrative slowly gathered force, began to resonate with implications and to ring true with its consistency of tone and vision, my resistance dissolved into interest and reflection. What in the end touched me most about *The Journeys of David Toback* was a certain rightness in this collaboration between an Orthodox Jew from Shumsk who was writing about a vanished world and his presumably assimilated American granddaughter revising it in Berkeley. In similar retellings and redactions, across cultures and generations, the narratives of Judaism came into being, beginning with the Bible. In saving David Toback's tales and memories from oblivion, and in developing her own mode of remembrance, Carole Malkin has maintained the continuity of Jewish consciousness, a continuity that lies deeper than local cultural influences, awaiting the touch of learning and imagination and love that retrieve and renew it.

The provenance of *The Journeys of David Toback* accords

with its main motif: the ups and downs of a Jewish existence through which an immanent spiritual design threads itself. This motif, a recurrent one in the central drama of Judaism itself, the drama of the Covenant, appears early in Toback's story. He grew up in a family so poor and isolated in backwoods villages of the Ukraine that he knew mostly peasants until he was thirteen. His father managed to find tutors for him, such were the obligations of Jewish learning even for a luckless miller and such was the penury of tutors; but eventually there was no money at all, and David had to educate himself. By the time of his bar mitzvah he had learned a good deal of the Talmud. That was his part in the unfolding of destiny. Another part was played by a set of phylacteries that had belonged to his great-grandfather, a famous *zaddik*, or holy man. In the midst of David's wretched bar mitzvah, which his family was too threadbare to attend, an expensive coach arrived and from it descended four men in fur coats: two of them were Hasidic princes; the third was a famous rabbi; the fourth was Alter Richels, a venerable disciple of David's ancestor who had once tried to buy the phylacteries and had now come with his distinguished friends to watch David put them on. The rabbi then tested him in the laws of damages:

"For each question a response would leap into my head and begin to develop, first one way, then another. All the ideas I thought of were new to me. I could hardly believe how quiet everyone was and how they stared at me, and I sensed it was with great respect."

Afterward, the rabbi kissed him and told his parents that their child had a rare intelligence and purity of heart and that he should be sent away to study with good teachers. Alter Richels took him aside and told him that now that he had worn his great-grandfather's phylacteries his life would change. And so it did.

In the next seven years or so David was to see and do and feel enough for a lifetime. He is one of those able and outgoing youths whom fortune seems to favor and one of the sensitive ones on whom nothing is lost. After he leaves his village for the town of Shumsk to further his studies, he is pulled in various directions by people who take a strong interest in him. A visiting seer is struck by his diligence and prowess and gives him a letter that will admit him to a yeshiva. The learned Alter Richels makes him his protégé and turns the duty to study the Torah into a lifelong passion (a passion that he believed inspired his memory some forty years later). But while he is being recognized as a potential prodigy of Jewish learning, he is also taken up by one Simcha Godels—a forty-year-old man supported by a wealthy father-in-law so that he can devote himself to learning. Godels introduces David to mathematics, Russian grammar, and gracious living, trying to point him in the direction of a secular education and the important career Simcha himself still yearns for. The Jewish community also comes to have designs on the boy, wanting him to replace their ritual slaughterer, who has died, and also to marry his impoverished daughter.

Alarmed by this development as well as by the scandal that has developed over David's relationship with the worldly Simcha, his parents send him to their one well-to-do relative in the hope that she will support him in the yeshiva in Proskurov, a city 170 miles from Kiev. Proskurov is a wonder to him. He falls in with a group of Hasidim, who adore his singing. A famous cantor offers to train him. But his aunt is a venomous woman who reviles him for his penury and country ways, from which she has only recently escaped herself; her husband puts him to work in the cellar of his store and tries to inveigle him into becoming a merchant. "It was thus that I learned patience," Toback says calmly, always ready to look for the uses of adversity.

Eventually David escapes to the yeshiva in Kishinev, fifty miles from Odessa, an even more amazing place than Proskurov: "Can you believe there was once a city where no Jews went hungry?" His patrons here are men with art collections and conservatories and private orchestra recitals; his best friend is a Jewish student, blond as any Russian, who is attracted to David by what he calls his "natural grace." But again fate intervenes, in the form of his conscience—he informs on Mendel, a hoodlum who befriended him during a cholera outbreak but who is now about to commit bigamy, which means that his lawful wife can never remarry. Spirited away from the vengeful Mendel, David ends up on a tobacco plantation in Bessarabia, where he advances himself until he is made the overseer. He becomes an expert horseman, sheds his pious gabardine for a dashing Russian costume, ceases to write home. Known on the plantation as "the Cossack," he courts the beautiful, wild Sasa, the niece of his employer. By now he is fifteen years old.

As David travels south—one of the legion of young and not so young Jewish scholar-gypsies who combed the Russian-Polish Pale—he brings a whole society, from bottom to top, into view. His sharp eye for the nuances of character and situation, for the cultural significances embedded in them—what Lionel Trilling called "the hum of implication"—along with his love of a good story, keeps the narrative of his journeys as expressive as it is eventful. I don't know of a better sustained account of the vicissitudes of Jewish life in the Pale during this critical era of the 1890s.

Like David himself, much of the Jewish society that he reveals to us was still bound by the traditions of piety and community that had sustained it for centuries. Also, like David, it was being pulled in all directions. He tells us of rabbis whose counsel and prophetic powers rescue this Jew or that from seemingly hopeless situations; of a stately elder who finds him doubled up with cramps in a study house, takes him home, and cures him almost immediately with his magic powders; of a cantor and choir whose singing is so beautiful that a Russian general has asked that they perform at his funeral. He also remembers the elders of Shumsk desperately trying to stave off a pogrom by bribing every official in sight after a Jewish merchant is caught giving short weight to a peasant. He witnesses a heated debate between a Zionist who speaks in Hebrew and an assimilationist who replies in Russian; they can agree on nothing except their hostility to Yiddish, the language they fall back on when they end by cursing each other. He returns to Kishinev at one point to learn that his blond friend has been snatched away and executed as an anarchist; later, on the plantation, David finds himself being seduced into an anarchist plot by the emancipated Sasa. Now and again his narrative trembles with reports of the Czar's new restrictions, anecdotes of the massive emigrations, rumors of new atrocities, as well as with his growing sense of frustration and outrage, which will culminate in his resolve to go to America.

By then he had long since returned to his family in Shumsk. On the plantation he had thought of himself as a latter-day Joseph, remaking his family's fortune while he cuts a fine figure and manages bumper crops. But for all that, he has remained the *shtetl* Jew formed by poverty, family loyalty, and Jewish law, and when he discovers Sasa fornicating with another anarchist he is overwhelmed. For all his Cossack airs, as he puts it, "I had become weak." He returns to his family, takes up the wretched life of a tutor to provide for his younger brothers. His efforts to find a wife whose family can give him a livelihood continually miscarry, and when he finally does marry, his in-laws turn out to be bootleggers on their way to prison. He manages to acquire a few woodlots during a building boom, but then a forest fire wipes them out. David has become something of a *schlimazel,* a luckless Jew. The occasional notes of loneliness and sadness on his travels, a kind of accompaniment to his resourcefulness and enthusiasm, now turn into a lamentation. He yearns to get back on an Arabian horse by joining the army: another Isaac Babel with heroism in his head and winter in his heart. His enthusiasm at the induction center—amid the other Jews, who turn up maimed, emaciated, or babbling—causes him to be rejected immediately.

Other misfortunes, along with his awakened anger over the condition of the Jews, strengthen his decision to emigrate, despite his young wife's opposition. Going alone, he reaches America, but bad luck continues to dog him. He is turned back at Ellis Island for insufficient means and has to return to Brussels and wait for his wife to try to scrape up another fare. In the meantime, he is offered a first-class passage by an attractive woman who wants him to accompany her to America as her husband. Once again he is "weak" and once again overcome with shame. He goes to America by himself, in steerage, a man whose soul has been sorely tested but again saved. As we know—from his opening words of grief about his daughter's suicide to his closing words of hope that his notebooks will somehow reach and help his grandchildren—his soul continued to be tested and saved.

A man of ready talents and sorrows and faith, David Toback stays in the mind as a representative figure of his generation who deepens our consciousness of it. Long after his moment of flamboyant success in Bessarabia, he continued to be a Joseph, one of the multitude of little Josephs who went ahead to bring their families out of the bondage of Eastern Europe and, as the Holocaust was to prove, to secure the survival of the Jewish people in a new land. His narrative stops short of his struggle to get out of the sweatshops of New York and to educate his children, but that is a familiar story by now. What is less familiar, at least to me, is the religious meaning he found in his journeys, his abiding sense of the one hundred generations of Jews and their God who stood behind him and in whose Law he continued to walk and to find his way. His faith is in his willingness both to be of use in the world and to serve Jewish virtue, come what may—a great willingness which begins in the determined studies of his youth and culminates in the writing of his journals, from which this remarkable chapter in the annals of Jewish faith has been made.

(1983)

A Text for the New Age

The Rape of Tamar, by Dan Jacobson, has received little notice and none that indicates that it is a brilliant retelling of the Biblical story as well as an important text for our "New Age," addressed to that blinkered condition most of us share called present-mindedness. In England, where the taste for fine narrative prose and the imagination of history both still live, *The Rape of Tamar* has had an excellent press. Here, its clarity and poise and beautifully paced intensity merely make it "literature"; the recipe for the fashionable novel these days seems to be to shake your head well and pour. And as for a novel about life three thousand years ago, when even World War II, except for the nuclear weaponry, has a kind of prehistoric status in many minds—well, who needs it? Rape, incest, fratricide . . . nothing new there. But before *The Rape of Tamar* falls completely through the coarse net of the fall book season, I'd like to call attention to its distinction and relevance.

The vanishing sense of the past at which Jacobson's book is aimed is due, as we are all told, to the great dizzying changes that engulf us. But it is also due to a certain vanity, as his narrator points out, that we, like the Jews of King David's reign, feel ourselves to be living in "the very time of times." We are like a man whom some sudden, dramatic love affair has lifted out of his life and into a realm of new, pressing possibilities. It is easy for him to feel that his past has all along been making toward just this state of being as its secret meaning and consummation, while, at the same time, his relation to his former life becomes tenuous and his attitude toward it somewhat scornful: all that drudgery, waste, inhibition, error, unawareness that no longer apply, that are now to be transcended. So with our sense of history: In our time of times, it is easy to flatter ourselves, particularly if we are young, with our "difference from the miserable, weightless rabble who crowd the spaceless chambers and corridors of the dead." Further, though the man of new possibilities isn't much interested in his memories, that doesn't mean his memories aren't interested in him—as he is likely to find out fairly soon. So with the lived experience, the collective memories, of the human past. The purpose and strength of Jacobson's novel is in reconstituting and pointing a few ancient memories, of making the shadow of some events three thousand years ago, and of the man who arranged them and those who suffered them, fall upon and frame the present.

A second and related reason for our present-mindedness is that history provides models of experience in which the principles of continuity, coherence, cause and effect, contingency, complexity, and necessity bulk large and limit the scope and force of the individual will. Meanwhile, word comes back from the frontiers of physics, philosophy, the arts, that our metaphysical underpinnings are made up of chance, randomness, senselessness, etc. This "set," with all its social and psychological ramifications, flatters the sojourner of being in us, whose "trips" are more real and significant than our abidances. Further, what interest is there in history, if the present itself is no more than what Hegel calls "the negativity of all singleness and differences"?

The Rape of Tamar is also aimed against this state of mind.

The tale Jacobson inherited from the Second Book of Samuel is unusually specific, sophisticated, and fateful: Amnon's revulsion after he has raped his sister, "so that the hatred wherewith he hated her was greater than the love wherewith he had loved her"; Tamar's freighted response—"this evil in sending me away is greater than the other that thou didst unto me"; her decision to make her humiliation public rather than conceal the act and prevent her ruin, and to go to her brother, Absalom, rather than to her father, King David; also Absalom's behavior toward Amnon—speaking "unto his brother neither good nor bad"—for two years until the time was ripe to kill him. At the beginning and end of the tale is the "subtile" Yonadab, who panders to Amnon's lust—"Why art thou, being a king's son, lean from day to day?"—who devises the stratagem that brings Tamar into Amnon's clutches, and who, after the murder of Amnon, far away from the palace, somehow knows and tells David that only Amnon has been killed by Absalom and not the other princes, as has been reported. In taking up the narrative, Jacobson artfully fills in the psychology and relationships of the five main figures and the relevant social ground and draws the strands of motive, act, and consequence into a binding web of paradox and necessity. The force of circumstances, the authority of *what has happened,* its foreclosure of other possibilities and of choice itself, inexorably overtake and bind the participants, from one event to the next. History is what hindsight calls destiny.

At the same time, David, his three children, and their betrayer are powerfully drawn in the way that Dr. Johnson found in Shakespeare's characters: "just representations of general nature," as modern as they are ancient. Also the narrative is embedded in a commentary, addressed directly to the contemporary reader and intended to ensure that no point of recognition will be lost on him.

The narrator/commentator is Yonadab, bound for all time to the story of his treachery and to "its one implacably unvarying routine." Yonadab speaks to us in character: sedulously deferential on the surface, all remorseless purpose beneath, and armed with a penetrating intelligence of men and affairs. His cynicism makes him an outsider in his world, ruled by a credulity that begins with David, whose power stems from his conviction that the Lord is his shepherd. Yonadab's inability to "believe in the worth or even the veracity of anything" puts him quite in touch with our world, not only with our fabled skepticism but with our own forms of conformity and credulity. The last thing he will grant is our sense of uniqueness, of enlightenment, of moral sophistication. He embodies the intelligence of the historian, and it is this, rather than his ghostly position in time, that enables him to shift tellingly back and forth across the gap of three thousand years, which as he reminds us is but 120 generations, and to make us see the continuum of human typology and of the "disproportion, strain, irresolution" of life.

David is portrayed as the aging king and empire maker, trying to conserve his authority, preaching law and order and cooperation to the young princes who yearn to take the great power he has created in the state into their own hands and put it to better uses. Absalom is ambitious, progressive, the prince of the people, already planning his rebellion, his reign of justice, which will commence with the murder of Amnon and the intimidation of his brothers. There is Amnon, lazy and fretful, whose passion for his sister becomes "the works": the great, liberating leap into the unknown and the forbidden, the moment at the very source of space and time, the act of "filth and impiety for the sake of a freer, more godlike piety," etc. Behind Amnon's adventure in blowing his mind is the Canaanite legend of Baal and Anat, the incestuous, rebellious children of the august

God, El; ahead of Amnon and Absalom is what Yonadab knows . . . unto the present. "The same story again!" he blurts out in disgust. "Always the same damn story—the same incitements, opportunities, and compulsions."

But the dark, resonating story Yonadab tells is presented as the outcropping of character rather than as a scheme to force analogies. He does not wish to be forgiven, for like his victims, he was what he had to be, and he is as shameless in telling the truth as he was in his treacheries, including that of instructing Absalom as he did Amnon. As he says, the real and the interesting are one and the same, and his saturnine morals are fashioned at every point from the manifold but contingent stuff of experience.

Take the rape itself. There is Amnon and beneath him Tamar, finally wrestled and half-smothered into submission:

> . . . at the fork of his body he has a pendule, a thick bud that must grow, rise, distend, reach and remain stiffly reaching, unable to grasp, fitted at an angle to him yet compelling him to fit himself around it, guiding him who has to guide it, a weapon that disables its wielder. . . .

And on through the night:

> Many times: driven still to reach a point that he seeks within her only because it is beyond his uttermost touch. Still beyond. Just beyond. Always beyond.

(1970)

Jacob at the Well

"And Jacob kissed Rachel, and lifted up his voice, and wept."
Genesis XXIX, 11

Why does Jacob weep in the high moment at the well of Haran? His perilous flight and awesome journey from Canaan have come to an end. A moment before, with a show of physical strength, a strength he has not been known to possess before, he has single-handedly lifted the large stone that covers the well, so that Rachel can water her flock. Then, following this virile and courtly gesture, he summarily kisses his beautiful young cousin, perhaps already claiming her as his bride-to-be. Indeed, throughout this scene of his arrival in Haran, Jacob behaves with a sort of lordly self-confidence, to the point of telling the local shepherds their business ("It is not time to gather in the livestock, so give the sheep to drink and go back, tend them"). All of which is the more remarkable considering that he arrives there not only a complete stranger but a penniless one as well. (The Biblical legends describe Jacob as being stripped bare by Eliphaz, Esau's son, after he has had to plead to the thirteen-year-old boy for his life.) And yet, for all this imposing of himself, he suddenly lifts up his voice and weeps. Why? From joy? From nervous exhaustion?

From some hidden spring of sorrow?

We have to be careful not to understand Jacob too readily. Because his life is fuller, more dramatic, and more concretely drawn than that of Abraham and Isaac, we feel we know him better: He is as familiar at times as a legendary family figure—the intrepid great-uncle, say, who started out in America as a presser and after twenty years of struggle and maneuvering had his own dress factory. However, Jacob has a far less unitary character than any such archetype, or that of his father and grandfather, or even that of his complicated son, Joseph. Just as he produces a dozen significant sons while the rest of the patriarchal line are confined to two each, so in his own personhood he comprises a much wider range of traits, talents, oppositions. Similarly, the plot of destiny he is in spins a much richer weave of passions than theirs. One might say that Joseph's coat of many colors is like a metaphor for his father's character or, better, that the multivalence of his being is emblematic of the diverse yet tightly knit nation that he will father and that will still bear his later name after thousands of years and so many changes.

The Bible tells us Jacob begins life as a tenacious younger twin who is marked by destiny. In his recent translation of Genesis, Everett Fox renders his name first as "Yaakov/Heel-Holder" but observes that it also may have originally meant "May (God) Protect." Jacob does not grow into an aggressive, competitive second son, hard on the heels of his brother. Rather, he gives up competing with the coarse, vivid Esau to become instead an *ish tam*, a plain or quiet man, and a *yoshav ohalim*, a tent dweller—not unlike his father. That he co-opts the birthright, and then its blessing, is presented more as a matter of his brother's brute impulsiveness, and then his mother's will and cunning, than of his own cold guile. Though he can simulate Esau's hands and neck, he remains nakedly his own shaky voice, afflicted by his own foreboding: "I will be like a trickster in his eyes, and I will bring a curse not a blessing on myself." Actually, as in many matters that concern him, that outcome is equivocal, for he receives both Isaac's blessing and Esau's curse, which takes the form of naming him, in Fox's rendering, "Yaakov/Heel-Sneak." The Jacob who received the blessing is a long way from the cool, patient, cunning manipulator of Laban's flocks, just as the young man who awakens from the dream at Beth-el, frightened by the images of angels rising and descending and of God's plan for him, is far from the patriarch who will wrestle with the angel until he receives his blessing, the name, as Fox translates it, "Yisrael/God-fighter."

The portion of Genesis titled *Vayyetze* more or less charts Jacob's growth and transformation. One can fill in the details for oneself—the tireless labors, the difficult marriages, the willingness to become a ram, as it were, among the flock of his wives and their handmaidens, the steely ability to turn the table on Laban, developed through twenty years of enduring heat and cold and little sleep as well as through an intimate knowledge of flocks and pastureland. One can say that Jacob the tent-dweller turns into Esau's equal as an *ish sadeh,* becomes, in fact, the kind of man he had once deceived his father into believing he was when Isaac said, "*R'ay rayach b'ni k'rayach sadeh a'sher bayra'cho Adonai*"—"See the smell of my son is like the smell of a field that the Lord has blessed." In short, one can watch him develop into the self-confident and prosperous patriarch who faces down Laban and will disarm Esau.

But I want to pass on to another dimension of Jacob, which both reinforces and complicates what we might call his evolved personality: that is, his spirit (destiny), which is both close to us and recessive, distinct and yet mysterious. Consider, for example, his service for Rachel, the seven years that "were in his eyes as but a few days because of his love for her." Love does strange, painful, and lovely things to our sense of time; but for most of us humans in Jacob's condition of waiting for the consummation of his desire, a few days seem more like years than the other way around. The phrase suggests that he could possess Rachel for the seven years by making her into the image of his desire, in Tolstoy's wonderful phrase, so that she accompanied him in the way that God at Beth-el had promised Jacob He would go with him.

For Jacob is like us and not like us. This is why he has for us what Walter Benjamin calls an "aura." By this he means (1) "the unique phenomenon of distance between the perceiver and the object" and (2) the latter "being embedded in the fabric of a tradition." Thus the American tourist who sends home a postcard of the Colosseum in Rome and wisecracks, "I wonder where they put the goalposts," has stripped away the aura of the monument by removing it from its tradition just as the postcard illustration itself brings the Colosseum too close in human terms to ourselves. We must be careful not to do this with Jacob—to bring him too close, as I started out doing myself, to extract him from his "tradition," which is, after all, the articulation of the mystery of God's purposes, a mystery which Jacob's destiny illuminates but into which it also recedes from us.

As I watch him change from Jacob into Israel, another way of envisioning this matter of "aura," I think of him as growing more aware that he has a spiritual destiny as well as a creaturely life. This development is marked first by the dream at Beth-el that overawes him, so much so that the next morning he more or less ignores the promise concerning his destiny—of the land, of his seed ("All the clans of the soil will find blessing though you and through your seed")—and seizes instead upon the immediate promise concerning his life: a safe journey and return, sufficient food and clothing. It is next marked in the night struggle at the Yabbok crossing, twenty years later. Here he recognizes his spiritual mission in the course of fighting for the angel's blessing, or at least senses the convergence of his life with his destiny: "For I have seen God, face to face, and my life has been saved."

Yet I don't want to make Jacob's life seem too much a steady uplift. One of the reasons he is so real to us is that despite (because of?) his destiny, nothing is ever settled for him. Even in his death in Egypt he remains a man of sojourns, contingencies, and vicissitudes, the great promise he has been given locked in a cycle of fraud and recompense, sin and retribution, poverty and wealth, exile and return, fulfillment and loss. He will pay for his deception of his brother by being deceived by his father-in-law; just as he uses Esau's appetite against him, so Laban will use Jacob's desire for Rachel; just as he disguises himself as his brother, so will his wife be disguised as her sister. Later he will find that just as he was favored over his brother, so will he favor one of his sons over the eleven others, as he will, like his father, also tamper with the rights of the firstborn and lose the favored son for twenty years.

Jacob/Israel's destiny is ultimately that of being inextricably caught up in a vast ironic drama stretching across the patriarchal generations, by which the moral order is being created out of the darkness and chaos of primitive human appetites. By the time he reaches Haran, I imagine him to have begun to glimpse this, however dimly. So that when he weeps after kissing Rachel, it may be because he remembers hearing of another meeting with a beautiful young woman at a well, perhaps this very one, which his father's emissary had come upon, bringing with him camels laden with gold and silver and all manner of bride wealth; while he comes to the same place and family and purpose on his own and empty-handed, attended and enriched only by some dream promises he has been given. And I imagine his sensing that this is the way it is to be, a destiny of great opportunities and uncertainties, in which much will be given and taken away and earned again, and taken away—as Rachel will be—and found again, as Joseph will be: a destiny in which deceptions and lies and mistakes will be both made use of and paid for so that they can enter the covenant and take their place in the moral order. No wonder, then, he lifts up his voice and weeps after the first touch of Rachel's lips—in sorrow and exhaustion and joy and who knows what else?

(1984)

Part Five

The Literary Campus and the Person of Letters

I

In a recent essay, "What Has Happened to the Publishing Business," I describe the widening gulf between it and the literary/intellectual culture. Increasingly ruled by corporate values and mass-marketing methods, the publishing business can be said to have moved most of its product and spirit to the shopping mall. Meanwhile, in response to the loss of its institutional home, the community of letters and ideas has been moving its product and spirit to the campus, where many of its books, magazines, and authors lead their dispersed but sheltered lives.

I see, for example, that John Hollander, one of our most sophisticated poets, is now being published by Johns Hopkins University Press. I learn that the fiction and essays of Isaac Rosenfeld, one of the important New York writers of the 1940s and '50s, will be reissued by Wayne State Press, after being out of print for fifteen years. The whole *oeuvre* of Harold Rosenberg—the eminent art critic and seminal intellectual, one of the great American prose stylists of the century—is being published by the University of Chicago Press, as are the essays of his chief peer and adversary,

Clement Greenberg. Nor is it an accident that *Habits of the Heart,* the most broadly illuminating study of the inner life of American society since *The Lonely Crowd,* was first published by the University of California Press. Twenty years ago, a list of new titles that included the prose of W. S. Merwin; the poet Grace Schulman's book on Marianne Moore; a reissue of Zora Neale Thurston's landmark novel, *Their Eyes Were Watching God;* an experimental historical novel, *The Greek Generals Talk: Memoirs of the Trojan War,* by Phillip Parotti; and the writings of Howard Gossage, the Ezra Pound of the advertising field, could only have come from a house like New Directions. As it happens, this list is from the University of Illinois Press and could be from one of ten or fifteen other university presses.

Most of the foreign literature that reaches America today is in the keeping of the university presses or of campus-based houses like Ardis in Ann Arbor. The recent revolution in American literary criticism, structuralism and its several branches, could hardly have come into being off campus. Similarly, the development of feminism, the most influential ideological movement of our time, has largely been undertaken by the women's studies programs and disseminated by the journals and books that come from the no longer academic press. (The influential Feminist Press, for example, is now sponsored by CUNY.) The universities and their fringe culture also publish most of our literary, theater, and film magazines and virtually all of the intellectual journals. Any issue of *The New York Review of Books,* both in its reviews and in its ads, provides ample evidence that the life of the mind in general and of the literary culture in particular would be severely curtailed without the communications network that the universities maintain.

So, too, would the literary and intellectual profession,

which by and large has packed up and moved to the groves and precincts of academe, as the one institution left in the mass society and consumer economy that values it and can afford it. Teaching provides a living for most of the serious literary artists and critics at work today as it does for our political and social thinkers. Moreover, the proliferation of graduate writing programs has meshed with that of the Ph.D. programs to form the principal training ground of the literary and intellectual vocations. A gifted young poet today can begin as an undergraduate at, say, Cornell; move on through the M.F.A. program at Syracuse; take up a teaching career at SUNY Binghamton, where s/he edits *Mss,* its excellent literary magazine; contribute regularly to *Salmagundi,* published at Skidmore; and publish poetry and criticism collections with the SUNY Press—a complete literary career without leaving upstate New York. Once the ivory tower of literature, perched so high above its time that it could view only the literature that began at a distance of fifty years and extended back through the centuries, the English and comparative literature departments, along with the writing programs, have become the refuge of novelists, poets, and critics in a culture that views literature as a rarely profitable, occasionally glamorous, and mostly dubious form of merchandise.

But as the history of the arts demonstrates, every gain involves some loss, and so with this development. The hospitality and security the academic community offers comes with its relative insularity and remoteness from the common life and its overt and underlying issues that are pressing for expression. (This is less true, of course, of the colleges and universities in urban areas, particularly the public ones.) Also the security of a teaching career, particularly after it is tenured, provides much more time to write than it does immediate need and incentive to do so. And as I shall suggest later, teaching may well begin to take over an important part of the writer's primary drive to make his thoughts and feelings known.

Certainly teaching has already significantly altered the practice of the writing vocation in America. By offering itself as a livelihood, it has been responsible in good part for the vanishing of the man of letters as of the freelance intellectual. Both of these figures are still visible in Europe, where the chances for a writer to earn his bread and butter by teaching literature are slim, and by creative writing, all but zero.

It is also true, of course, that European newspaper, magazine, television, and film culture provides an alternative mode of income that hardly exists any longer in America as a major one, at least outside the pages of *The New Yorker.* A few other magazines pay well but not to contribute to letters. Edmund Wilson could both do his work and make his living at a magazine like *Vanity Fair.* It's unlikely, to say the least, that he would be able to do the former at today's *Vanity Fair,* which, one can fairly surmise, would cut his essay on Fitzgerald's last years to the juicy parts and title it "Scott on the Rocks." As for movie and TV money, many are called, few cash in. The rest is the occasional book review, think piece, travel article, which earns a night out but hardly room and board.

V. S. Pritchett speaks of himself as coming at "the tail end of a long and once esteemed tradition in English and American writing." As he says of himself and his dwindling brethren: "We have no captive audience. We do not teach." Instead his livelihood depends upon writing books and articles that the common reader wants to read. But this bread-and-butter writing has traditionally had a wider objective in view, which preserves the freelance literary person from becoming a hack: this is to keep the torch of letters lit and circulating, even in a time as windy and dim as our own. In Pritchett's words:

> We do not lay down the law, but we do make a stand for the reflective values of a humane culture. We care for the printed word in a world that nowadays is dominated by the camera and by scientific, technological, sociological doctrine. We still believe, with Dostoevsky, that "without art a man might well feel that his life was not worth living."

Words like these, so modestly phrased, so deeply felt, are like the colors of a regiment whose brave last members are still holding their position, though the others have been killed, wounded, taken prisoner, or are missing in action. Though we have many literary writers at work today in America, many more than at any time in history, we have few men or, to bring the term up to date, persons of letters. Were it not for Gore Vidal, John Updike, Elizabeth Hardwick, Susan Sontag, Hayden Carruth, Diane Johnson, Eric Bentley, Robert Bly, and a few others, one would be hard put to know what the phrase has meant.

According to Pritchett, the person of letters knows two things: that "literature is rooted in the daily society" and that "it springs out of literature itself." These two points will seem like platitudes to us. For the functioning person of letters they constitute a lived truth, for there is no lofty separation between their daily life and literature. The one is the other: they write in order to live, they live in order to write. Moreover, one cannot readily speak of literary matters to the common reader without approaching him or her from the direction of the common life. Here, to take an almost random example, is Pritchett talking to us about Nathanael West's *The Day of the Locust:*

> The artificial lights of the freak show are off in this book and we see human absurdity as something normal. This is a novel about Hollywood. West worked in the hum of the American dream generators and he chose those people who have done more for American culture than their coevals in Europe have done for theirs: the casualties, the wrecks, the failures, the seedy and the fakes. They are the people to whom the leisureless yea-sayers have said "No."

It is only a long stride of attention from the common life to the public sector of society. Pritchett has generally refrained from taking it; his leading American counterpart, Edmund Wilson, was prompt to do so when the age or his own outrage provoked him. As the tribune of public consciousness and conscience, the person of letters has a lineage that goes back as far as Voltaire and Milton; in this country, it was associated with the literary vocation from the start by the example of Emerson and Thoreau and was taken for granted by writers as otherwise dissimilar as, say, Howells and Twain.

During the 1960s there was a great deal of this direct public writing by persons of letters which both defined and influenced the character of the age: Paul Goodman's *Growing Up Absurd*, James Baldwin's *The Fire Next Time*, Norman Mailer's *The Armies of the Night*, Philip Roth's *Our Gang*, Susan Sontag's "Trip to Hanoi," Mary Ellmann's *Thinking About Women* and Kate Millett's *Sexual Politics*, Allen Ginsberg's *Planet News*, Robert Bly's *The Light Around the Body*. But this kind of public prose and poetry, political in its thrust but literary at its core, was found everywhere. Such writing today turns up now and then in a piecemeal way, barely rustling the stare of apathy that letters turns toward the public sector. A notable exception is Jonathan Schell's *The Fate of the Earth*, which eloquently and powerfully portrays the total horror, from the personal to the ecological to the ontological, of a nuclear war, and in so doing reminds us how desperately such writing is needed to cut through our stupor. Of the prominent novelists today, only Gore Vidal persists in writing strong public prose, and among the critics it is only the neoconservative ones who play cultural politics with a passionate intensity. Indeed the most telling sign of the passivity of most of the community of letters is how little opposition there has been to the extraordinary politicization of literary judgment that has been conducted by the militant anti-Communist, high-bourgeois ideologues such as Hilton Kramer and Norman Podhoretz and those who write for their respective magazines.

Much of the noncombativeness of the so-called adversary culture can be attributed to the liberal/radical malaise of the past decade rather than to its affiliation with the academy. But that some of it is due to the privatism and insularity of the campus-based writer can be inferred from the decline of interest and controversy not only in the public sector of letters but in the literary one as well. As Pritchett reminds us, the person of letters keeps the other foot in literature. He or she makes readers conversant with the significant literature of the time, provides a bracing and aggressive standard of judgment, and keeps the literary tradition visible and perking by transmitting the energy of his or her own interests in it: in short, minding and defending the fort at least part of the time.

This was a function that serious writers until the recent past took for granted, partly because they made some of their income from doing so and partly from the felt need to stake out and protect ground on which to cultivate interest in and taste for their own work. The tradition of modern poetry, for example, was virtually charted by the critical and ruminative prose of Rilke and Valéry, Pound and

Eliot, Yeats and Auden, Tate and Ransom, Louise Bogan and Randall Jarrell, et. al. All of them were active poets and position takers. The only comparable figure I can think of in our own time is Robert Bly. During the thirty-year history of his self-published magazine, Bly has tried to rechart the mainstream of American poetry to show how it runs through his own work and that of his kindred poets, has maintained a provocative and coherent line of judgment of his peers, and has significantly internationalized contemporary American poetry by publishing his own and other American translations from various languages. In sum, Bly is an inspiring example of what one person of letters can accomplish on his own—provided, as Bly himself would be quick to add, he doesn't teach.

From my vantage point as a literary editor in New York, which has its own insularity, I'm mainly conscious of a huge expansion of the writing population and a continuing decline of literary community and authority since I wrote about it twenty years ago in *The Red Hot Vacuum.* The general state of letters pretty much resembles that of the society at large in its dullness, diffuseness, crowdedness, perplexity, and privatism. In a remarkable long essay, "The Post-Modern Aura," Charles Newman places these conditions in a perspective that combines the inflation of literary productivity and value with the fragmentation of the modernist heritage. "In such a situation," Newman writes, "both the critical and aesthetic intelligence often relinquish their traditional claims, preferring to explore what they imagine to be the richness of their own limitations."

Well, yes and no. Postmodern criticism continues to play its elaborate games of removing the author's presence from his work to make it more habitable for the critic and the limitations of his "discourse." Also much of the higher discussion of contemporary fiction has been dominated by the metafictionists and their admirers. Meanwhile the Bellows and Updikes and Carvers, who have been writing most of the fiction of the age, go on trying to get at the truth in their outmoded way. The really interesting and relevant literary talk that I've come across in recent years has not been in texts but at readings and panels and in conversations. It's Robert Bly saying that the trouble with the young writers today is that they're afraid to attack the older ones because some of them have been their teachers; that writing programs cool out this necessary opposition. Or it's Lynne Sharon Schwartz talking about the difficulty women writers have had in writing subversively. Nor do I find that writers generally are more indifferent to or imperceptive of political and social conditions than they were in the past. And when I listen to their talk, I often wish they would develop this strong point of view, that sharply angled opinion, their clearheaded sense of the literary situation, and publish it in order to clear the air, stir the pot, get the juices flowing again. And the truth that comes to me is that they don't because they teach: that is, they don't write in the main for their keep, and the public and literary sides of their sense of vocation are expressed and probably pretty well exhausted by the process of passing on their concerns and standards and provocations to their students. And the rest of their spirit, energy, need to impose themselves and have their say goes into their own fiction, poetry, plays, on which their careers depend.

I also sense that this is so from contending with my own feelings of anomie (i.e., "an anxious awareness that the prevailing values of society have little or no relevance to one's condition"). When the muddle of greed, hypocrisy, mediocrity, and hype of big-time publishing gets to me, I find myself wanting to teach again, to close the door on the muddle and get in touch again with the spirit of literature and try to pass it on. So I teach a writing course or a seminar, and after a few weeks the atmosphere of sweetness and light descends, and I think that the literary community has taken refuge on the campuses rather as the early Christians took to the catacombs—to nurture faith, reinforce belief, tell one another the gospel, promulgate the word, and prepare the missionaries.

II

Still, if the writing programs and English departments and university presses are to become the home away from home of the writer, they will need to strengthen communication and communion with the common reader and the common life. I hope that one or two of the more ambitious university presses that have been expanding into trade publishing will see their way to creating the kind of broadly interesting and lively magazines that the publishing houses once took to be their responsibility and opportunity, from *Harper's* and *Scribner's* up to the days of *Evergreen Review, Noble Savage* and *(New) American Review.* There are, of course, various literary reviews emanating from the university presses today, but they tend to be rather narrowly literary, the poems and stories sandwiched between thick slabs of academic-type literary criticism, and to be parochial rather than national in scope and tenor. The type of magazine I have in mind stations itself at the crossroads (which need not be bloody) where literature and politics meet; where the main action is a "lively dialogue between private imagination and public concern," in Geoffrey Wolff's apt formulation. As the example of *Granta* in England testifies, there is nothing like such a magazine to begin to pull a literary culture together by the breadth of its quality, interests, and timeliness and the readability of its prose. If a magazine like *Granta* gets going here, I think it will be because the right young editor, probably at a university press, insists on starting it and keeping it going by his vision, his will, and his gifts, not least of which is his ability to hustle.

The other way that the university community can provide a better home for letters is to professionalize its writing programs. By that I don't mean bringing more editors and agents to campus to talk about how to get into the big time. What I mean is developing the training and values that would inculcate a commitment to the profession of letters: i.e., the equivalent of the general professional training a medical school or a law school or a Ph.D. program provides.

If the graduate writing program is at its best a sanctuary and a staging area, it tends more often to have the torpor of a boondoggle and the cynicism of a scam; also, in the poet Greg Kuzma's words, "the ecstasy of being associated with a growth industry." Thirty years ago, when there were only a few graduate writing programs, their loosely structured curricula, revolving around the fiction and poetry workshops, made more sense than they do today because of the presence of the genuinely gifted. In John Berryman's class at Iowa in the early 1950s were W. D. Snodgrass, Philip Levine, Donald Justice, Robert Dana, Donald Petersen, Henri Coulet, Jane Cooper all of whom went on to have significant careers. Today, with twenty-five or thirty prestigious programs and another seventy-five that are looking to become so, the talent and seriousness of the students and their ability to teach each other become spread very thin. As Kuzma puts it, the writer "no longer teaches the few who really are dedicated to the art but the average and the many . . . the contentedly mediocre." Even in a workshop in a top-ranked program today there will likely be among the fifteen students only a few who have the talent for a literary career, only one or two who have the determination; so it is hard to avoid a congenial tolerance of the ordinary, that is to say unnecessary, poem: what Donald Hall calls "the MacPoem." So, too, with fiction writing.

The tacit deal that is cut with the students whose enrollment pays for the program and its faculty is that since we can't give most of you a career, we won't ask much of you. We will mostly let you "critique" one another's work and sit in a few seminars where you'll have to do some reading but that will still leave you with plenty of time to concentrate on your handful of stories or poems, perhaps teach an introductory writing course, and hang out with the other writers. As for the talented few, about the best we can do is to steer you in the direction of writing publishable work so that you can get a job teaching writing too. More or less divorced from the standards and demands of the English department, having lost, in Kuzma's words, "the old sweet antagonism between the academic and creative writer," the creative writing industry becomes in part a curious division of the consumer economy, academic branch, promoting not the culture of letters but the culture of narcissism. For a devastating account of how the industry works and the typical work it rewards, see Kuzma's essay in *Poetry* (Winter 1986).

Some programs are more strenuous, some teachers more stimulating, but the workshop institution is limited not only by its popularity but also by the immaturity of many of its students, often just out of college; by the brevity of the program, that is two years at most; and by the narrow and more or less calcified curriculum. Why not, then, develop a program that addresses these problems and also might begin to replace the missing persons of the literary community, the persons of letters?

First of all, the persons of letters program (PLP) would not admit writers—except in rare circumstances, such as having had extensive military service, managed a farm, raised a child, or experienced some other mode of precocious maturation—until they are twenty-five or older. Along with probably having developed another skill besides writing (Gary Snyder has said that the best preparation for becoming a poet is being a good carpenter or mechanic), the older student brings to a writing program a stronger hand of experience to play, a more settled character with which to develop a voice, and a mature attitude, which regards the program not as a pleasant option to take a crack at but as a privilege that has been earned.

Along with choosing writers on the basis of their gift and their experience, the PLP would require them to have a personal literary culture, which is not often the case today. They should know well the work of at least twenty-five writers, distributed through literary history and the several genres, and of at least a few foreign ones in their original language.

The PLP, then, would depart from the current practice of producing prematurely specialized poets, novelists, playwrights, and instead provide a training that would be both more broadly based and more rigorous. My model is the European practice of the profession, in which it is taken for granted that the writer is able to address the public in several forms, as do Grass, Kundera, Graham Greene, Fowles, Handke, Calvino, et al. The first year's writing course would be devoted mainly to the fundamentals of the different genres: a student would choose an experience that has a strong personal significance and write it as an essay, a story, a novella, a poem, a one-act play, a film script. The emphasis would be on the basic techniques and resources of each genre.

How would such a course be taught? By team teaching in a rotational way: a poet and a playwright, say, teaching the poetry phase. The advantage to this arrangement is that it replaces the dialogue of one, the coaxing of responses, that makes teaching writing often a dulling experience for everyone. Also it would be stimulating and challenging for the teachers to think in other genres than their own, and the principle of rotation would lessen the burden of their own banality and reduce burnout. Team teaching would bring the faculty together in a common effort to develop a pedagogy of teaching writing, which at present rarely progresses beyond the catch-as-catch-can group criticism of the workshop.

The PLP would also rejoin the writing program to the English department and extend it to the comparative literature one, so that each could benefit from the other's resources. Donald Hall has written about the value to the writer and student alike in turning the former loose in a literature course, where s/he can show the different character a literary work takes on in the hands of a writer who is looking for its source and circuitry of power rather than schematizing its meanings. By the same token, I've known literary scholars who would have been magical in a workshop. And again, both types of teachers would benefit from this interplay. The PLP should enrich and revitalize the teaching of writing as much as it does the learning.

So, too, with the foreign-language component. With the exception of the structuralists, American letters has been losing companionship with other languages and literatures and becoming more provincial with each decade. Hence one of the requirements of the PLP would be that each student translate at a professional level at least one work by a foreign writer and be conversant enough with his or her *oeuvre* and that of contemporaries to write a publishable introduction to the translated work. The idea would be to use the requirement to tutor the flow of the student's interests rather than to prescribe what they should be. Also, access and intercourse would be encouraged from the other side of the language barrier. The M.F.A. writing courses would be open to gifted writers from the other departments, as they would be to those in English Lit.

Good curricula possibilities proliferate once the writer and the university begin to take each other seriously rather than regard each other in the mutually distrustful, resentful, and exploitative way that often obtains today: the undergraduate course in poetry writing having to add another section, while the one in the seventeenth-century lyric is canceled for lack of enrollment. Why not let a course like the latter be a requirement for the former and put some of the writing program poets into it to strengthen the discussion? The PLP would also bring literature and writing students together to learn from a professional how to write a publishable fiction or theater or film review. The writing student in, say, a Melville seminar would be enabled to write an essay for his term paper that weaves recent scholarship into a literary essay as a Kazin or Hardwick would do.

I'm sketching some organizing principles and values for an innovative comprehensive writing program rather than specifying a curriculum. It departs from the current Ph.D. in creative writing, which the more strenuous programs offer, because we need more persons of letters and not more English professors who write fiction or poetry. The PLP would offer training in travel writing and children's book writing, in manuscript editing, to give its graduates a better chance to survive by their pens instead of having virtually no alternative but to teach or to do something unrelated to writing.

Just as it would flow easily between the different departments, it would maintain easy access to and from the society. Students would be free to leave for a year or two in the middle of the program to write on their own and to try to get by. Along with the core teachers, who would provide continuity, professional writers and editors would come for a semester or two to teach their craft. Though broad in scope and loose in structure, the PLP should be as busy and intensive as a medical school or a law school: writers with too much to do, just as they're likely to be, if they're productive, for the next twenty years.

Yes, much of what I'm proposing is impractical as matters stand. What students in their mid to late twenties would be attracted to such a program? Only the few who are gifted, serious, and mature enough for it. What universities would initiate such a radically different program? Only the creative few that would sponsor the kind of magazine for the common reader that their writers would in time write for. What writers and academics would work harmoniously together in such a program? Only those, in V. S. Pritchett's words, who "do not lay down the law but make a case for humane values."

(1986)

What Has Happened to the Publishing Business

I

As an editor who works in trade PUBLISHING, I lead a dual life. On the one hand, I come from the world of letters, a vague but real place that has given me my standards and shaped my skills, and that keeps a record of my performance. On the other hand, for the past twenty years I have been reporting, as we say there, to the world of publishing, a specific but increasingly unreal place where I earn my living and produce my goods, and where a different kind of record is kept.

Though these two worlds have probably never lived on easy terms with each other, they have traditionally shared a certain common ground of desire and function: the pen yearning for the press that disseminated and rewarded its words, the press yearning for the fine pens that enabled it to move upward in a society from the business to the profession of publishing as an institution of culture.

So matters stood some twenty years ago, when I came to work at New American Library. Hardcover publishing was still largely a genteel profession. The "houses" were, like the homes of the gentry, distinctive, stable, guided by tradition or at least precedent, inner-directed in their functioning values. They characteristically bore the names of their founders—Norton, Knopf, Scribner, Harper & Brothers, Farrar Straus, Simon & Schuster, and so forth—and had developed along the lines of a kind of idealized self-image of the founders: their vision, taste, and interests, and those of successors who were generally chosen to maintain the reputation. The identity of the house was remarkably stable for an organization as subject to the vicissitudes of the times and the market as a publishing house was.

The main reason for this stability was that the identity of the house was framed and its profitability was stabilized by its backlist—the well-established titles that more or less sold themselves from year to year. This endowment, as it were, enabled the publisher to refrain from the promiscuous pursuit of best-sellers. Moreover, profits were expected to be modest and variable, given the nature of the business. In hardcover publishing, the ratio of the cover price to the acquisition and production costs of a book was a little better than four to one; when the high overhead of a labor-intensive product and a 40 percent discount to the seller are added in, one can see why a publisher who showed a net profit of 8 percent a year judged himself to be doing well. The publisher and perhaps the few other officers derived incomes sufficient unto Fifth Avenue or Chappaqua; salaries otherwise were perhaps a bit better than at a university or some other nonprofit organization.

Thus a publisher like Alfred Knopf, relying upon a franchise author like Kahlil Gibran and an occasional bonanza like Camus's *The Stranger* (which he bought for $750), could develop a list of authors of international standing, ranging from England to Japan, from South America to Canada. Publishing for Knopf, a not untypical son of the risen Jewish merchant class, was a means of joining commerce and culture in a cosmopolitan way, just as he cultivated a refined life-style and an autocratic deportment. (He is supposed to have said that he did not care to publish any author whom he would not want to invite to dinner.) With certain deviations for temperament, one could point to the younger leading hardcover houses—Viking, Simon & Schuster, Random House, Farrar Straus—as similar examples of Jewish newcomers' using family money to establish houses that conformed to their desire and drive to play an important cultural role in New York, much as their counterparts were doing in Vienna, Berlin, and London. Even Simon & Schuster, whose principal figures had something of the pizzazz and uninhibitedness of the Hollywood moguls about turning a buck, had its own touch of class, as well as a shrewd awareness that quality paid, which quickly made Pocket Books, its paperback subsidiary, preeminent in the ragtag field of reprints that existed before the Second World War. Viking and Random House, which began in the late 1920s, soon established themselves as leaders in literary and intellectual publishing by virtue of their aggressive pursuit of important writers (Random House brought the famous court action that enabled *Ulysses* to be published in America, and Viking published Joyce's other books) and their innovative marketing, which produced the Modern Library and the Viking Portables. Farrar Straus, which began after the Second World War, was another bright star in the publishing firmament. When I came to New York, in 1960, it had much the same aura as *Partisan Review,* than which there was none brighter.

The older houses were typically more conservative in their behavior, less eclectic and more domestic in their interests. For many decades, Harper's had been guided by its commitment as a book and magazine publisher to serving as an arbiter of mainstream American culture, particularly its political and social concerns. By virtue of its magazine and its editors, culminating in Maxwell Perkins,

Scribner's had been a force in American fiction ever since its great New York edition of Henry James. W. W. Norton was more or less the publisher of record in psychology and music; E. P. Dutton was known for its Americana and nature books; Houghton Mifflin, Little, Brown, and the Atlantic Monthly Press maintained the Yankee Brahmin strain in American life and letters. Of course, these were all general publishers as well, much of whose lists for a given season might not seem readily distinguishable from one another. But the perceived tradition and character of each house was important in selecting editors and manuscripts, in determining priorities and taking risks, in packaging and marketing a book. Because each book is different, or at least used to be, publishing is full of contingencies and guesswork; hence, in uncertain circumstances it pays to know who you are and what you do well.

A strong sense of their identity and role was particularly apparent in two houses—New Directions and Grove Press. Though neither named his house after himself, both James Laughlin and Barney Rosset stamped their lists of authors with their own signatures. The scion of a steel fortune and a poet himself, Laughlin was the best kind of patron, the one who supports his authors by publishing them, and he devoted New Directions mainly to discovering and disseminating the canon of the modern tradition. Rosset, a well-to-do Irish-Jewish American with a bohemian streak, made Grove and its magazine, *Evergreen Review,* into a forum for the international avant-garde of the 1950s and 1960s—though "forum" may put the matter too passively. As iconoclastic as his authors, Rosset aggressively promoted the work of Beckett and Genet, Robbe-Grillet and Brecht, William Burroughs and Henry Miller, Frantz Fanon and Malcolm X. He went to court to appeal the Post Office's banning of his unexpurgated edition of *Lady Chatterley's Lover* and subsequently defended his right to publish

Tropic of Cancer and *Naked Lunch.* Kenneth C. Davis, a publishing historian, regards Rosset as being "almost single-handedly responsible for the rewriting of censorship laws in this country." Pursuing his various interests in erotica, in profits, in modernism, in freedom of the press, in showmanship, Rosset was withal a bookman. In Davis's *Two-Bit Culture,* Nat Sobel, Grove's marketing manager, recalls asking Rosset why he was publishing a bilingual edition of Neruda's poetry "when I can't sell poetry, let alone bilingual poetry." Rosset replied, "Because it's important. We made a lot of money with this and that and we've got to give a little of it back to the business that made us the money.' "

In his personal style as well as in Grove's format, Rosset belonged more to the paperback side of publishing circa 1965 than to the hardcover one. That's where most of the crusaders and plungers were—the mission and the action, the classiness and gaminess of the "paperback revolution." This was still in full swing when I came to New American Library to start a literary-intellectual paperback magazine. As it happened, NAL was going through some strange and, as it proved, prophetic times, which I shall touch on, but the vestigial spirit of its two founders, Kurt Enoch and Victor Weybright, was still operating, though both had departed a few years before. The office I was given had just been vacated by David Segal, who had launched in the previous two years, as part of NAL's fledgling hardcover program, the novelists John Gardner, William H. Gass, and Cynthia Ozick. In the next office was Arabel Porter, the tutelary spirit of *New World Writing,* which had demonstrated a decade before that editing a big little magazine for the mass market was not necessarily an oxymoronic idea. Down the hall were the editors who worked on Signet Classics and Mentor Books, which had brought much of the best that had been thought and said into corner drugstores and transportation terminals. There was the kindred spirit of Sylvan Barnet, who edited NAL's superb Shakespeare series.

What surprised and then instructed me was that though NAL also made a big thing out of publishing Mickey Spillane and Ian Fleming, among other "downmarket" authors who largely supported the enterprise, this practice mattered much less than I would have thought. Coming there, as I had, from *Commentary* and the New York intellectual scene, where the distinctions between high, middle, and low brow were rigorously and disdainfully preserved by the elite, I was struck by the degree to which at NAL the right hand of commerce and the left hand of culture each knew and even respected what the other was doing. Indeed, they imparted a kind of synergy, the hustle and the aspiration each pulling its oar.

E. L. Doctorow, who had preceded me by a few years, likes to recall that he was responsible for signing up Ayn Rand and Ian Fleming as well as for overseeing Signet Classics and NAL's science books, the last because "Victor found out that I had gone to Bronx Science, which he'd heard was on a par with MIT." Bringing in "the good read," I soon learned, was not simply a way of earning your room and board, as it were, but also an opportunity to stay in touch with the adolescent reader in yourself, the very same person who went with you to American movies and ball games and who knew how to discriminate between the interesting ones and the dull ones.

This kind of discrimination was also a part of the Enoch-Weybright legacy. Enoch, a refugee, had been a pioneer of paperback publishing in Europe. His Albatross Books, marketed for the English-reading audience of the Continent, had put Joyce and Lawrence and Virginia Woolf side by side with Ellery Queen and S. S. Van Dine. This vision of the broad market for inexpensive books that were the best of their kind had lit up Weybright's mind. A farm boy from Maryland who had made his way through journalism to the Office of War Information in London. Weybright was a man whose status drives were matched only by his reading habits (he claimed to read two thousand books a year). Brought together by Allen Lane to run the American branch of Penguin Books, Enoch and Weybright soon found themselves cramped by Lane's toniness and priggishness, and founded NAL to go after the mass as well as the class market.

Enoch's efficiency in production and marketing and Weybright's ability to keep himself on constant alert for the next opportunity made them a formidable team. But what drove NAL in the direction it took was their combined energy as very ambitious and cultivated men who demanded to be taken seriously—not as "reprinters," the somewhat derogatory term that the hardcover side used to mask its dependency on those who did cheap editions of its books, but as culturally important and valuable publishers—indeed the new movers and shapers of the industry. Dealing in the rough-and-tumble and still somewhat shady world of the magazine distributors who handled most of their books no doubt gave Enoch and Weybright a motive to polish their image. So, too, did the congressional investigation in the mid-1950s of the alleged violent and licentious influence of paperbacks. But the main point remains that these two publishers had built their house in their idealized self-image of cultural missionaries to the masses. "Good Reading for the Millions" was the motto they stamped on the cover of each of their books: Walt Whitman's *Democratic Vistas* come true.

To be sure, conditions were right and ripe. There was the virtually continuous expansion of the economy after the Second World War through the next two decades. There was the dramatic spread of higher education because of the

GI Bill and, later, the federal subsidies that poured into the colleges and universities between *Sputnik* and the Great Society. Together, these influences produced an educated middle class and a serious reading public that had hardly existed before, as well as a huge campus market that was supplementing and increasingly replacing hardcover textbooks with paperbacks. Moreover, the nature of paperback distribution, in which the publisher set the quotas for the wholesalers, enabled a house like NAL to force its quality books into the market in the same "drop" with its westerns, detective stories, romances, and its reprints of the previous year's bestsellers. True, a lot of these books were returned unsold, but since mass-market books cost only a few cents a copy to produce—the ratio of cover price to production and distribution costs being more than double what it was in hardcover, and the royalty rates about half—one could afford to take risks.

Another advantage of paperback publishing at NAL was that its editorial group was small, versatile, quick on its feet, and trusted. Weybright, who in other respects put the *mega* back in *megalomaniac,* gave his editors their head, trusted their intuitions and enthusiasms, and stimulated their venturesomeness. Doctorow tells a more or less typical story of jumping on the news of Adolf Eichmann's capture, calling up a knowledgeable journalist friend, and getting him to write a quick book. In a few weeks the manuscript of *The Case Against Adolf Eichmann* was delivered, photographs were pulled together, and Doctorow rushed off to Chicago to see the book through the press. A month after the event, the book was in the racks and went on to sell 500,000 copies. The success is less to the point than the venture itself. Good publishing at NAL was neither a crap shoot nor a market analysis: it was taking sensible risks in the pursuit of what was interesting. Edward Burlingame, another young NAL editor at the time, recalls Weybright's enthusiasm for as worthy a project as the poetry and prose of Giacomo Leopardi, a figure as towering in Europe as he was unknown here.

The reason I had come to NAL was that this pursuit was still going on, and I had all the freedom and backing I could ask for, when I began. It would have been much the same if I had worked for Peter Mayer, at Avon, or Oscar Dystel and Marc Jaffe, at Bantam, as I did a few years later, or Ian Ballantine, at his house. They were all astute rabbis of the paperback book and fervent in its cause. Weybright himself summed up their careers:

> I had run the gauntlet and emerged with proof, widely acknowledged, that widespread cultivation of new and habitual readers of inexpensive books does not lead to vulgarization and the lowest common denominator of quality. In relation to the literary scene there was scarcely a notable author, contemporary or classical, who was not listed in the current volumes of paperback books in print. . . . Our paperbacks gave new prestige and importance to books as compared with popular periodicals, and we had widened the availability of good books to older intellectual readers as well as to students.

II

As it fell out, Weybright's words were a valedictory not only of his achievement but of NAL's as well, and, in time and in good part, of the revolution Weybright had helped to lead. He and Enoch were already diminishing legends when I arrived at NAL, because seven years earlier they had sold their company to the *Los Angeles Times Mirror,* a junior-size conglomerate. Each man has given different reasons for his decision and for the other's, but it is pretty clear that the allure of the big time was the tacit one they had in common, an allure that was to work its will on other independent publishers, to much the same outcome. As it happened, Enoch and Weybright were like a couple that stays together for the sake of the child and whose relationship disintegrates rapidly when the child leaves home. But it was to prove not untypical that the accord that had prevailed in a privately owned company was displaced by rivalry and jockeying in a subsidiary one, that the golden apple of corporate acquisition would produce discord. It was also not untypical that the man from the business side would prove to be the more effective conglomerateer. As the head of the *Times Mirror's* book division, Enoch went from apparent strength to strength, acquiring World, whose highly successful bible and dictionary provided a solid foundation on which to build; Harry Abrams, the leading art-book publisher; and a small English house, which was renamed New English Library and was to be Enoch's beachhead in the United Kingdom.

Meanwhile, Weybright steadily lost ground. He had little or no influence in Enoch's acquisitions, which worked much better in the theory of acquiring them than in the reality of managing them, Weybright found his autonomy vanishing in his own sphere, and he had to take on the responsibility for World's new titles when its editors resigned en masse. The brief but disastrous history that followed, which led to the fall of NAL from the top place in paperback publishing to one deep in the second rank in little more than a decade and to the virtual demise of World and NEL, is sketched in gall in the chapter "From Dream to Nightmare" in Weybright's memoir, *The Making of a Publisher.* Its story of misconception, mistrust, mismanagement, and mediocrity, a later chapter of which I was to witness, forms a paradigm of the fate of many of the trade publishing houses that in the next two decades climbed the magic beanstalk of increased operating capital shares of stock, and reassuring promises, only to end up in the land of the hungry giants.

The theme that runs through Weybright's account is more to the point of my subject than are its details of personal conflict and tragedy, at least for the moment. This theme is the subversion of publishing planning and practice by the expectations and methods of the corporate mentality. At one point toward the end, Weybright recounts a meeting with the executive of the management consulting firm that was now overseeing the book program:

> "You are a purchasing—a procurement—executive," Jack Vance said, "and you *must* be responsive to marketing." Since it had been my talent to anticipate marketing by five years or more in my publishing program, I was shocked but concealed my sense of outrage.

There, in embryo, is the story of much of trade publishing in the next twenty years. The main supporting characters are the conglomerates that bought publishing houses, the "procurement executives" who replaced the Weybrights (he resigned a month later, never to return to paperback publishing), the bookstore chains, and the new breed of American book consumers. Together they have worked like a pincers movement to narrow the scope and prospects of literary and intellectual publishing in the book trade; then again, they have worked like a flanking movement to capture and exploit the new mass market of the age of consumerism and the culture of narcissism.

The typical publishing corporation or conglomerate subsidiary is only nominally interested in providing "good reading for the millions." At the management level it works, breathes, and wills like any other big business. Its paramount concern is not the integrity and value of its product but the value of its shares, which is keyed to its short-term profits, derived from the number and profitability of books it sells. The result has been to expand the volume of the product (from 1965 to 1985, the number of published titles increased by close to 25 percent in each decade) and to tailor the product to the demand. This is more pronounced in paperback publishing, where the invisible hand of the mass market is more coercive. But it has increasingly affected hardcover publishing as well, both as the supplier to the reprinters and as a merchant looking for its piece of the action at the chain bookstore in the shopping mall. The action is in the books that service either popular needs for information, instruction, entertainment, and fantasy, or merely consumerism itself: that is, the need to keep buying, or preparing or just wishing to buy, that has turned the shopping mall into the church where many families worship each weekend. This explains the overwhelming shift in most publishing houses to consumer-oriented titles: the proliferation of cookbooks and dieting books; physical, mental, and spiritual self-help books; investment guides; crafts manuals; hobby and other leisure books; and advice books on all stages of the life cycle, from infant care and child rearing to retirement and estate planning. It also explains the corollary development in fiction, the domination by the masters of the categories—occult, romance, detective, spy, western, horror, and so on—and the other brand-name entertainers.

The pursuit of trendy, fast-moving titles has contributed to the decline of backlist publishing and its conserving, stabilizing influence. The mass market of the shopping mall has proved to be the Great Leveler of the publishing business. With a few exceptions, such as Knopf, Viking/Penguin, Norton, Pantheon, Farrar Straus & Giroux, and Ballantine, the major houses today are virtually indistinguishable. (Here, as elsewhere in this essay, I exclude Harper & Row, my present employer, and Bessie Books, my publisher, from the discussion.) Like members of a football team in the huddle, the publishing players are distinguished from one another mainly by their size and numbers (that is, volume of sales). The long-standing identities that derived from the houses' traditional interests and purposes have eroded, along with their backlists. So, too, for the most part, have the differences even between the hardcover and paperback publishers. Authors, publishers, and editors move from one house to another without dropping a stitch, missing a beat. Why shouldn't they? The discourse they've left is the same kind they find: the demanding novel is a "tough sell," the one that isn't immediately topical is "marginal," the crudely written, heavily plotted one is an "easy read," the slick one, in which, typically, a gimmick meets a fad, is "popcorn." So, too, with nonfiction, in which the complex and learned study of a subject is elbowed aside by the one that approaches its subject and audience with outflung arms, the main idea on its author's mind being money. By attempting to standardize their product, most of the publishers have succeeded in standardizing themselves.

III

How does the corporate mentality infiltrate a publishing house? Let us begin with a not so hypothetical example. Telcom, a far-flung media empire of newspapers, magazines, and TV and radio stations, decides it wants the prestige and entrepreneurial possibilities of owning a New York publisher. It looks into Harbinger House, a distinguished publisher of mostly quality books, which has been hit by high interest rates, soaring manufacturing and overhead costs, a flat book market, and the IRS's recent policy of taxing inventory, which has driven backlist publishing further to the wall and many important books out of print. Harbinger has been losing some authors, and failing to acquire others who belong on its list, because of the inflated advances for quality books "with commercial possibilities," which almost everyone wants to publish occasionally so they can look themselves in the face while laughing all the way to the bank. Moreover, Harbinger needs financing to capitalize on what it does well—particularly to expand its trade paperback line by acquiring undervalued titles from other publishers. This looks good to the chief executive officer of Telcom. Wanting to impress the Harbinger people with his urbanity and himself with his high-mindedness, he assures them that the house's autonomy will be fully respected.

For a time not much changes except Harbinger's cash flow. Then Telcom buys Premium Books, a mass-market paperback house, to "mate" with Harbinger, the thinking being that they will now be able to compete with similarly positioned companies for the super best-sellers that seem to make all the difference. To coordinate his new companies, to place them more symmetrically on Telcom's organizational chart, and to "goose" their managements, the CEO sets up a new division and places it under the supervision of Howard Green, a Telcom executive who has no experience in book publishing but was successful as the number-two man of Telcom's magazine division.

Green moves in with his team of financial and marketing analysts, who quickly discover that book publishing is a very irrational and uncertain business. For example, only 12 percent of Harbinger's list is responsible for 78 percent of its profits. But the main problem they discover is what Harbinger *doesn't* publish. Breaking down its list and comparing its "major" titles (fifty thousand copies or more sold) with the *Publishers Weekly* hardcover and trade-paperback best-seller lists for the previous year shows that Harbinger was weak in occult fiction (one title), suspense fiction (two), and romances (none). In nonfiction it was even worse: inspirational books (none), diet books (none), cookbooks (one), humor (one), exercise and fitness (one), pets (none), business and investment (none), health and child care (two), psychology and sexuality (one), and so on. In sum, the analysis not only explains why Harbinger is still showing a negative ROI (return on investment) after two years but also confirms Green's belief that its management may have an incurable case of "egghead tunnel vision."

A similar analysis of Premium Books shows that it is cluttering up its inventory with books like *Doctor Zhivago*, *The Hedgehog and the Fox*, and *The Last of the Just*. It should eliminate all titles that aren't moving at the rate of a thousand copies a month and should not acquire any for which this rate of sale cannot be anticipated. Premium, too, needs many more consumer-oriented titles, a line of "clean romances" like Harlequin, biographies of celebrities, and especially more "blockbuster" novels (a million copies or more). Also, Telcom's ROI would be substantially improved if Premium would acquire and co-publish more of its major acquisitions with Harbinger. At the next Telcom board meeting it is agreed that a Robert Ludlum, a Carl Sagan, or a Stephen King comes high, but that's where the investment should be; acquiring King and doing him in both editions plus a movie tie-in is a license to print money. It's almost as exciting as picking off an undervalued corporation.

But the following year Harbinger's return on investment has barely improved. The publisher explains to Green that most of the new, high-priced authors he has acquired are still finishing their books and that his expanded paperback line is running into heavy competition in the burgeoning field of trade paperbacks. Green needs more than that to take to the board meeting. To show that *he* now is in charge, he demands a major commercial acquisition before the meeting (for which Harbinger will badly overpay); all new acquisitions of fifty thousand dollars or more will henceforth be cleared with him; operating overhead for the next fiscal year will be cut by 15 percent; and the quota of "major" titles will be doubled. After trying unsuccessfully to meet with Telcom's CEO, the publisher resigns and is immediately replaced by an aggressive treasurer from another house with whom Telcom's "headhunter" agency has been negotiating. He brings in his own editor in chief, from one of the big book clubs. After a few months the new publisher easily convinces Green that Harbinger will be viable only if its entire operation is moved to and merged with Premium; Harbinger will maintain its editorial independence, though joint ventures by the two houses will be more vigorously pursued.

In fairly short order, a new Harbinger House begins to emerge. Poetry is cut back to a few authors who command substantial anthology fees; literary criticism departs; history and biography become more popular and up-to-date home-and-family titles begin to proliferate. Fiction in particular comes under the new editor in chief's scrutiny: does it have a page-turning plot, sympathetic characters, a punchy style, a topical subject, erotic steam? Is it, in short, a novel that he likes to read and can sell to a reprinter for at least double its advance? Collections of stories are highly dubious unless the author has been consistently published in *The New Yorker* and preferably in one or two of the women's magazines. Social and political criticism is similarly subjected to the standard of popular appeal: is its point of view widely shared, immediately accessible, both controversial and reassuring? In short, is its author likely to be invited to be on the Phil Donahue show? So with psychology, biology, religion. "Don't tell me how good it is. Tell me who is going to buy it."

All of which has a conditioning effect on even the most independent, venturesome, quality-minded editor. He finds that his value to the house has been quantified: his salary and overhead are now expected to produce X times their total in the net sales of the books he acquires. The pressure as well as the changed atmosphere of Harbinger affects the way he reads, judges, and even edits manuscripts. His attention and evaluation begin to shift from the characteristics that make a book unique to those that make it readily identifiable ("the new anti-yuppie novel"), from those that make it risky and interesting to those that make it promotable ("a cross between Jay McInerney and Robert Stone")—in a campaign that starts within the new Harbinger itself.

If the former characteristics significantly outweigh the latter, which is generally the case with original or otherwise difficult work, he becomes less and less willing or able to take the book on. In the new marketing environment of Harbinger, he feels that the credibility of his judgment is always on the line and that to prevail with the moderately unusual and complex manuscript he must forget about doing the esoteric and demanding one, even though he knows in his heart, if he has any heart left, that the author could be the next Italo Calvino or Susan Sontag or John Berger.

In other words, he has to trim his sails to take advantage of the countervailing winds that can help to keep him from drifting completely off his previous course. Even commercial-minded publishing doesn't lend itself all that readily to the kind of controls that corporate managers like to employ to tailor the product to the market. The reading tastes and interests of the serious book-buying public are still too idiosyncratic and unpredictable for any computer to track.

Once you get past the best-selling authors and the trashier categories and "lines" of pop writing, you're in a gray area of crude comparisons and hunches and surprises. That is one reason the beleaguered, compromising editor at Harbinger House remains haunted by the spirit of art and ideas. Along with maintaining his morale, he knows that the literary or intellectual work that strikes it rich can strike it very rich indeed, and for years to come. First novels may generally lose money, but how would you like to have passed up *The Bell Jar* or *The Catcher in the Rye* or *Catch-22* or *The Naked and the Dead* or *Invisible Man?* A writer whose first three or four novels didn't sell is hard to justify to the sales force and the bookstore buyer, but how would you like to have turned down *The World According to Garp* or *The Golden Notebook* or *The French Lieutenant's Woman?* So the literary editor tries to persuade his new publisher and editorial director to keep a margin of imagination and seed money available for at least a few of those unlikely submissions, like *Gödel, Escher, Bach* or *The Man Who Mistook His Wife for a Hat* or *The Name of the Rose.*

Even so, the new and strong pressures at Harbinger will likely continue to push the editor in the direction of the "major" titles. Since the authors of such books are already being well published and cherished elsewhere, he finds himself in the new role of raider and seducer for Harbinger. Apart from the effect that this behavior may have on his morale, it tends if he is successful to curtail his independence and compromise his editorial role and skills as much as the new marketing criteria do. Besides more money, he doesn't have much to offer the best-selling author except his flattery and Harbinger's fading prestige. But if he enters on his knees, how is he then to stand on his own two feet and edit this author? If he has reservations about the author's glibness, which he wasn't about to reveal during the courtship, how is he to establish the ground to criticize this in the new work? Moreover, acquiring writers because they write best-sellers means that the editor must continue to trim and misrepresent his own judgment of their books in hyping them at marketing meetings and sales conferences, in writing catalogue and flap copy. An editor can't do much accommodating and falsifying and, in some cases, groveling without losing respect for his own judgment, which is what he mainly edits with. This is one reason that less and less serious editing will be done at Harbinger.

There are other subtle but determining changes that will likely mark the change at Harbinger. Arthur Samuelson, of Summit Books, who is one of the more astute younger editors, speaks of the benefits of learning the business at a small house, where the editor is close to the various phases of the publishing process, takes on diverse books, and is often left on his own to improvise. At a large house he is remote from much of the process, and his purview is much more specialized and routinized. Under Bennett Cerf and Donald Klopfer, Random House solved this problem brilliantly, by making its senior editors in effect publishers of their own books. Such a policy is virtually unthinkable in a comparable house today, except with the handful of editors who have been given their own imprints. These editor-publishers, such as Helen Wolff, Seymour Lawrence, Elisabeth Sifton, James Silberman (with whom Samuelson works), and the late Henry Robbins, have been responsible for a disproportionate share of the distinguished books in the past twenty years of trade publishing. Their achievement—indeed, their very survival—points up the prowess of individual taste, independent judgment, personal marketing savvy, and professional standards. Like the small family farm and the small serious bookstore, imprint publishing is where much of the memory, will, and intelligence of a cultivating type of work goes on leading its precarious life.

Samuelson makes the interesting point that the big-time house doesn't seem to have a memory, which limits its intelligence and distorts its will. Because it is always thinking and rushing ahead, chasing its sales and profit projections, little appears to be learned and applied beyond the obvious successes and failures. In a small house, all sorts of know-how is retained and used, and memory is its guiding light. With its limited cash flow and credit, the house can't afford to forget either its mistakes or its right moves, and so they naturally become part of its mentality. Similarly, its sense of risk is more judicious, being founded on its past judgments and performance as well as its limited resources, rather than being prompted by the round-robin derring-do of the agents' auctions and the elastic projections of sales and subsidiary income that the "heavy hitters" use in competing for a book. Like a stable person, a good small house respects its experience.

An excess of memory may, of course, be confining in its own way, particularly when coupled with a scarcity of operating capital. But at least the issues of the house's functional identity and the editor's scope are clear. The editor likely earns less money, but he can regard the difference in his early years as tuition and in his later ones as the dues one pays to be one's own man. In big-time publishing, the editor tends to be more uncounseled by himself and others. The functional identity of the house is both more diffuse and more assertive, communication is more formalized and abstract, and the atmosphere comes to be that anxious state between the present and the future known as limbo. It's hard to know how to function, and the editor comes to rely upon signals from the best-seller lists and the in-house authorities to counter a chronic low-grade panic. This is one good reason that many younger editors today know a great deal about market trends and promotional ploys but are either glibly or poignantly at a loss when asked about their ideas for interesting books.

Let us assume, though, that the editor at the new Harbinger still has some margin left in which to persist, and some will to do so. He manages to acquire, say, a remarkable collection of coarse, enigmatic, but cumulatively powerful stories about low life in Glasgow. He does everything right for the book as an exciting and important literary discovery, including finding six prominent fiction writers who call it one, only to encounter in the marketplace an even more onerous version of the books-as-product mentality.

Two major developments in bookselling are at work here. The first is the phenomenal growth of the bookstore chains, which now control 30 percent of the market and counting, and powerfully influence the rest of it. An article in *Publishers Weekly* a few years ago described the outlook at Waldenbooks, which now operates some one thousand stores.

> All of its top executives strongly support the mass merchandising concepts (that is, of treating books like a product in the same way a manufacturer would merchandise a bar of soap). Hoffman [the president], who views romance titles with as much respect as literary works, experienced the selling power of mass merchandising techniques when he was an executive at Bell & Howell.

More recently, in *The New York Times Magazine*, Harry Hoffman amplified his view of the book market. One of his more telling points was that

> people are interested in what's happening whether it's diet or sports. I don't think publishers are taking into

> account that time is a factor. People want something short that they can read in a night.

One can easily imagine the response the salesperson from Harbinger will receive when she presents our editor's unique book about some lost souls in Glasgow in their own idiom, for which the editor has fought to get an advance quota of five thousand copies but no advertising budget. Even if the salesperson shares the editor's enthusiasm for the book, buyers at Waldenbooks and at B. Dalton, the other major "full-line" chain, will order no more than a few copies for 15 percent of their stores.

Let's assume that this "slow read" and "tough sell" receives major critical acclaim. A rate of sale deemed acceptable for it has already been plugged into a central computer. If the book doesn't meet it in ninety days, it won't be in most of the stores when its reputation catches up with it, and when the author's next book comes along, assuming the editor still has the credibility and heart to take it on, 30, or perhaps by then 35, percent of the market will be closed to it.

A phenomenon even more ominous for quality publishing is the advent of the discount bookstore chains, which narrow the market even further by restricting their inventories to the quick and the dead—best-selling types and remainders. The main trouble with both kinds of chains is not that they exist (no one in publishing is opposed to bringing more of the public into bookstores) but that by expanding omnivorously they make it difficult for many of the independent booksellers to survive, particularly in communities where serious readers are not legion. It's not only that the full-line chains have taken to discounting some of their best-sellers to pull in customers but also that because they buy books on a chain-wide basis, they get discounts 6 to 8 percent higher from the publisher, even though it pays the same freight costs to send five copies of a book to B. Dalton in San Jose as it does to supply the independent there. More important, their purchasing capacity enables them to receive many times more money for co-op advertising and promotion from the publisher. Along with killing off competition, they further distort the book business by driving the larger independent stores to adopt their methods.

One of the ways the outpriced and outgunned independent bookstore has fought back is by countering the impersonal, supermarket, "I just work here on Saturday" service of the chain store with increased attention to its clientele and with the programs of readings, discussions, and other events that enable the store to serve as a center of the local literary community. This has worked well in places with high concentrations of serious readers, like Minneapolis and Berkeley, but it's hard to put across in Saratoga Springs or Tucson without some significant help from the publishers. The endangered state of the local bookstore is a particular problem for quality publishing, because the store provides the advice, information, and service to readers, including a congenial atmosphere for browsing and book talk, that give the original collection of stories set in Glasgow a better chance to find its readers and vice versa. And as independent bookstores vanish like sentinels whose positions have been overrun, and the chain merchandisers move in with their store traffic control and target marketing plans, the reverberations are registered back in New York, where, amid talk of "cutbacks" here and new "lines" there, the transformation of publishing from partly a profession to wholly a business broadens and accelerates.

In recent years the diversified conglomerates like Telcom have for the most part departed from the business of book publishing, spinning off Harbinger and Premium as being stale and profitless, the Hamlets of their subsidiaries in the magical morning of the electronics age. But their impact is still to be reckoned with in the many houses that they badly destabilized and the several that they killed (notably Fawcett, a major paperback publisher) by their demands for unrealistic and quick returns on the money they poured into them; by their arrogant and/or ignorant meddling in publishing judgments, programs, and practices; and by their firing, demoting, and undercutting sound bookmen in the course of bringing in their conglomerateers or empowering those who rushed into their embrace within the house. The advent of the conglomerateer, obsessed with ROI and market share and corporate politics, along with his deputies and fellow travelers, has bred an atmosphere of fear, cynicism, rapaciousness, and ignorance, and shortsightedness that has been as destructive to sound and serious publishing as any of the other developments I've described. Its cost can be reckoned in the substantial number of sagacious and dedicated publishers, editors, and marketing executives who, like Victor Weybright, lost their occupation, whether by being driven out or demoralized or corrupted.

The conglomerates' ravage of the publishing industry was compounded by the stagflation of the late 1970s and early 1980s. The paperback houses fared particularly badly, and their cutbacks severely reduced the subsidiary income many hardcover houses needed to make ends meet. The books that were most adversely affected were the so-called "midlist" ones, which included most of the quality titles by authors who did not have major sales, who were not "brand names." If more of the wiser heads of the industry had remained in charge, I think that publishing would have come through the crunch of those years without abandoning so much of its identity as an institution of culture. But the older management tended to be replaced and its natural heirs to be superseded by a new managerial class who fell in smoothly with the book-chain executives and buyers and store managers, being uninhibited by convictions, other than that publishing was profits and losses and books were "product." In this climate, in the late 1970s, of inflated advances and reprint sales and a declining interest in most literary and intellectual titles, it also, sadly, became true that some important publishers and editors who had been committed to quality were more or less overcome by the mass marketeer in themselves. The intense competition for established or even potential "market leaders," which Thomas Whiteside describes in his book *The Blockbuster Phenomenon,* also gave new scope and impact to the wheeler-dealer literary agent and lawyer. They plugged the high voltage of Hollywood into the delicate circuitry of established author-publisher relationships, shorting out a good many of them and creating overloads of publishers' advances and authors' expectations from which both groups are still recovering.

In the latest round of the mergers and acquisitions that are much with us these days, the publishers who have adapted most successfully to supplying the demands of consumerism have been using their surplus capital to take over those that have not adapted as well. Because these print conglomerates are more experienced and efficient, their effect is likely to be that of rationalizing and strengthening the tendencies I have been describing, which reward commerce and impoverish culture. If you want to observe these tendencies in action, I suggest you watch what happens to Doubleday now that it has been bought by the multinational firm of Bertelsmann, which has presided over the transformation of Bantam from the brilliantly balanced purveyor of commerce and culture that I worked for in the 1970s to a megamerchandiser of both hardcover and paperback products, most of whose huge monthly order form reads like a tour through a shopping-mall bookstore. It is only fair to observe that part of Bantam's former spirit may be reviving in its new imprint for publishing new writers, if it doesn't prove to be another flash in the pan of trendiness.

IV

One can say, of course, that it's a free country, and that the big publishers and booksellers are giving consumers the books they want. One can also say that there is no reason to expect books to be spared from the economic, social, and cultural forces that continue to massify all the other media. One can also argue that relative to the products of the radio and television networks, the film industry, and the newspaper and magazine chains, there is still much quality of thought and art to be grateful for in book publishing. One can also talk about the twilight of the print era, the culture of narcissism, the rock-bottom state of the *Zeitgeist* during the past decade, in which the best have lacked all conviction and the worst have been filled with passionate intensity. One can say all this and also believe that there is more to be said.

Speaking for myself, I think that in viewing its proper place in the society as the big time, much of the publishing business has sold itself a bill of goods. In so doing, it has largely sold out its cultural purpose to its commercial one, thereby losing the vision and synergy and realism that guided and empowered publishers like Knopf, Cerf, Klopfer, Harold Guinzberg, Cass Canfield, Kurt Wolff, Ballantine, Enoch and Weybright, and others. The truth is that the basic economics of the trade book have not changed since the days of aggressive cultural ambition and modest economic expectation. If anything, the spread between costs and receivables has contracted because of the chain stores' higher discounts and promotion charges. It's true that publishers have been able to put out many more of the mass-merchandise titles for which the chains have expanded the market, but they are also taking book returns that are three and four times what they used to be, so by corporate standards profit margins remain slim and capricious.

Yet because they are corporations, the bigger houses have big-time overheads—six-figure salaries for the officers, many of whom have little or nothing to do with publishing books, and substantial fees to the directors, skyscraper rents for office space and executive apartments in the city, limousine service and the other perks of the boardroom. It's no wonder, then, that there has been the frantic pressure for blockbuster books by name-brand authors and by celebrities from politics to entertainment, the competition for which leads to bloated advances, bloated promotion costs and services, and bloated risk. When a few putative blockbusters —in some cases, even one—fail, the effect on the rest of the list can be grievous indeed. Just as when the market softens for a time and annual earnings and value per share show a loss, the drive to reduce operating expenses follows as the night the day. Quality books are the most grievously affected, for they lose the pittance of advertising money that their authors count on to develop a reputation that may sustain their careers. Moreover, the attitude toward acquisitions hardens against the gifted, serious, inexpensive submission but grows starry-eyed about the big commercial property that can be published quickly. As the CEO and his number-crunchers exert themselves, publishing decisions are likely to be more reckless and shortsighted: not just the micro decisions, regarding this piece of merchandise or that, but the macro ones—to take over weak houses, to increase market share, or to diversify into areas of publishing that they know next to nothing about. In the past couple of years, as trade publishing has consolidated further, the lords of the market share, the counselors of the quick fix, the true believers in the divine rights of the ROI, have been laying waste lists and careers in trade publishing in an even more relentless way. Where will it end? Meanwhile, what can be done to keep the profession of publishing alive as an institution of culture?

Obviously, the giant houses aren't going to take themselves off the big board or otherwise become small again. But it's not too much to ask their CEOs and other top executives to mull over some serious questions. Given the narrow profit margins of trade publishing, is it sound business to saddle it with the bloated salaries that corporate officers receive—four to five times those of senior editors and marketing people? The latter are willing to work in publishing for less money than they would earn in a more profitable business—not to mention the junior staff, who can barely subsist on their salaries. Why should officers not accept the same facts of economic life? Along with improving morale, it would make them better publishers. Does a publishing house really need the towering midtown location that pushes its overhead further through the roof? Are the new breed of executives in the right to flood the market with nonbooks that may or may not increase their market share but will surely drive out genuine books and distort and degrade the publishing business? Does sound publishing follow from the pressure to increase short-term profits and return on investment levels that belong to a more profitable and stable business? The truth is that the opulent corporate style reinforces the expansionist corporate mentality, institutionalizing the motive energy of greed and envy, which, far from fostering rational publishing, usually turns out to be the driving force behind the disastrous decision and the distorting policy. E. F. Schumacher wrote, in words that the high rollers and their dice bearers should take to heart,

> If human vices such as greed and envy are systematically cultivated, the inevitable result is nothing less than a collapse of intelligence. A man driven by greed or envy loses the power of seeing things as they really are, of seeing things in their roundness and wholeness, and his very successes become failures.

Envy and greed lead one to think big; respect and care lead one to think small. Thinking small pays attention, in Paul Goodman's words, to "the object, the function, the program, the task, the need," while thinking big pays "immense attention to the role, procedure, prestige and profit." What would thinking small, or at least smaller, be like? It would ask if this cookbook or that travel guide is really useful or just another packageable and promotable piece of merchandise. It would evaluate the quality of the advice a book purports to give. Instead of cynically predicting the market, it would ask if this book of pop psychology or spirituality is one the sponsoring editor and publisher would give to a troubled friend or family member. Is the guide for the small investor one they would give to a colleague? Thinking smaller would mean asking if the scheduling of the number and kinds of books is in keeping with the house's resources of professional skills, time, and money. In other words, is it acquiring and scheduling more books than it can publish well—that is, edit, produce, package, and promote carefully? Does the house habitually disrupt its publishing program and undermine professional standards by rushing out books in the fourth fiscal quarter to inflate its annual volume and profit figures?

Thinking smaller also leads one to ask if the climate and procedures of the editorial group foster independent judgment, cooperation, initiative, painstakingness, and pride—or power roles, committee decisions, crass opportunism, pressure, rivalry, fear and the depreciation of editorial skills. Are editors encouraged to be the allies or the exploiters of their authors? Is the house promoting the big books unduly and the small ones hardly at all? Do the house's marketing meetings and sales conferences have the human tone of a town meeting or the atmosphere of a cross between an ad agency slide presentation and a Soviet Party congress? Are its salespeople able to sell its list effectively as well as those of the other publishers it distributes? Does at least 20 percent of its list (the figure publishers used to use to justify the other 80 percent) make a significant contribution to genuine culture and public enlightenment?

In these and other ways, thinking smaller puts one in touch with the values that probably led one to come into publishing in the first place, as well as those that were found in the good publishing houses twenty years ago. By the same token, if you are a CEO or an officer or an editorial or marketing executive and these values mean little or nothing to you, why then do you persist in such a low-margin and capricious business? Is it to bask in the lingering prestige of publishing while at the same time undermining the management and work ethic of the profession that created this prestige?

In asking the corporate publishing executive to think smaller and more seriously about his purposes and methods, I am trying not to turn the clock back to 1965 but rather to take account of the facts as they now stand. I am pleading with him not only to moderate the heedless momentum in the direction of the mediocrity and unreality of the newspaper chains and the networks but also to make better use of the capital and other resources that are available. The truth is that a big house can spend more to promote a worthy book and author than a small one can. Why doesn't it do so as a matter of course? Why behave like the patron Dr. Johnson described—the person who complacently watches a man struggling in the surf and then overwhelms him with attention when he finally reaches shore?

It costs about fifteen hundred dollars to put a young or little-known author whose book has received compelling reviews on the literary map by taking out an ad in *The New York Review of Books,* where the map is partly redrawn every fortnight. The same amount will buy full-page ads in four leading little magazines, which also position an author in the world of letters; such advertising is also the best way of supporting the literary and intellectual culture. When you realize that this very modest budget is about 3 to 5 percent of the budget for the big commercial book by the name-brand writer, which will soon be shouting for attention all by itself in bookstore windows across America, you can see why the hearts of editors sink in dismay and frustration. The big ad budget has much less to do with selling the book than with impressing the buyer for the chain and appeasing the vanity of the author. Would 5 percent less make any real difference to either of them? It can make all the difference to the author who badly needs—for teaching jobs, fellowships, and likely his battered morale—the recognition that his book has earned. You don't even have to go back to the good publisher's formula of budgeting 10 percent of anticipated net income to advertising and promotion. Half of that would provide enough for the collection of poetry that you expect will sell four thousand copies in hardcover and paperback, or the novel or other prose work that you expect to sell five thousand copies.

The big publishing house can afford to innovate. Less than one percent of a typical annual ad budget would pay the salary of a young publicist assigned to put his literary passion to work in developing a program of readings, panels, book signings, and so forth for the house's quality authors. Such events would bring the authors and their audience together in bookstores, on the campus reading circuit, and on college and listener-supported radio stations. They would feed into the efforts of the independent booksellers to compete with the chains by serving the culturally literate community, and campus and other local media would publicize them. Poets have been selling most of the copies of their collections this way for the past fifteen years. Why not give them a hand in arranging readings and other appearances and do the same for serious fiction and nonfiction writers as well? Co-op advertising money that was allocated according to last year's billings instead of on a book-by-book basis would help the small, creative independent bookseller get behind the serious books. Again, what would be a little seed money in publishing terms would go a long way, as would a slight reallocation of priorities. It's shameful for an editor at a big house to tell an author over a sixty-dollar lunch that there's no budget to advertise his book. Give editors the free use of every dollar they save from their entertainment budgets, matched by one from the house, to promote their first novels and other budgetless books, and see what happens.

I once had an argument with an editorial director who believed that the most exciting kind of publishing was to spot a writer you wanted to publish, wait while another house did the first three or four books, and then move in for the killing. I made a list of authors who, at that time, were still with the house or the editor or both that had taken on their early work. It included John Hersey, James Baldwin, Robert Lowell, Allen Ginsberg, Susan Sontag, Robert Penn Warren, Reynolds Price, J. D. Salinger, Samuel Beckett, Thomas Pynchon, Truman Capote, Flannery O'Connor, John Updike, John Steinbeck. I remember stopping at thirty or so. It doesn't take much to make most quality authors feel that they are appreciated and supported: an accessible, responsive, honest, and skilled editor, a classy book jacket, well-written flap copy, and a few ads that show the flag. Such treatment is what good writers mean by a good house, and if they receive it, they're likely to remain loyal. All the rest is money and flattery and the aura of the big time. When these widely become the terms of appeal, there comes about the collapse of author loyalty over which publishers have been wringing their hands, however slippery those hands may be. By the same token, a facilitating freedom, trust, and a say in marketing decisions create the working conditions good editors need. When those depart, so likely, will they—an outcome that has also become one of the major destabilizing symptoms and effects of corporate-style publishing.

Too much destabilizing of professional practices and superseding of higher values tend to make things unreal. A good example is the way the publishing business has come to honor its achievements. Until ten years ago, the National Book Awards were prizes of one thousand dollars, given to the most distinguished work in each of six or seven major areas—fiction, poetry, science writing, current affairs, biography, history, and translation—as determined by a jury of three eminent figures in that area. The ceremony was generally held at Avery Fisher Hall, in Lincoln Center, and most of the professional personnel of publishing turned out to listen to a speech by a public figure, which was usually respectable and to the remarks of the winners, which were often eloquent. Then everyone attended a congenial reception. All in all, it was an appropriate and even inspiring occasion. But then the big-timers moved in, notably the mass marketeers from the paperback industry and from one of the bookstore chains. Their idea was to make the National Book Awards just like the Academy Awards. So there came into being hosts of prizes for reprints (as well as original books), for jacket illustrations, book designs, and what have you, as chosen by jurors from all walks of the book trade and market, and the reception turned into a black-tie event that was attended mostly by executives.

This circus was supposed to capture public attention, sell lots of books, and make the entire business proud of itself. When, within a few years, it collapsed of its own inanity, the sponsoring organization, the Association of American Publishers, cast about for alternatives. Soon only three prizes were awarded: for fiction, nonfiction, and, to show that everyone's heart was still in the right place, the first novel. Last year the awards for distinction were raised to ten thousand dollars and reduced to two—fiction and nonfiction, with consolation prizes of one thousand dollars for the "short list" contenders. The celebration was held at the Starlight Room of the Waldorf-Astoria, and the whole thing financed by selling tables for $750 a crack. Afterward the AAP sensibly decided to stop sponsoring the event, which is slated to grow even gaudier. This year the prizes will be larger still, to attract more attention, which they won't. Thus an industry that is rapidly losing its claims to distinction, in both senses of the word, has turned its back on the ritual event that appropriately honored it and has instead taken to making a pass at the Muses by flashing its money and glitz. It was more or less predictable that the mood of the authors at the Starlight Room last year would be one of either opposition (Peter Taylor) or self-irony (E. L. Doctorow), for they realized that the real tribute that the publishing business was paying that evening was to its own hypocrisy.

The Association of American Publishers should take back the National Book Awards and return them to the original format, as a competition and an event for which there is an important need and purpose. I would like to make one other suggestion to the AAP. This one would even give it an opportunity to think bigger, if it wishes to publicize serious books effectively. American educational television has never had the type of serious book program that is taken for granted in England and France. I suggest that the AAP set to work to sponsor a really interesting program for PBS television, which could be rebroadcast on National Public Radio. What would such a program be like? It would have a personable, articulate bookman as moderator. The format would be a lively and informed discussion of a current provocative book. For example, it might put Richard Gilman together with Mary Gordon, Wilfrid Sheed, and Father David Tracy to discuss Gilman's new book about his journey through Catholicism. Philip Roth and, say, Robert Coover, Diane Johnson, and John Updike might comment and argue about Roth's experiment with metafiction in *The Counterlife.* And so forth. The AAP should fund a pilot and then turn the project over to a producer to seek government, foundation, and corporate support.

Such a program would promote a serious book and its author by appropriately willing its end, the wide enlightenment of the reading public. It would show how the hand of commerce and the hand of culture can work together again. The trouble with having an event like, say, Stephen King reading Dickens in a B. Dalton store—an idea that recently came out of a meeting of publishers and writers considering how to address the crisis in marketing serious books—is that, like the American Book Awards, it makes the book business that much more unreal. It doesn't integrate imagination and intellect with their public but with their nemesis, namely hype, thereby aggravating the condition it seeks to remedy.

The picture of the book business I have been painting is

the bleak side of it, which needs to be emphasized because it is dominant and spreading. Of course, many good books continue to be published in New York and Boston, and some of them are marketed well despite the weak or negligible performance of the chain bookstores in their one third of the market. Of course, those editors who care about the literary and intellectual culture continue to find ways to function in the space where the margin of risk meets the margin of pride that most publishers still take to a greater or lesser degree. And of course, there are still the publishers and editors who, whether they work in a big house or a small one, remain the lords and owners of their faces. Andre Schiffrin, Harry Ford, Ann Freedgood, Richard Seaver, Robert Giroux, Aaron Asher, Robert Wyatt, Robert Gottlieb, come quickly to mind among those who have been able to survive and even flourish because of their convictions and prowess. As models of high conduct and the cause of it in others, they enable the publishing business to still honor its claim to being a profession.

And there is, thank God, the alternative press. As I have written elsewhere, much of the party of letters—particularly its experimental and traditional wings—has been moving to the campus. *The New York Review of Books* demonstrates by its ads and increasingly by its reviews that the literary and intellectual culture is finding in the university presses a home away from home. The campus-based publishers have been widely occupying territory that the trade houses have retreated from in the arts and sciences or all but abandoned, such as foreign literature and thought. Meanwhile, the small-press movement continues to lead its dispersed, precarious, seminal life. And shrewd and reasonably well funded presses such as North Point, Algonquin, Ardis, and David R. Godine; like surprise witnesses at a trial, testify persuasively that the future of independent trade publishing may well lie in regional centers like Berkeley and Ann Arbor, Chapel Hill, and Austin. May all the publishers and editors of the alternative press, like their dwindling brethren in New York and Boston, continue to think small and ambitiously, to believe that a good book is an opportunity rather than a problem, and to welcome the fine pens that need and confirm their work.

(1987)

Index

Copyright Acknowledgments

Solotaroff. Copyright © 1983 by Ted Solotaroff. Reprinted by permission of Harper & Row, Publishers.

We also wish to thank the copyright holders for permission to quote from the following poems:
"September 1, 1938": Copyright © 1940 by W.H. Auden. Reprinted from *The English Auden,* edited by Edward Mendelson. Used by permission of Random House.

Sonnet from China from "In Time of War": Copyright © 1945 by W.H. Auden. Reprinted from *W.H. Auden: Collected Poems,* edited by Edward Mendelson. Used by permission of Random House.

"The Novelist": Copyright © 1940 and renewed 1968 by W.H. Auden. Reprinted from *W.H. Auden: Collected Poems,* edited by Edward Mendelson. Used by permission of Random House.

"The Love Song of J. Alfred Prufrock" in *Collected Poems 1909–1962,* T.S. Eliot, copyright © 1935, 1936 by Harcourt Brace Jovanovich, Inc.; copyright © 1964 by T.S. Eliot. Used by permission of Harcourt Brace Jovanovich, Inc.

"Facing Sentence" and "St. Roach" by Muriel Rukeyser. Reprinted by permission of International Creative Management, Inc. Copyright © 1973, 1976 by Muriel Rukeyser.

"The Fundamental Project of Technology" by Galway Kinnell from *The Past,* by Galway Kinnell. Copyright © 1985 by Galway Kinnell. Used by permission of Houghton Mifflin Company.